Praise for Pro[illegible]

'One of the most complex and uncompromising heroes since Harry Bosch.' *Weekend Australian*

'The best thing about this book is that it looks like there will be a second one.' *Australian Bookseller & Publisher*

'Chilling and memorable: top-notch Aussie noir definitely not for the faint-hearted.' *Graeme Blundell*

'For crime fans thirsty for an Aussie voice.' *Woman's Day*

'Tony Cavanaugh's searing debut marks the beginning of what should be a very promising writing career.' *Canberra Times*

'Cavanaugh's capacity to crawl inside the mind of his killer character, Winston Promise, is convincing and frightening, walking the reader in graphic detail through the acts of stalking, abduction, torture and killing.' *Herald Sun*

'Compulsive reading, *Promise* itself is more menacing, more disturbing and much more confronting than any other crime thriller on the shelves. It is brutal. It is terrifying. It is a brilliant book.' *Rob Minshull, ABC*

'The good part of any crime story is an intricate yet totally authentic plot, allowing the reader to suspend any disbelief for the entire journey. Mr Cavanaugh manages this with the deftness of a tightrope walker – all the while retaining his own unique approach to the characters and backdrop.' *The New York Journal of Books*

# DEAD GIRL SING

TONY CAVANAUGH

This is a work of fiction. All characters are fictional, and any resemblance to actual persons is entirely coincidental. In order to provide the story with a context, real names of places have been used, but there is no suggestion that the events described concerning the fictional characters ever occurred.

Isosceles quotes from 'The Charge of the Light Brigade' by Alfred Tennyson on page 27, and from 'To His Coy Mistress' by Andrew Marvell on page 267.

hachette
AUSTRALIA

Published in Australia and New Zealand in 2013
by Hachette Australia
(an imprint of Hachette Australia Pty Limited)
Level 17, 207 Kent Street, Sydney NSW 2000
www.hachette.com.au



National Library of Australia
Cataloguing-in-Publication data:

Cavanaugh, Tony.
Dead girl sing / Tony Cavanaugh.

ISBN 978 0 7336 2788 0 (pbk.)

Ex-police officers – Queensland – Fiction.
Detective and mystery stories.
Gold Coast (Qld) – Fiction.

A823.4

Cover design by Luke Causby/Blue Cork Design
Front cover photograph courtesy of Trevillion Images
Back cover photograph courtesy of iStock
Author photograph courtesy of Jasin Boland
Text design by Kirby Jones
Typeset by Kirby Jones
Printed and bound in Australia by Griffin Press, Adelaide, an accredited
ISO AS/NZS 14001:2004 Environmental Management System printer

The paper this book is printed on is certified against the Forest Stewardship Council® Standards. Griffin Press holds FSC chain of custody certification SGS-COC-005088. FSC promotes environmentally responsible, socially beneficial and economically viable management of the world's forests.

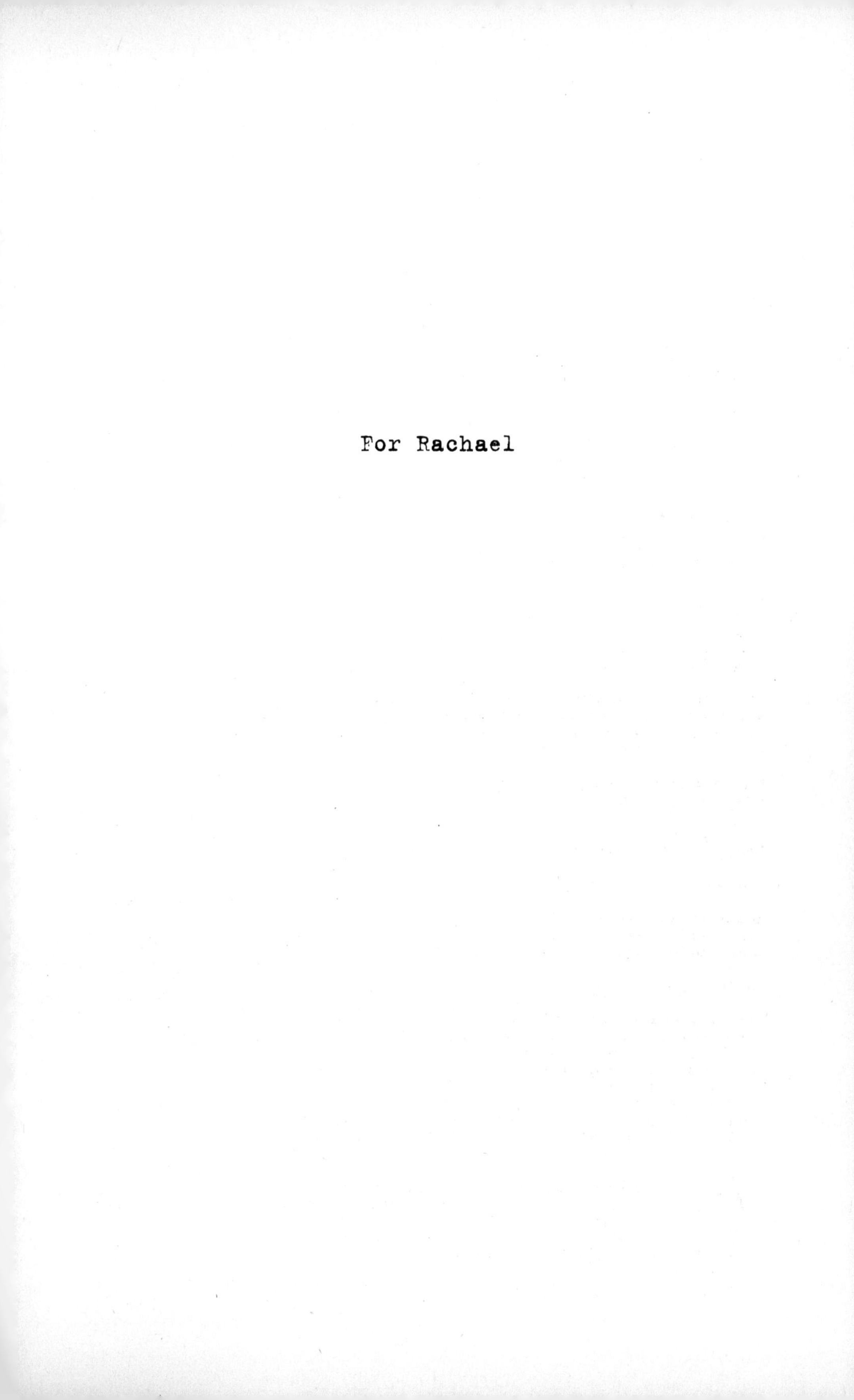

For Rachael

'If you are in hiding, don't light a fire.'

Ashanti proverb

# 1

# No Eye Contact

MAYBE SHE WAS TWELVE.

All we'd been told was that a girl had been stuffed into a plastic wheelie bin, one of the large ones. Olive green with a bright yellow lid. The lid hadn't been properly closed. That's because plastic wheelie bins aren't made to hold people.

It was the 1980s and metal rubbish bins were starting to be phased out; plastic and recycling bins were new. Only a few councils had begun to introduce them. People didn't get the recycling thing, me included, but I knew they weren't meant for throwing out human bodies.

It was my first body. Until then I'd been running down petty crims, attending domestic disputes and too many drunken fights in aimless streets of ruined houses built by a generous postwar government in the suburb of Springvale, far from the heart of Melbourne, a flat, sprawling city just north of the Antarctic. Down behind a small, seedy shopping plaza that advertised a sex shop, a noodle bar and a discount chemist was a gravel lane. A yellow neon strip at the back of the sex shop spilt a dirty light into the gloom of night. Beyond its reach, a seemingly endless carpet of low and flat suburban streets, spreading across to a distant ocean. I could hear the low rumble of the highway, six lanes that led to the heart of the city an hour away. It was cold and late. It was a Thursday.

A fat guy – the guy who owned the sex shop and who'd called it in – was bouncing on his toes as we walked towards the girl. At first he looked suspicious. Then he looked impatient. He was waving at us.

'Down here,' he shouted.

We'd parked at the end of the lane and got out to walk the distance. My partner, Eric, an old cop, liked to walk and slowly observe as he entered a crime scene.

I could see part of her body sticking out of the bin.

The cold made the gravel harder. The sounds of our feet crunching down the lane carried like sharp echoes.

'Kid?' said Eric.

I hated being called 'kid'.

'Yeah?' I replied.

'How long you been in uniform?'

'Four months.' I was nineteen.

'Ever seen a DB?'

'What's a DB?' I asked as we drew closer. Crunch, crunch.

'Dead body.'

Cops love shorthand.

'No,' I said. 'Not people, that is,' I added, as if the clarification might be helpful.

'Don't look 'em in the eye,' he instructed.

The sex shop owner was already talking before we got to him. 'So I come outta the shop, you know, to go home, it's late, you know, and pow, there she is. I mean, what fucking loony goes and shoves a kid in a bin? I mean, you know, what the fuck?'

What the fuck indeed.

Eric was old school, a walking police department. He'd done it all, seen it all. Forensics, traffic, CIB, community liaison, missing persons – each of these areas has its own department now, but back then they were just an everyday part of the job. The two-way was in the car, at the mouth of the narrow lane. Mobile phones were something I'd seen in a *Lethal Weapon* movie and they were the size of a small suitcase.

'Let's check her out,' he said. 'Lie the bin down, kid.'

She was slumped inside, like she'd folded in on herself. An arm was sticking out. Whoever had put her in had shoved her feet first. I took the bin and rolled it back towards me. One of the wheels had come off. My mum would have complained to the council. Guess the fat guy didn't care; we were out the back of a sex shop where nobody usually bothered to venture.

I tilted it backwards and gently laid it down on the gravel lane. The yellow lid flipped open and her body flopped out. She had brown hair.

'Drag her out, kid,' said Eric.

'Can I go now?' asked the fat owner.

'No,' said Eric.

I reached in.

The yellow-lid bins are for recycled stuff: paper, bottles, cans. She smelt of cardboard. I gently eased my hands under the girl's shoulders and slowly pulled her out, over the lid, onto the gravel.

She was still warm.

As I lay her on the cold, hard ground, her hair fell away from her eyes, and there we were, face to face. I exhaled, and my breath hung before her in a white mist.

The DB. Eighties shorthand. Now we call them 'vics'.

Maybe she was twelve, I thought. Not much older than that.

'What do you think her name is?' I asked stupidly.

Eric ignored my question.

'Kid? What did I say to you?'

I looked up at Eric, then back down to her face. Our eyes met and I held her gaze.

Don't look 'em in the eye, he'd warned. Because, if you do, you'll connect.

It was good advice from a seasoned cop. Advice designed to help a young rookie survive, advice that I ignored.

You do connect. But not only with the victim. The last person they see alive is the person who kills them, who extinguishes life. And the next thing their dead eyes see is you.

That's the common bond between you and the killer. He's stared into her eyes as the door on her life closes and you pick up after him. You find him. You close the case. Close her eyes. Put him away. Let her rest. If only there was rest for you. If only they stopped coming. I was young. Later I'd learn they'd never stop coming.

—

IT WAS ADVICE that I ignored yet again, many years later, as I stared at two sets of eyes belonging to two young bodies, laid out like patchwork, an entwined mosaic of limbs and a ribbon of hair, floating in the shallows beneath me.

# 2

# 'You Cannot Retire'

SOMEWHERE A PHONE WAS RINGING. FAR AWAY, BURIED, ITS ring tone an annoying and vaguely familiar song. It stopped. I pretended it hadn't happened. I continued on with the wise business of river-staring. For those of you uninitiated, this involves sitting in a comfortable chair or, in my case, a hammock, staring at the flow of the Noosa River on an incoming tide. Occasionally you may see a plank of wood float past or pelicans with accusing looks that say, 'Where's my food, pal?' or, every now and then, a boat full of tourists, or one of the local fishermen who trawl the long river for anything that swims around under its brown, quick-flowing surface.

River-staring is one of my main occupations now. I used to be called 'the Gun'. People said I was the best homicide investigator in the country. Used to be. I resigned over two years ago.

The phone rang again – the same annoying pop song – and then, after a brief pause, it started up one more time. The song had been designated to a girl who was, at the time, in mortal peril of being taken by a serial killer called Winston Promise.

Promise was dead. After a hunt, I caught him, watched as my so-called partner shot him and then buried him in an unmarked grave that nobody would discover. So it wasn't him trying to make contact.

I had four phones during the time I was searching for him, all of them with songs specifically designated to potential victims so I would instantly know, if one of them rang, who was under threat.

It stopped. This was now the third time it had rung. It meant someone wanted my help. It meant someone thought they were in trouble.

I have little memory of what happened after Maria and I emerged from the dark forest where Promise lies buried next to an unnamed creek and called it in. An empty killer's house, no sign of the owner, lots of questions from suspicious cops, but no charges. I recall coming home in a daze. I recall the walls of my home covered with pictures of Promise's victims. I recall tearing them down. I remember staring at the river and waiting for the glow of dawn. I remember it rained. I remember putting the phones away in a cardboard box. Along with my gun. I'd kept the phones on charge, connected up to a powerboard. Even though Promise and the threat that he posed to those girls had been erased. Why did I do that?

It rang again.

I walked in through the wide open doors of my old wooden shack on the river and looked up at the roof.

The house I lived in had been built in the 1920s by a fisherman who was, I'm convinced, either permanently drunk or extremely eccentric. When the wind blew hard – which it did nearly every day, as the river's mouth to the ocean was barely a mile away – the house swayed as if inebriated. The fisherman builder either got bored, ran out of money or decided that a ceiling was unnecessary. Above me were exposed hardwood beams and sheets of tin metal. When people were polite they said it looked rustic. It didn't. It looked unfinished, but I didn't care. When I bought the house all I wanted was a place to escape. And after my initial reaction – what the fuck is that all about and why did the real estate agent fail to mention there wasn't a ceiling? – I stopped looking up and eventually forgot about it. The hardwood beams had become a useful place to store things. Among which were a number of cardboard boxes, and in one of them, a phone that wouldn't stop ringing, a girl in need of my help.

The old fisherman had installed a power point in one of the beams above me. Cords snaked from it to the ceiling fan and an air conditioning unit that didn't work and an extension cord, which disappeared into one of the twenty-seven boxes above me.

Why had I kept the phones on charge? Why hadn't I turned them off? Buried them, like I buried the killer? Now that the danger had passed, did I really want these girls to stay in touch? In case there was future trouble? All teenage girls have trouble. Why did I keep the lines of communication open? Was it the buzz? Was my friend Casey right when he handed me the Beretta and told me I'd never get rid of it, that it was part of me?

I'd retired, left the force, turned my back on the darkness. I'd come out of retirement to cleanse the Sunshine Coast of a killer, but since then I'd been just dandy, happy sitting at the end of my jetty. Hadn't I?

—

'Darian, is that you?'

I was tempted to say: no, wrong number, sorry, and hang up, but one of the unfortunate by-products of designating ring tones to certain people was that you could picture them. I knew, as soon as

I saw the phone – bright pink – vibrating with some long-forgotten song we'd chosen over a year ago, that it was eighteen-year-old Ida from Vienna, backpacking her way around Australia. She'd been left on the edge of my lawn by the river one night, naked and terrified, swathed in a cocoon of about sixty-five layers of cling wrap, a gift from the serial killer to me. Against her will I'd forced her to leave Noosa and lied about how beautiful the Gold Coast was, how happy she'd be down there, and dumped her at the Nambour railway station. I did the right thing; she'd been targeted by Mister Promise and he would have gone back to her cheapo motel room and finished her off just for the fun of taunting me. Had she won the hours-long argument she would have ended up literally joined to a string of other victims in a macabre and perverse display of his glory.

'Ida? What's up?'

Mistake number one: don't invite a problem. I quickly tried to make up for the error.

'I'm sitting out by the river. I'm really enjoying not having to be a cop or be involved in any crime. It's great. I'm catching a lot of fish,' I lied.

Didn't work.

'Darian, you must come. Only you can help. There are so many bodies–'

And that was it. I thought I heard some sort of swift movement from behind the words, like a person grabbing the phone off her, but maybe it was my imagination. I looked at the pink phone in my hand and checked its battery level; maybe it had died. But no, it was still fully charged.

I redialled.

'Hello, this is Ida, please leave a message.' And then, '*Hallo, hier ist Ida. Bitte hinterlasse eine Nachricht,*' which I took a wild stab at being the same, but in German.

I stared at the phone and felt the emptiness at the other end. I tried not to see her, but that was as useless as trying to stop breathing.

I stared at the river. I stared at the hammock. I stared at a flock of seagulls on my front lawn. I told them to fuck off. They didn't move. They never do. You have to run at them, physically intimidate them, otherwise they'll stand and stare at you, hoping or expecting that eventually you'll succumb and feed them a crust or a soggy potato chip.

That's me, I thought. Like a dumb seagull. Programmed to react and respond in a certain way. *Help*, she'd said. *Only you can help.*

No, I thought. I don't do that anymore. I've retired. That's all behind me, remember, as instinct took over and, without even thinking, I reached down to the very bottom of the box in which the phones had been tossed. Under them and some old rubbishy LPs by Deep Purple, as if buried from sight and mind, was the gun.

The Beretta 92. I felt its cold metal, gripped my hand around it and pulled it out, tucked it into the back of my jeans and rang my colleague in the glass tower.

—

'I'M BUSY, I cannot talk. What is it you require? I am in the employment of the CIA, temporary, of course. High-level paranoia. Their remuneration is rather good, I might add, better than yours, dear colleague. What is it you need? I am in your rapture.'

This was Isosceles, a brilliant computer genius I'd dragged out of court some years ago. I made sure that the charges against him – about 875 breaches of the telecommunications act – were dropped, then I hired him to be the analyst/computer guy for all the crews working homicide under my watch on the eighth floor of Victoria Police HQ.

'I need you to track the location of this number,' I said as I squinted at the little screen on the mobile phone.

'Ida from Vienna,' he said as I heard his fingers tap dancing across his keyboards. 'The first woman to travel around the world on her own came from Vienna, did you know that, Darian? Her name was Ida too. Ida Pfeiffer. Tremendous achievement considering women weren't even allowed visas in the 1850s. Labrador.'

There was silence on the other end, the sort of silence that says, 'Done, task over'.

'Labrador?'

'Labrador. Not the hound but the town.' He giggled. Isosceles brought his rather eccentric sense of humour to every murder investigation he worked on. It didn't exactly endear him to the homicide crews but usually nobody said anything. The guy was a genius and routinely supplied information that led to the successful conclusion of an investigation through arrest and conviction.

'Thanks,' I said. 'Can you get me the exact location in Labrador?'

'Indeed. That will take just a little while longer.'

'Call me back.'

'Just a query. Before you go. Does this search for Viennese Ida represent social activity? By which I mean, are you intending to go visit her? She is very young, too young for you to be engaging in sexual activity, I would have thought. Or are you in fact coming out of retirement, again? By which I mean is she in peril?'

'I don't know.' I paused. 'I think she's in trouble.'

'Darian?'

'Yeah?'

'You cannot retire.'

He hung up before I could respond.

Moments later my mobile buzzed.

'Yep?'

'Tell me I'm a genius.'

'You're a genius.'

'I know. The signal from Viennese Ida's phone has not ceased. It might be turned off but the battery has not been removed, therefore I can tell you with complete certainty that she is in the Coombabah Lake Nature Reserve, a large forest of dense bushland on the northern side of the Gold Coast Highway, close – in fact approximately two hundred metres – from Coombabah Lake itself. She is, in fact, dead smack in the middle – pardon me, Darian, I do apologise – she is smack in the middle of what was a crab farm, until its closure in 1972. I wonder what happened to the crabs after they shut down the farm? Do you think they just left them to die? I've emailed you the coordinates. It's not as remote as the Sunshine Coast, but it's off what you might call the beaten track.'

I looked at the map. The town of Labrador was on the right-hand edge up near the top of the Gold Coast. I'm not good with directions, but I do left and right pretty well.

—

THE GOLD COAST is like a brother or a sister to the Sunshine Coast. Each is a resort playground full of tourists and itinerants, a series of towns and villages strung along a magnificent coastline that connects them and seems to never end. Hundreds of miles of pristine white sand and surf. In the middle of these tourist meccas is the capital city of Queensland, Brisbane, a town of some two million people. Forty years ago you'd be driving down a Brisbane street and have to stop and give way to sheep. Now it's a hot city, cool and groovy. The big difference between the Sunshine Coast and the Gold Coast is that one has a thousand skyscrapers, numerous 1970s high-rise brick apartment blocks and an angry violent stretch in its heartland called Surfers Paradise, home to bikie gangs, hookers, Russian mobsters, endless thousands of drunken teenage students and equally violent and nasty cops armed with tasers and batons. I drove through it once. It reminded me of Tijuana.

The other is a gentle, beautiful – some might call it boring – place where the greenies insist the tallest building can be no taller than a palm tree. The Sunshine Coast.

The twin playgrounds on the surf are joined by the Bruce Highway. It takes at least two hours to drive from one to the other, more likely three or four, depending on the urban snarl of Brisbane traffic.

I thought about driving down there, to see if Ida was all right. That was my next mistake: thinking. I should have just relied on my instinct.

# 3

# Connections

'I THINK IT'S BEST IF WE DON'T EVER TALK TO EACH OTHER again.'

Maria was a sergeant at the local police station. She had hooked up with one of my only friends, Casey, and had been my unofficial partner in the hunt for Winston Promise. She was career-minded and liked to play it by the book. I didn't. It wasn't the best of partnerships. In fact, since she blasted Promise into eternal damnation she'd barely spoken to me. Taking a life, even that of a serial killer, is a momentous step in a person's journey. It places you within a rarefied society, in which many of the inhabitants are evil; it redefines you and makes you – forever – consider who you really are. If you have the propensity to extinguish life once, for whatever reason, you'll never stop worrying if you will do it again. Maria didn't talk about it but I knew she was shaken to the centre of her identity. As I was the one who contrived for her to take aim and pull the trigger she had, since, carefully chosen to avoid me, keep me at a faraway distance. Casey still tossed out the dinner invitations when we spoke on the phone but if I ever said yes I think he'd collapse with shock.

My role in the investigation of serial killer Winston Promise had also caused some excitement with the boys on the hill, especially

Maria's idiot boss, Fat Adam. I'd broken one cop's arm and laid out two others in the very public arena of a nearby highway. I was best avoided if you wanted to climb the ranks at the Noosa station and Maria was ambitious.

I ignored her opening line. After all, she'd taken the call. 'Do you know anyone stationed on the Gold Coast?' I asked. 'I just had a call from a girl who seems to be in some distress.'

'Call them yourself,' was the answer.

'Thanks, never thought of that. It's a simple call, it'll take three minutes of your day.'

Cops are clan-like. As long as you wear the uniform you're part of the special elite. If I called I'd be put on hold for an hour and then passed on to some dummy who'd log the report and go back to sleep. I might have been one of the clan two years ago but now I was a civilian.

'Please,' I added, remembering she was a well brought up girl.

'What's the distress?' she asked.

I told her about the call and gave her Isosceles' coordinates.

'I've got a friend,' was all she said before she hung up.

I went back to the river.

I wasn't aware I'd just passed on a death sentence.

# 4

# Connectivity

'WHAT THE FUCK HAVE YOU DONE?' SCREAMED MARIA.

I checked the time. It was five in the morning. I was in the kitchen, on my third black coffee, and she was on the other end of the line.

'What are you talking about?' I asked.

'Johnston is *missing*,' she said.

'Who's Johnston?' I asked.

'Johnston is the officer I rang, at the Gold Coast. He told me he'd check out your Ida story, told me he'd drive out to have a look. They've been on the phone to me. He's disappeared and they're blaming me because that call was his last. It was a favour, it wasn't even official, he didn't log it in and now he's missing.'

'Who's they?' I asked.

'Stop asking questions and give me answers.'

'Answers to what?' I asked, not very helpfully.

'What exactly did the girl say to you? What's there, at that place you said she was calling from? Who is this girl? What's she mixed up in that would lead to a cop going missing?'

'I can answer questions one and three but they're not going to help; it's questions two and four that need to be investigated.'

'What the fuck? Questions two and four? What are you talking about?'

—

A FEW YEARS ago it used to be that thirty thousand people were reported missing in Australia every year. Now it's thirty-five thousand. Most are found. About sixteen hundred are not.

One thousand, six hundred people missing. *Every year.*

They've either successfully created a new life having escaped a bad one or they've been abducted and killed. Body dumped and buried somewhere. In ten years that's over fifteen thousand people, an unknown number of them the victims of killers.

When a person gets reported missing cops react accordingly with reassuring phrases like 'They're bound to come home, just wait' and a recitation of the stats. It makes sense. No-one wants to spend time, money and resources on a kid who's out joy-riding, off the radar for thirty-six hours, only to turn up hung-over and hungry.

If they don't turn up, though, the cops don't have another playlist. It's the same refrain: 'They're bound to come home, just wait.'

Things are a little different if it's a cop who's gone missing.

—

I RE-DIALLED IDA'S phone. This time it rang.

'You Darian, right?' said a man's voice. Rough, laconic, European maybe, young.

'Can I speak to Ida?'

'Ida. She dead girl sing,' he said.

Then hung up. The next call went straight to voicemail.

He must have not known to take out the battery of her phone or didn't care. It was still sending out signals, from the Coombabah Lake Nature Reserve, from the exact place where, forty years ago, a crab farm had been situated by the side of a dusty road, now a highway, three hours' drive away, according to the Navman that rested on the dash of my car.

—

'IT'S YOUR FAULT,' Maria had said to me on the phone. 'I'm going down there and you're coming with me,' she had said. 'I'll pick you up from your place in forty minutes.' She hung up without waiting for a reply.

I left without her.

# 5

# Place of the Cobra Worms

I WAS DOING SEVENTY MILES AN HOUR IN MY STUDEBAKER. Even though Australia embraced the metric system many years ago I didn't. Kilometres are lame. They suck. I was passing jerks in grey suits driving anonymous cars. They were all doing k's, cruising to work. I was driving. I was doing mph.

I have two cars. One is a Toyota. It goes. It's nice. No attitude. It's good when I want to be anonymous. In it I'm cruising. It drives itself. I could have a smorgasbord lunch while driving the Toyota. The Studebaker is a car. It snarls and grumbles. In it I'm driving and after about an hour behind the wheel, as the city of Brisbane began to loom ahead of me, awash with dawn's golden light reflected off the city towers, after the sheer thrill of the joy-ride began to wear off, I thought: *What am I doing?*

I'm not a cop anymore. I'm not a private detective. I left that world behind. Why am I driving hours down a congested highway, through sugar cane and pine plantations, passing a rapidly exploding sprawl of housing estates and industrial zones, which hug a string of beach communities along the Pacific Ocean coast in south-east Queensland?

Why didn't I call the cops? They'd take my call. They'd listen. They'd probably even go check out the old crab farm. They'd probably find my missing Austrian girl. They'd know what to do and where to look. They'd have the inside running.

So why, I wondered, as I sped past Caboolture, towards Bald Hills, did I decide to play the hero?

I knew the answer but I didn't like it. It was why I'd left those mobile phones connected, and on charge. It was why I kept the Beretta, hidden, safe, waiting.

I'd returned to the gun. It was my life, my code, no matter how hard I'd tried to leave it behind.

And in my heart I knew that the Gold Coast cops would be like all other cops.

They'd be bothered by my call. It was work. It'd mean they'd have to drag themselves out of the office. It was inconvenient. Chances were it was nothing. So many of the calls lead to nothing or, worse, a domestic. Maybe, I speculated, I just wanted to be a hero. But one thing I did know: I wanted to make sure Ida was safe.

*Only you can help*, she had said.

—

DRIVING FROM THE Sunshine Coast to the Gold Coast is easy. You point your car in the direction of down and stay on the wide highway.

After passing through Brisbane – or driving around it via a massive eight-laned highway bypass – the traffic became more intense. The Gold Coast is only forty-five minutes' drive away from Brisbane but a lot of people commute. While the speed limit on this stretch of highway is 60 mph or 100 k's or, in some parts, 110, most drivers seem to think that somehow they are in Germany, hurtling along the autobahn. The average speed seems to be 140. I'm not big on speeding fines, and I counted three speed cameras on the way down, so I kept to the limit. At this pace I could observe the hysterical weaving in and out of lanes by the fast drivers in my rear-view mirror then, as they roared past me, ducking in and out of the three lanes as they mowed on ahead.

After passing the city of Logan, which is known, probably unfairly, for its population of bogans, my car started to creep up on a blue Holden that looked as though it had just come from a wedding. Streamers and balloons adorned it, stuck to the edges of the windows. Staring at me through the back window were three teenage girls. The car was packed with another three girls in the front. It was being driven by a P-plate driver. As I passed it I noticed the side panels were covered in large scrawls of handwriting.

FINISHED SCHOOL, said one of the messages. OFF TO SCHOOLIES, said another and finally, scribbled where there was some space left: YAY!

The girl driving the car was holding on to the wheel with great concentration. The windows were all up and inside I could see the other five singing to a song that must have been playing loudly on the car sound system.

The five girls all waved at me and yelled, but the driver didn't take her eyes off the road and kept her foot on the pedal at exactly 100.

Schoolies week is an annual drink and fuck fest where kids who have just graduated from high school, mostly about seventeen years old, descend on the Gold Coast for one long, endless party at the beach and in the clubs. It was notorious, loathed by parents, adored by kids across the country. Between twenty and forty thousand teenagers, like the six girls in the car with the windows up, singing happily to a song on the radio, were about to hit the beach.

As was I.

I wondered how long their innocence would last as I overtook them.

—

I TURNED OFF the highway and carefully drove to Sea World, one of the numerous Disneyland-type theme parks. I had already driven past Dreamworld and Movie World and Wet'n'Wild, which was a waterworld.

Sea World, I knew, was nowhere near the Coombabah Lake Nature Reserve. I had, as usual, gotten tremendously lost. Rather foolishly I'd turned off the GPS. I truly hate being spoken to by a friendly computer who has a better sense of direction than I do. I turned it back on.

'Perform a U-turn where possible,' it helpfully told me.

Kids and parents spread out from the entrance to Sea World. They were laughing and holding stuffed toys and eating ice-cream cones or hot dogs or burgers. Empty tour buses waited. Another car park was swollen with empty cars, baking in the sun. Behind me was a forest of tee-tree that opened onto the beach. I could hear the pounding of the waves on the other side of the scrubby green thicket. I turned at the nearest roundabout and went back in the direction I'd come from. On my left was a five-star Sheraton Mirage, on my right was the Versace Hotel, the only one in the world, I seem to recall. Flashy cars, fake breasts and big teeth dazzled me from both sides of the road. I sped on. I was beginning to regret having told Ida to come down here.

I drove back onto the highway and turned right. Gleaming high-rise apartment blocks were everywhere. Canals of brilliant blue water weaved between them. The sunlight radiated from the waterways onto the facades, sparking off the windows like scissor-mirrors. This was definitely a place for sunglasses.

For about twenty minutes I travelled back the way I'd already come, driving along a winding four-lane highway that snaked along the water, turning inland and back towards Brisbane. Isosceles had been following my journey and, appalled by my progress so far, decided to call and guide me on the hands-free. I had him in one ear, the atonal GPS in the other. At least he provided me with a narrative of the landscape.

'Did you know that Coombabah means "Place of the Cobra Worms" in the local Aboriginal language?'

'No. I didn't actually.'

'Do you know what a cobra worm is, Darian?' he asked. I had at least another ten minutes, according to the GPS, before I reached my destination, time that was going to be filled by his idiosyncratic questions and my ignorant responses.

'No. I don't.'

'Little wood-borers. Apparently they are a delicacy when soaked in water. Isn't that interesting?'

No, not really. 'Fascinating,' I replied.

'Don't be patronising, Darian, it demeans you.'

'My apologies,' I replied.

'Accepted,' he said. 'Turn right at the next lights, do a U-turn and then turn left at the next road.' And I did, turning the GPS off and now allowing myself to be guided by him.

'I'll tell you when to pull over. The signal from her phone is approximately 145 metres from the road, in the middle of the bush. Is it hot and dry there? There might be snakes.'

The road was narrow and the forest of dry scrubby bush rose up on either side. It was hard to believe there was a lake nearby. There were tourist signs indicating bushwalks and what animals and birds one might see on these walks. I climbed out of the car and looked around me.

I was yet to find out exactly where Johnston might have parked his car, but it and he were nowhere to be seen. For the time being I wouldn't worry about the missing cop and would focus instead on finding Ida. It was, after all, still uncertain that the two were connected.

I was starting to feel and act like the desk idiots when a missing person gets reported: don't worry about it, they'll turn up.

Well, the likelihood of an officer vanishing in response to a girl missing was pretty remote, I told myself. Most likely Johnston's disappearance was related to something random like getting drunk or running off with a new lover.

I was ignoring my own basic first rule of an investigation: there's no such thing as random.

I looked in at a deepness of swamp oak and paperbark trees, wild grass and native bush. I'm not fond of the wild; even though I grew up on a small farm I prefer footpaths and streets.

As I pushed aside low branches and entered the forest I heard and felt a swampy floor – the place was moist with salt water, oozing from the nearby lake that was fed by estuaries and rivers, all of which merged into the Pacific Ocean which, Isosceles reliably informed me, was only a few kilometres away. Broken shards of sunlight dappled across the trees; the canopy above was thick and undulated slowly as a wind gently buffeted the leaves.

Isosceles guided me. I climbed over fallen tree trunks and sank into pools of stagnant swampy water and crossed saltmarsh pockets of dry land until he finally said:

'Here.'

I looked around me. I was standing in about three inches of murky black water that was seeping from the ground below. Paperbark trees, bent and gnarled like old men, stretched away from me, as far as I could see. Larger blackbutt gum trees sprang out of the ground, towering up into the impenetrable sky above. It was gloomy and dank. No snakes but lots of mosquitoes.

'I can't see anything but trees and more trees,' I said.

'I can only get you to an accurate radius of about six metres. Her phone is close by.'

The last time I did this I found a teenage girl's skull, shorn of her face, hanging in a tree above me. Instinctively I looked up and saw lots of branches and leaves. Nothing human in any direction.

I closed my eyes and tried to imagine being here in the shadow of a teenage girl from Austria. Or as a killer. Or as somebody who had abducted her. That was part of my problem. I didn't know who or what I was stalking. What had happened to her?

Forget the phone I said to myself. Look for the person.

I stepped back and focused on the shape of the bushes and the flow of the ground. The pattern of nature is perhaps as chaotic, or structured, as the pattern of a person's life but I tried to see if what was laid out before me showed signs of intervention. I looked for moulds of footprints, for broken twigs and branches, for anything in the unspoilt tangle of bush that might give me a direction to follow. This was much easier in the streets of a city or in a victim's house or, especially, in the face of a possible suspect. Still, I tried to place myself within the surroundings and get a sense of the lines and forms around me, the lines of the trees and the grass.

After what seemed like two decades I noticed that an area of tall hard grass seemed to have been flattened. I walked over and began to flatten it myself, in the hope that I was on to something.

I was.

I'd stepped onto a hard firm part of ground, dry. With the denseness of the bush around me I hadn't noticed that it was like a small hill and gave way to an expanse of mangrove-infested swamp that ebbed darkly under tree roots and overhanging vines, the water sparkling with pools of sunlight that managed to penetrate from above. The swamp reached away from me until it was swallowed up by a black wall of trees in the near distance. Sitting on the ground, on this hillock, was a pink Nokia mobile phone.

But it wasn't the phone that got my attention. It was the bodies of two naked girls, their hair flowing gently into a matted web, floating just beneath the surface of the water. They reminded me of Millais' painting of Ophelia or, more recently, Nick Cave's video clip where Kylie Minogue is lying face up, dead, in a small pool of water. In both the clip and the painting from the 1850s, the dead woman floating in water seemed serene, as if her death and the surroundings of the gentle pasture and shallow river were at one.

Not so with these two girls. Their mouths were open in a frozen scream of terror and their eyes were bulging out, as if imploring me to stop their anguish. I've seen a lot of dead bodies in my time and none of them were at peace, not even my father's, who fucked and drank his way to death in a shabby Bangkok hotel room. No matter how many you see, no matter how prepared you are – and I certainly wasn't at this moment – they are shrill in their horror which has an insistent ability to wrap itself inside you and not let go.

The girls seemed to be young, about eighteen or nineteen, maybe a little older. There was no indication of how they'd died but one thing I was certain of: it was murder.

There were no bullet wounds, no apparent bruising, although that was hard to tell from where I stood, and no sign of blood, although that would have been swept away by the gentle swell of the tides. Their arms were outstretched as if they were appealing for help or reaching out in an embrace. I couldn't tell if there were indentations around their wrists, which would indicate they'd been tied up.

*There are so many bodies.*

What had Ida meant? Were there more bodies? In this watery grave? Elsewhere?

A body under water will decompose at half the rate of a body left above ground. These girls looked like they'd been killed within the past forty-eight hours, meaning that Ida's frantic call to me had come at a crucial time close to their death.

—

I'D DRIVEN DOWN here to find a missing girl. I'd ignored her cry about 'so many bodies', tried to push it out of my mind. I don't know what I expected but I hadn't been prepared for this. Now I'd discovered a double homicide and no sign of the girl I was actually looking for. Still, I had her phone. I put it into my back pocket and called Isosceles.

'No Ida, but I found her phone . . .'

'Brilliant work.'

'. . . and the bodies of two dead girls.'

'Oh.'

'Not Ida. Can you trace her incomings and outgoings?'

'Done. I've already emailed it to you but, Darian, I don't know if this is her primary phone. You gave it to her for the specific purpose of triggering an emergency and loaded it with enough credit to keep it going for a while with minimal use. She has certainly been using it but nowhere near as much as a girl her age would normally be accessing such a device. And it's registered in your name, with your address, which means I haven't been able to find her address. What's her surname?'

Good question. I had no idea.

'She was just Ida from Vienna,' I replied, aware of how lame that sounded.

'Very helpful,' he said. '*Cannon to right of them, cannon to left of them, cannon in front of them, volley'd and thunder'd, storm'd at with shot and shell, boldly they rode and well,*' he added in an upbeat manner, quoting one of his favourite poems about the ill-fated charge of the Light Brigade during the Crimean War, an obsession of his.

I didn't respond but took it to mean that he would keep on with the search for Ida's identity despite the significant obstacle of not even knowing her name.

'Are you going to stay down there? You'll need to be connected; I can do that for you but I need a place of abode, an address, a place where you'll be sleeping and rising in the morning so we can communicate.'

I hadn't thought that far ahead. I hadn't planned on staying on the Gold Coast for longer than the day. Hero that I was, I imagined I'd arrive down here, find Ida within a couple of hours and be back home on the Noosa River before midnight.

'No problem. I'll let you know when I have it. I'm going to email you a photo of the girls' faces. It might help identify them.'

As I leaned down and snapped shots of the dead floating girls a thought crept through me: was this what Johnston saw? Before he went missing?

Had I inadvertently sent him to their watery grave at a time when the killer was still in the area? *No such thing as random.*

I was afraid I had.

—

THERE ARE SEVEN major police stations on the Gold Coast. Major as in big two- or three-storey bunkers, each one full of cops, each one a concrete warehouse. They like to do it big on the Gold Coast. It's a splashy, in-your-face city. In October they close the streets and run an Indy car race. They have million-dollar horseraces. The first casino in Queensland was built here. Dino De Laurentiis, the larger-than-life movie producer, built Australia's first movie studio here. The tallest apartment building in the southern hemisphere is here, sitting on the beach. The beach is big. The waves are big. The surfies are big. The drugs and the sex trade is big. I didn't know it at that time but the education industry is big here too. There are over forty institutions selling graduate education of some sort. Two major universities. One of them has over fifteen thousand students. The other was built by a white-collar criminal billionaire who spent years in jail for defrauding millions from his investors. The university is still named after him. No shame here. I felt the boys in the seven bunkers could more than easily handle the two girls floating beneath me.

I was wrong on that.

I expected the boys in the bunkers, with the massive amount of crime on the Coast, would respond with professionalism, albeit of the testosterone type, in regard to the floating bodies and the crime scene.

I was wrong on that too.

I knew the boys in the seven bunkers had put away some of the most aggressive and violent gangsters in the country. I knew they were tough. I'd driven past one of the courthouses. It looked like an industrial complex. I knew they'd be a different breed, different from the boys on the Noosa hill, back up on the Sunshine Coast. Up there it's Japanese tourists and stoned rich kids. Little guys growing dope and drink-driving. It's tourism crime. Down here, on the Gold Coast, it's hardcore. It was sleepy and laid-back in 1954. Now it's a hellfire inferno. The waves kept crashing against the beach and the corks kept popping; it is a tourist playground, after all, but there's a rumble-fuck not far below the surface. Step back from the beach and you can feel it, hear it, see it. The cops more than meet the need. They're known to show off their guns to teenage girls. They don't mind a bit of jackboot.

I had a choice: I could either walk away from the crime scene and let someone else find it or I could call it in and suffer the endless questioning about how and why, in the middle of ragged bushland,

I just happened to stumble across two floating bodies. Cops can't help themselves; they love to make connections, especially obvious connections like a dead body and the person who discovers it. It's a default mechanism: person finds a dead body, same person must be responsible. It's an automatic connection as if logic and common sense are ignored. You call it in, you invite scrutiny, suspicion.

I had a job to do: find a girl called Ida. If I called in the double homicide I'd invariably get tangled in the investigation. What were you doing there? How did you just happen to find them? Aren't you the ex-cop who, it's rumoured, has killed over a dozen guys, good and bad? Aren't you the ex-cop who broke about a thousand laws up on the Sunshine Coast while that serial killer was on the loose? The same cop who assaulted three fellow officers? What are you doing here, so far south of where you live?

And what were the answers? I'm looking for a girl called Ida from Austria who called me with a vivid and most likely inflated description of bodies …

And what *did* lead her to this place? What *was* her involvement? An innocent bystander, someone who stumbled across darkness, that's what I was hoping. Maybe she wasn't so innocent. Maybe she was responsible, in some way, for the bodies.

I wanted to protect her but I wasn't sure who it was I'd be protecting.

And now with their colleague missing, from the same place, all those cop suspicions would be seriously amplified and these cops liked aggro. Recently a young guy, a father of one, was arrested on the Gold Coast for creating a public nuisance, which meant he was probably pissing in a narrow street or yelling too loudly; he was dragged into one of the police stations and beaten up by the uniformed cops – who knew the CCTV cameras were recording it. In response to a question by the press, after this was made public, asking if this was appropriate behaviour, the Queensland Police Commissioner said, 'Of course.'

I really didn't need the hassle and the inevitable delay and frustration.

But.

I'd connected with their eyes. I shouldn't have looked when I was a rookie kid with Eric, after he warned me on our walk down the dark alley. I hadn't learned even all these years later. I should have looked away as soon as I saw those bodies floating in the water. I shouldn't have made contact.

But I had and I was going to pay for it.

I called it in.

# 6

# Wraparound Squad

EVERY COUNTRY HAS ITS OWN THREE-DIGIT EMERGENCY CALL number. Ours is 000. It takes you to a call centre where the nature of the emergency is defined. Is it really an emergency or are you trying to avoid paying for a taxi to get to an appointment at hospital? That's stage one. Stage two is: where is the location of the emergency? You haven't called nearby. The person you're talking to could be thousands of miles away. It's a big country, Australia, the size of the US, with only six mainland states. But at least you're not talking to New Delhi. Stage three is dispatch and stay on the line until they arrive. In a vast land of few people and remote communities, of raging bushfires and terrible floods, it's a good system.

I didn't use it.

'Homicide,' said the voice on the other end. Zero enthusiasm. Funeral parlours sound more interested.

I had all the direct numbers to the homicide units across the country embedded in my brain. There's only one in Queensland, in Brisbane.

'I have two bodies. I need a crew. I'm on the Gold Coast, in the Coombabah Nature Reserve.'

'Who's calling?' He sounded like he was on Xanax.

'My name's Darian Richards. I'm ex-homicide, out of Melbourne.'

'Two bodies?' He could have been reading me back my pizza order.

'Coombabah Nature Reserve. Gold Coast. Two bodies. Female. Recently deceased. As in the past forty-eight hours.'

'Hang on.' Even the Livestock Squad would have sounded more interested. But it was a detective I was talking to. Homicide doesn't have receptionists and if there's a course on how to talk to the public I don't think anyone attends. This guy sure as hell wouldn't have passed.

I waited. I kept my back to the floating dead girls below me. I could feel their eyes on me. Leave me alone. I'm doing the job, I'm calling it in, the crew will arrive and they'll investigate and find the creep who's responsible. I'm retired. I don't do this anymore.

I don't think they were listening.

'Did you call triple-o?' asked the voice.

'No. I called direct.'

'How'd you get this number?'

'I used to work in homicide. In Melbourne. For a long time. Have you dispatched?'

There was a long silence. Followed by:

'Hang on.'

For the first time I heard an attitude. It didn't sound good.

I took a deep breath and began to walk back towards my car. I'd called it in. I hadn't eyewitnessed anything. I had a missing girl to find.

'Who's this?' Another voice, also male. More authority mixed with some curiosity and cynicism.

'My name's Darian Richards. You've got two bodies in a shallow water grave at the Coombabah Nature Reserve.' I had walked back out of the bush and was standing by my car, on the road. I looked around me and saw, in the distance, a dog pound.

'Near the dog pound.' I was spectacularly bad with directions. 'Near a fence. On the left side.'

I heard a car approaching behind me. It was driving fast. Before I turned around I knew it was the police.

'Don't move! Put your hands where we can see them!' they screamed.

—

HERE'S A VERY important rule in the world of policing. It's especially relevant in territories that used to be, in recent memory, redneck. If a cop is pointing a gun at you, raise your arms slowly and do what he says, regardless of what he's saying or how you might believe that you've somehow been teleported into an episode of *Dragnet*.

'Someone will be there soon,' said the voice at the other end of the phone.

'They're here now,' I replied and signed off, holding both my arms out wide so they could be certain I wasn't going to pull an Uzi from my back pocket and mow 'em down.

They were constables, both heavy buffed guys in wraparound dark sunglasses which I guess they thought made them look more menacing.

'What's your name, buddy?' one of them asked. Queensland cops have been wearing name tags since 1990, when they became a service, not a force. His name tag read Connor.

—

NEVER TALK TO cops. It's a basic rule of interaction between civilians and police. It gets ignored all the time. By cops who like to hear things and think they have the right to ask you anything and receive answers to their questions. And by civilians because people, for the most part, are innocent of crimes and want to assure the constabulary that they're good, upstanding citizens. Forget it. Cops think the opposite. They think all civilians are guilty of something and the truth is, of course, we are.

When a person babbles a cop will think they're covering; either they're nervous because they're guilty or chatty because they're guilty. When a person is silent a cop will think they have something to hide and that silence is confirmation of guilt.

The downside of not talking to cops is that it unnerves them. They expect civilians to babble, they thrive on it. Silence freaks them out. Silences beg to be filled and only the most stalwart of us can accommodate them without losing some sort of control.

That all said, in Queensland you have to, by law, state your name and address. And nothing else.

'Darian Richards. I live in Poinciana Avenue, Tewantin.'

'Did you call in a homicide?' asked the other cop, whose name was Larkin.

I didn't respond.

'Is that your car?' asked Connor, pointing to my Studebaker.

I stayed quiet.

'How did you find the body?'

I wondered how many questions they'd ask before realising I wasn't going to answer.

'I want to see some proof of identity.'

I didn't move. Four questions, no answers; this was about the time when one stretches the patience of a cop. The next beat was for the cop to realise the person they're questioning is upholding their rights under the law and providing only the most basic information or that the person is being a smart-arse and needs their head kicked in. Most cops default to the latter. These heroes were no exception, which was a shame, as I didn't want to break any more police officers' limbs. They really get annoyed about that sort of behaviour and I can do without the grief that follows.

Still, it was their call.

'We're talking to you, mate,' observed Larkin.

I could hear the fast approach of another cruiser. More uniforms. Homicide detectives drive fast but not as maniacal as these sorts of heroes. Homicide detectives understand patience. They've seen a lot of dead people, not like these constables. A good homicide detective moves slowly and takes it all in. A not-so-good homicide detective is the type of guy who drives like a speed-freak to a crime scene where the killer's presence was a mere drop in a story that lasted days, possibly weeks before the actual incident.

Larkin and Connor looked around to see the second cruiser arrive, one of the new breed of highway patrol cars, decorated in vibrant pink stripes and lots of chequerboard prints; logos promoting good driving adorned the doors and the roof was home to a bunch of antennas that reminded me of *My Favorite Martian.* The car screamed to a stop and two guys climbed out. If possible they were even more pumped than the first two. Another set of wraparound sunglasses. They must be handing them out free at graduation. More biceps and flexing muscles and brawny attitude.

It was as if we'd all gathered for a morning work-out to be followed by a beach sprint.

I decided to break the vow of silence and turned to the four muscular heroes and said, 'There are two bodies.' I turned and pointed into the bush. 'That way. About a hundred and fifty metres in.'

'Show us,' said Connor.

I led them in, like a tracker up front, bashing through the bush, towards the watery grave.

We got lost a few times, which seemed to agitate them; I think they imagined I was doing it on purpose. I could have called Isosceles and asked for directions but there was no way I was letting them in on who I was or who I was connected to. We trudged in silence. The boys sounded like a clutch of American mortar bombs with their thick black boots and wide shoulders as they crashed through the bracken and tore off tree branches. When we finally arrived I stepped back and let them peer down and see the girls. Their bodies had moved, just a little, the current beneath had rearranged them like clothes on a washing line.

I waited as they registered shock, watched as they pretended that they were used to seeing dead bodies. Their focus of attention would be coming back to me with the inevitable questions – with suspicion – but I was prepared.

'How did you find them?' asked one of the cops who rode up in the second cruiser. He was the biggest and toughest of them all. His name was Keevers and he asked the question with attitude.

I didn't reply. Just stared at him.

'This prick didn't answer our questions either,' said Connor.

Keevers didn't acknowledge Connor but his gaze bore harder into mine. In one of those snap decisions he decided I was an enemy and he stepped towards me. Normally I would have taken him down, and the rest of them, but I didn't need to make a point. I needed to get on my way. They could intimidate me as much as they liked, as long as I could get on with the job of finding Ida.

'You think you're real fuckin' smart, don'cha?' he said, eyeballing me, so close I could smell the Big Mac on his breath.

I didn't say anything, just held his gaze.

He and the other three really, really wanted to beat me up. But they couldn't. It was outside their jurisdiction. If I'd been pulled over on the side of the road and acted in this way they would have but this was homicide and pretty soon these four boys would be handing over the crime scene – and me – to detectives, guys with more power, guys who could make their life difficult.

I could feel the hostility. One of them was giving me a look that said I was a sorry excuse for a human and the others had that simple, elemental rage, bursting with testosterone and, understandably, an uncontrollable emotional response to the dead girls. They hadn't experienced murder, they didn't understand it and it offended them in a most primal way. It doesn't help when the victims are pretty young women. These feelings had quickly coalesced into feelings of impotence. All they could do was stand and stare. And get information from me. Anything – if I was talking at least the vacuum would be filling up, at least they'd be thinking: we're doing something, we're on the job, we're responding. My silence was badly compounding their inertia and that, to their very core, was offending them.

There wasn't much I could do about it. With every passing moment I was aggravating the situation but I wasn't about to start up a chat to defuse it. It was bad enough that I had placed myself in their hands and, soon, the hands of the local Criminal Investigation Branch, who'd take me back to one of the bunkers and hammer me for answers and information; I didn't need to exacerbate it by providing answers to questions that would be mulled over, re-asked, pondered, considered, re-asked again until the statutory time allowed in custody had elapsed. The two dead girls were tragic but I'd done my duty, called it in.

'We lost one of our own around here last night. You wouldn't happen to know anything about that too, would ya? Because from where I'm standing it looks as though you know things.'

For a moment it seemed as if he was going to take a swing but his brains got the better of him and he stepped back. Or maybe it was the faraway sound of another police siren approaching us.

—

I WAS DRIVEN to the bunker at Southport, taken in through the side gates, led through metal doors and up a lift onto the second floor, placed in a small interview room with all the charm of a public toilet and told to wait. I'd already called Isosceles and told him I was in the hands of the local constabulary – which was no surprise to either of us – and that I'd make contact sometime in the next few years, when they deigned to release me. Reminding myself that doing one's public duty is actually a good thing, I leaned back in my hard chair, put my feet on the table, crossed my arms and began to hum 'Don't Think Twice, It's All Right' by Bob Dylan. Surprisingly I hadn't even got to the chorus before the door opened and a man dressed in black suit pants and an open-necked white shirt, tucked in neatly, stepped inside.

He was smiling like we were brothers and strode towards me with an arm outstretched.

'Darian Richards, we've met before. At a convention down in Hobart. You probably wouldn't remember me. Dane Harper,' he said. Gone were the threats and intimidation. Now I was part of a happy family. We shook. I didn't remember him but I assumed he was in charge of CIB.

'We have a situation,' he said as he sat down opposite me. 'And it would be pretty foolish of me not to ask for your help.'

I wasn't used to being treated with respect by other cops since I'd resigned from the job and didn't really feel like I wanted it to start now. Who knew where it could lead? Nowhere good, I was sure of that.

He wasn't being nice, he was being territorial. The homicide squad from Brisbane would be arriving soon and taking over the investigation. Cops like Dane Harper love publicity, love seeing their photo in the paper accompanying a story about how they busted a big investigation, but the squeeze from the boys from Brisbane was going to make that impossible. If Dane had me working for him, like a shadow, he might have a shot at breaking the case ahead of the homicide squad. But I wasn't inclined to be helpful.

I just smiled. I was going to ask if he had a pair of wraparound sunglasses but decided to check the wit and stay silent.

'Two dead girls, a missing police officer, which may be connected. And you,' he said.

I kept smiling and said nothing.

'I'm not sure how all this fits together. Yet. It would be a real help if you could fill me in.'

He waited for me to speak. When I didn't he went on:

'One of my police officers, Johnston Connelly, went missing after taking a call from your colleague, Maria, from Noosa. She's told us that you'd rung her about a girl in some sort of trouble. Maria told us she asked Johnston if he wouldn't mind checking out the place where, according to you, this girl had made contact. The same place that we now have two dead girls.'

He waited. I said nothing.

'Can I ask you this: the girl who rang you, the girl that Johnston was checking out – was she one of the girls found dead this morning?'

'No,' I answered.

'What can you tell me about this girl? What's her name, to start with?'

'Am I under arrest?' I asked.

'No, of course not,' he replied, as if such a thing would be tantamount to treason.

I got up and walked out of the room. I didn't catch his reaction but I don't think it was positive.

—

DANE WAS STILL standing. It was an instinctive action; every time somebody older or important stood up from a chair, he would too. It was something his parents taught him. Respect your elders. Respect those who know more than you.

As Darian had stood from the interview-room table, so too did Dane. What did he expect? A pat on the back? A handshake? He didn't expect what he got: a walkout. Didn't even bother to say goodbye or nod or give any form of farewell. Simply got up from his chair, turned and walked out of the room.

Leaving Dane standing, feeling foolish.

Feeling embarrassed. Feeling angry.

He watched Darian leave and he felt shame. He'd extended his hand of friendship, of respect and what did he get back? Ridicule, disdain. Darian had dismissed him, ignored his genuine offer of help, walked out, back turned to him, without even a smile or a thank you or a note of respect.

He'd gone to Darian's talk in Hobart, he'd shown him respect, he'd listened to the great homicide investigator as he illuminated the audience about criminalistics *his way* but Darian hadn't remembered him, even though he'd gone up to him at the end and told him how much he enjoyed the talk.

He'd show him. He'd make Darian Richards remember him. He'd make Darian respect him.

# 7

# Blond Richard and the Jimi Hendrix Experience

I STOOD OUTSIDE THE FORTRESS AND CHECKED MY PHONE. While I was in custody I could feel it buzzing. People had been calling; Isosceles, hopefully, and no doubt my jilted travel companion, Maria. The first of her angry unanswered calls had come through when I was on the highway, soon after dawn had broken. I hadn't bothered to listen to her messages as I knew what they contained. She'd called me about once every half-hour, no doubt to blast me for having left before she arrived. I didn't want a partner and I hate sitting in somebody's passenger seat. I was hoping to have found Ida and skedaddled out of here before she found me.

'Do we even have her surname?' I asked Isosceles. Ever since I came out of retirement to find Winston Promise I knew I was rusty but this adventure had already been seriously hamstrung by my initial 'take action, ask questions later' approach.

'No, but I can surmise she is a university student and I do have an address.'

Brilliant. Progress.

'I've been trawling through her text messages, feeling somewhat like a voyeur I might add, and found one where she's invited a friend called Fiona over to watch *The Biggest Loser*.'

'How many contacts does she have?'

'Thirty-two.'

That was thirty-two phone calls I'd be making if I didn't find a direct link to her whereabouts at where she lived. For all I knew she was home and in bed. Safe.

I didn't think that was likely.

'Do you know what university she's studying at?'

'Not yet. She's only mentioned being late for a lecture.'

—

I HAILED A cab. Half an hour later I was back at my car. The entrance to the Coombabah Reserve was cordoned off with yellow police tape and an emergency response team had begun to set up. The coroner's van was parked next to the red Studebaker, wedged in between a forensics vehicle and one of about six other police cruisers.

Nobody spoke to me but a few of the constables watched warily as I crossed to my car, climbed in and drove away.

A hundred metres up the road I pulled over. The dog pound was to my right, the forest on the other side. As I took out my phone I could hear howls and barking from inside the shelter. Lost dogs, homeless dogs, dogs in cages, behind bars, about to be rescued or about to be put down.

'Yep?' said the voice at the other end.

'It's Darian Richards.'

'Is it? You in town?'

'Yeah. I need a place to stay for a night. Maybe two nights. A motel room.'

'It's schoolies week.'

'Yeah, that's why I'm calling you and not driving to every hotel and motel to find out what I already know.' With the teenagers descending on the Gold Coast to celebrate the end of school with a rampage of dancing, fucking, drinking and chucking, every hotel room had been booked out for months in advance. The Gold Coast is like this. If it's not schoolies, it's the Indy or the Big Day Out or one of the weekly expos at the massive convention centre next to the casino.

'Gimme an hour. You wanna drop by the shop?'

'Not really.' Blond Richard owned and ran a second-hand record store near the beach in Surfers Paradise.

'Yeah you do. I've got a copy of Neil Young's feedback record – come over and have a listen.'

'I don't want to hear that.' It was called *Arc* and entirely consisted of amplifier feedback. Not exactly his biggest hit album.

'Where you calling from?'

'The Coombabah Reserve.'

'Creepy joint. Used to be a crab farm in there. You're fifteen minutes away. Come on over, listen to some rock'n'roll.'

'Maybe later. I've got a place to visit.'

'Your loss. I'll text you the name and address of the hotel when I've found you a room. It may not have an ocean view.'

—

TWENTY YEARS AGO Blond Richard was a bass guitarist in a Melbourne band no-one remembers. They never broke out beyond pub gigs on the Mornington Peninsula. He was also violently active in one of the Persian gangs, occasionally breaking open a head in a suburban car park after midnight. He rode a Harley and was always mistaken for a bikie. People were scared of him and he enjoyed that reputation. He was a tough guy and often had to be pulled into line. Well over six feet tall, he had skin and hair so pale he was almost albino. With long scraggly lank hair tied into a knot, he was covered in tatts. He looked like Johnny Winter, the awesome Texan bluesman. About as thin as Johnny Winter too. But unlike the bluesman, who looks as though he could snap in the wind, Blond Richard was full of muscle and flex. Sometimes he was called the Knife Dancer because he would put a silver coin on the end of his nose, while lying down, then spin the point of his knife on the coin so that it twirled like a ballet dancer, round and round, and just before it teetered and fell, he'd grab it with his hand. Never cut himself once. The sort of trick albino muscle men play, I guess.

Ten years ago he was wrongly put in the firing line as the main suspect in the killing of an eight-year-old boy, his nephew. A couple of my homicide investigators had taken a dislike to him and, convinced he was good for the killing, spent a lot of time ignoring the evidence and built a case around him.

He had a girlfriend at the time named Debbie who claimed to have fucked Jimi Hendrix when he was in London. She broke into his hotel and seduced him, or so the story went. She broke into my house after spending a bit of time tracking me down and left a long letter on my kitchen bench detailing the innocence of her lover and the set-up by the homicide squad. I dunno why she thought I'd read it but I did. I busted her for breaking and entering and then went on to bust my two investigators for being lazy and setting up an innocent man. Blond Richard certainly didn't qualify as father of the year but he was never a killer.

I didn't believe the story about Debbie and Jimi Hendrix but after Blond Richard was exonerated I received a copy of his *Electric Ladyland* LP, signed by the great man himself. Go figure.

It was justice plain and simple but I guess Blond Richard thought it deserved recognition. He made it clear that if I ever needed help, no matter what, he was there to provide it. He stayed in touch, an email or a message or even a Christmas card, to let me know where he was and that his debt of gratitude was still owing and would always be. A few years ago I heard that he'd relocated to the Gold Coast, went surfing every morning and had the best record shop for rock'n'roll in the entire country. He sent a note saying that if I was ever in the area he'd look after me.

I don't imagine he thought I'd be asking him to find me a hotel room in the middle of schoolies week. It was probably going to be harder to achieve than busting a bad guy's head open.

I turned onto the highway and drove towards the address Isosceles had given me.

# 8

# The Boyfriend

I DIDN'T GO TO UNIVERSITY. IT DIDN'T OCCUR TO ME AND I was working at the time. But I have a passing knowledge of the life of uni students. I dated a psychology student once and I've been to a few universities to question witnesses. I sort of know what students look like, what they do, how they work and what to expect from them. Lots of drinking and parties, huge stress levels when an assignment is due – and a certain degree of poverty is also part of the package. Not only do they have to take out a huge loan and pay back the government for letting them get educated, university students are poor. They do part-time jobs to pay the rent and fill up the car, if they have one. I've been to a few student houses and apartments in my time as well. They all share a common thread: the fridge is bare, but for some generic frozen food and cheap vodka; there's hardly any furniture; the floor is covered in mess and no-one has cleaned since the last landlord inspection.

I try not to allow myself to be subject to preconceptions, ever, but I was surprised at Ida's apartment, as I padded down the soft carpeted hallway. Actually I was surprised when I pulled up at the address that Isosceles had texted me.

I'd gone to the Marrakesh Apartments expecting a fibro dive in a shantytown street. Instead I was staring up at a twenty-storey modern luxury resort. It even had four stars out the front, on the sign that also advertised weekly rates, cable TV, in-house movies, a pool and spa. There were three complexes of apartments, in a lush garden of thick grass, golden cane palms, frangipani trees and carefully manicured bougainvillea. Sprinklers gently watered the garden and young men and women wandered through this paradise in skimpy bikinis and board shorts. It was a block away from the beach, two blocks off the main highway that threaded through all the towns and communities of the Gold Coast.

I'd driven over vast rivers, the sun gleaming off their surfaces, boats and yachts dancing on the water, pine trees lining the road, snaking my way through Southport, over a bridge that led to a narrow stretch of land called The Spit, past Main Beach and into Surfers Paradise where the highway got narrow and tall imposing concrete-and-glass structures loomed up from the water's edge. Five-star resorts next to old 1920s dumps. Trendy outdoor bars next to old tourist dives like a wax museum and a miniature golf course, complete with model dinosaurs.

I turned off the highway and drove towards the beach. It was vast and surf thumped in, onto the expanse of golden sand. Endless cafes and bars and pubs and malls full of buskers and teenagers and the occasional family on a sunny outing and busloads of Asian tourists littered the place. It was pumping. It was the sort of place that didn't look like it would go to sleep. Uniformed cops were in abundance and seemed to be doing an excellent job of advising tourists where the nearest public toilet was. Like all the other local cops I'd seen they were buffed and pumped and wore those giveaway wraparound sunnies. They looked like they all belonged to a hit team with the marine corps on holiday.

Winding my way along the beach, on the narrow tree-lined coast road, I turned off as Surfers blended into the next town, Broadbeach. I could see the white buildings that comprised the Marrakesh from a distance.

—

I STOOD IN the doorway and tried to get my bearings on the place.

Ida's apartment was on the tenth level. It was modern, with bland but expensive-looking furniture. The walls had been painted in an off-white, the colour of dead coral. Mass-produced paintings of palm trees and girls in bikinis were pretty much all that were on the wall. A desk sat on the other side of the room, by glass double doors that opened onto a balcony.

Everything looked normal. No signs of distress, no upturned furniture, not even any mess. It looked like a poster ad for Ikea.

I stepped in and closed the door behind me.

I'd left the Beretta in its shoebox that I kept tucked under the front seat of the car. The apartment seemed to be empty. I'd come in quietly and hadn't heard any movements since I'd been standing at the door.

I began to search the place.

It had two bedrooms, a large open-plan lounge room with kitchen, a balcony that overlooked the pool and gardens below and a view of the ocean. You couldn't quite see the sand of the beach from the tenth floor. It was spotlessly clean. No mess in the kitchen or lounge room and the granite tiles were free of dust. Someone had done an excellent job of cleaning.

The bedroom was like all young women's bedrooms, full of clothes scattered across the floor, cupboard doors open to reveal even more clothes in jumbled piles, make-up and a hastily made bed.

I went through her drawers and found nothing. Went back into the lounge room. On a table near the doors leading out to the balcony was a laptop and textbooks. She was studying journalism.

I'd looked in every room. No signs of struggle, no signs of mayhem.

The computer was off. I booted it up and wandered into the kitchen to see if there was any food while I was waiting. I like to look inside people's fridges; it tells you a lot about them. Her fridge was almost bare. There were three tomatoes. Old, squishy. Half a container of milk that was almost yoghurt. An unopened packet of vege burgers and a bottle of vodka in the freezer. The bread in the cupboard had mould on it and its use-by date was a week ago.

I looked around me. The computer was requesting a password and I didn't think I'd be able to get into this girl's head to comply.

The only indication of her personality, aside from the clothes in the bedroom, was by her desk. Above it was a small framed photo of her and a guy. They were at the beach and had their arms around one another. They were laughing at the camera and it looked as though it was recent. I crossed over and looked more closely. Ida was tall, almost six foot. She had shoulder-length blonde hair and wide, saucer-shaped eyes. She reminded me of a young Jane Fonda, in *Barbarella*. Behind the smile I thought I detected a hard edge, maybe a sense of caution about the world or maybe an uncertainty about the guy she was with. Maybe I was wrong; I've sat across the table from monsters who you could walk past on the street and think they were sweet and generous. The guy was also young. He was clean-shaven, had black hair that waved in a sexy Latino way. He looked like a sashaying type of guy. He reminded me of Antonio Banderas. He was either Italian or maybe from somewhere in South America. I never paid any attention to the classes on racial profiling; people are good or bad, regardless of where they come from.

What exactly had I learned about this girl? Not much, I realised as I sat and looked out at the view through the glass doors that led onto the balcony and, beyond, past tall palm trees, the ocean. From somewhere down below I could hear the sounds of kids splashing in the pool.

Her name was Ida. She came from Vienna, was backpacking around Australia and had now settled on the Gold Coast. From the textbooks on her desk I could see that she was studying at one of the universities in the area. Griffith, not the one created and named after the billionaire who went to jail. Either she or her parents were wealthy enough to afford this level of student accommodation.

I still didn't know what her last name was. I called the man in the glass tower.

'Did they bash you?' he asked.

'No, I managed to avoid the pleasure,' I replied. 'I need to know everything about this girl. Starting with her name.'

'Ida Faerber. She's nineteen, was born in Vienna. She has a brother, Stefan, who's studying law in Boston. She likes Johnny Cash and her favourite movie is *Gone with the Wind*. Am I a genius?'

'Yes, you're a genius. How'd you find that information?'

'Most of her messages are to an Estefan.'

I'd already seen that name when I glanced at her phone. Isosceles continued: 'So I just took his number, checked the name on the contract and found him on Facebook.'

I was scrolling through the messages on her phone as he talked.

'Did you know she has 428 friends on Facebook? That's rather a lot, don't you think? I have three. Somehow I feel tremendously lonely. I think I might send friend requests to a thousand random people this afternoon. What do you think, Darian?'

Estefan and Ida spent a lot of time talking to each other. Ordinary stuff mostly, but on the Tuesday she disappeared she had texted him:

*really really sorry*

Estefan hadn't texted back.

I looked up at the framed photo on the wall. 'Can you see what he looks like?'

'Of course. I'm on his page now. Not a chap who says very much. He only has forty-six friends. His name is Estefan Marquez. He's a student at Griffith University, as is she.'

'Can you text me a photo of him? Now?'

'I can but it would be remiss of me not to mention that you could actually do what I am doing yourself; your mobile phone plan allows you to go onto Facebook, Darian. That said, I'd probably rather not wait a few hours as you try to determine how to do that, so let's do it the old-fashioned way. Check your texts. I've just sent it through.'

I did. I was looking at the same guy who was on the wall, his arms wrapped around Ida.

'Should you call him?' asked Isosceles. 'I'm tracking him as we speak.'

'Where is he? I'll pay him a visit.'

—

IDA'S COMPUTER WAS a laptop, a MacBook Pro. I decided to take it with me. Isosceles might be able to crack into it, even though he was over a thousand miles away. Whatever, I didn't want to leave it there. I knew it would contain secrets, vital in my attempt at unlocking the girl and then finding her.

As I picked it up I saw two things underneath, as if the laptop had been placed to conceal them. The first was a handwritten list of names. There were about twenty. All girls. Their age and mobile phone number on the same line for each. Five of the names had ticks next to them; whatever the list meant, the ticks seemed to designate some form of completion.

The second thing I saw was blood.

—

I WAS A pretty messy kid. Every week my mum would shout at me to clean up my room and I'd comply by shoving clothes into the bottom of drawers and cupboards, stacking papers and books on top of each other so it looked like an orderly pile. And I'd shove extraneous stuff, from comic books to shoes, under the doona on my bed. Whoever had been through Ida's apartment cleaning had the same sort of approach. Clean what you see. They'd forgotten about the space on the glass desktop under the laptop. I was staring at a handprint of blood, smeared as if it had been dragged across the surface.

Ordinarily, upon the discovery of a potential crime scene like this, you'd call it in, it would be cordoned off, neighbours would be interviewed, the blood would be taken and analysed, the place would be dusted for prints and the evidence would start to narrow down the list of suspects and identify a possible victim. I wasn't going to do any of that. I wasn't going to call it in. That would simply invite way too much aggro and most likely a spot inside a jail cell. If the cops ever found out that I'd been in here and neglected to pass on the fact that a crime seemed to have been committed they could come after me. But by then I would've gotten out of Dodge.

I wasn't going to go door-knocking either, asking the neighbours what they'd seen or heard. The news of that sort of investigative work would also lead directly back to me. I needed to keep the cops off my back and to stay ahead of them. I was doing just fine on both counts so far, albeit breaking a few laws every time I moved.

I took photos of the apartment, I took the laptop, took photos of the smeared handprint. It was dry, otherwise I would have tried to stencil off a replica and see if we could, somehow – I didn't know but could've asked Isosceles – check for ID on the print.

I eased out through the door quietly and went on my way.

# 9

# Impulse

AT FIRST HE LIED. THAT'S NOT UNUSUAL, I WAS EXPECTING him to. But then, after I kept asking him questions about the girls, little questions based on his dumb answers, it became clear – to him, not just me – that it was of no use, not anymore. I knew, he knew, and with every dumb answer to my questions he was digging himself deeper and deeper into the ditch, so it was just easier to confess and tell me everything. And then, as always, to say sorry.

Carlos had fucked up. His sorry was meaningless. Instead of bringing the two girls to me, safe and secure as always, he'd gone and abused them. That was his first stupidity. Then he panicked because he knew he'd broken the rules so he cut them. Killed them. That was his second stupidity. Then he panicked even more because he knew the girls were due to be shipped out so he took them in the back of his van and dumped their bodies in a swamp at Coombabah. That was his last stupidity. Actually no, it wasn't: the last stupidity was lying to me and the first stupidity was not calling me, not asking me how to sort it.

And he got Ida involved. Again.

That was his fourth mistake; telling her too much. Revealing his blood crime. Now she's on the run and neither of us know how to find her. And then, the absolute dumbest, biggest dumb thing:

He kills a cop.

Stupid Ida, who was never to be trusted in the first place, never, never, never, goes and calls some friend of hers and then, somehow, a cop turns up a few hours later. Who is this friend she called? Before she got away from Carlos he managed to get her to talk a bit.

A bit.

If it was me, she would have talked a lot.

That's what being in love does to you. I told him to watch his emotions, I told him not to get involved with a girl that he might end up liking. He called it love. For fuck's sake. There's no time for that.

So before Ida ran away, while Carlos's guard was down she told him a bit: she told him that her friend was like a saviour, that he helped her escape being killed last year, that he was an amazing cop or ex-cop. Great – now he's probably hanging around too, looking for her.

His name is Darian.

This we don't need, not with cops searching everywhere to find the killer of two girls and another cop. Bodies are so messy. Carlos is an idiot, even though he is my brother; you just don't leave bodies around for the cops to find. They haven't found the dead cop's body yet but they will. It won't take them long. How do I know? Because Carlos is an idiot.

He thinks he's still in Brazil, he thinks he can act like he did when he was in the gang, be the hero on the streets, living without fear. Back there you can kill with impunity, you can take anyone's life and not get caught, or if you do, just pay someone or threaten them with further violence and it all goes away. Back there you make what you want; Carlos would have killed many people, including cops, and gotten away with it. He thinks that sort of behaviour caught the flight with him to Australia. He doesn't care about his actions, he didn't seem concerned when I yelled at him. He just shrugged and smiled and said sorry, not even like he meant it. More like, what would I know?

This makes him dangerous. Most people in his position would be scared and hiding; he'll be bragging and drinking and thinking about ramping it up. He might even be out there searching for more girls to fuck and slice open, just for the fun of it or maybe just to taunt me, as if to say how he's the one who really knows what's going on in the world, not me, he's the one who understands, not me.

A little bit of fear helps. It focuses the mind. I have a little bit but not very much. I know everything will be all right but I also know that I could be smug and silly and become a target for the police.

My plans are totally screwed. It's a disaster. All because Carlos didn't think and acted on impulse. Panic then impulse.

# 10

# Ashanti

ORIGINALLY A STRING OF BEACHES ALONG A STUNNING coastline, the Gold Coast found its heart in 1925 when the Surfers Paradise pub opened across the road from the beach. Beer, waves and the golden sun. One of the country's first beach apartment blocks was erected and suddenly the place became a magnet for tourists and surfers along the east coast. In the 1940s real estate developers decided to push for a new name for the entire area and the Gold Coast was born, comprising all the towns from its northern tip to the New South Wales border. It wasn't surprising I thought, as I drove down the wide highway that traversed the flat, monotonous landscape dotted with KFC outlets, Putt-Putt golfing ranges, sex shops and mini marts, that town centres here were defined not by a park or a council office or a square, but by a shopping complex. Money rules big-time even though it seemed to me that a lot of people walking the streets or waiting for a bus looked far from wealthy.

The 1940s was a time when the British Empire was fast winding down, a time when the American influence, beginning with MacArthur and the Pacific War, was about to take over the Australian landscape. It could have begun here, on the Gold Coast.

At that time, around 1940, there was another Gold Coast in the empire. I was blissfully ignorant of this fact until Isosceles, who enjoys peppering my travels with obscure facts, decided to give me a history lesson while I drove along the four-lane Gold Coast highway, approaching a town called Miami, proudly announcing itself with a huge sign on the side of the road.

'The other Gold Coast was in West Africa, Darian. I don't suppose you know that but I do suppose you can guess why it was so named. It wasn't because of the sunshine.'

'The gold, as in precious metal?' I asked, as I considered the panorama in my rear-view mirror, waiting for the lights to turn green; this place sure looked like a mini version of the Florida Miami.

'The gold indeed – but prior to that the Gold Coast was called the Ashanti Empire. Did you know that the Ashanti were one of the most sophisticated people in Africa?'

I didn't reply. I could have turned up Bob Dylan's *Together Through Life* full blast but it wouldn't have made any difference; he would have kept chattering.

'The English fought four, Darian, that's four, major wars with the Ashanti before they subdued, or one might say bludgeoned, them to submission. Interestingly the Ashanti would often marry their slave girls. This is a curious fact, is it not?'

It wasn't curious to me, I wasn't listening.

'It was considered wise, by some, to marry one's slave girl because it then allowed any inheritance to flow directly to the children without having to bother about the wife's family. Slave girls not having any family that mattered. In that respect the modern Ashanti look upon their slavery as a sort of humane one; what do you think, Darian? I'm not sure I accept that.'

'No, you're right,' I said without thinking.

'You weren't listening, were you?'

I kept driving.

—

ESTEFAN LIVED IN one of the towns down near the border – Burleigh Heads. It was recently voted to have the best beach in Australia and I could see why; a stunning headland jutted out into waters that gave up amazing waves for dozens of surfers, crashing onto a vast, long beach that was ringed with pandanus and pine trees. The vista was all-encompassing, sweeping. In the distance, shrouded in the salt from the surf, were the glass temples of apartment blocks and high-rise hotels.

Most of the Gold Coast seemed to have been built in the last twenty years although every now and then you'd find an exception: a spectacularly ramshackle house teetering on wooden stilts or a 1950s retro shop, hidden among palm trees and overgrown tropical gardens, wedged in between multimillion-dollar houses and one of the thousands of motels that I seemed to have driven by, each one showing 'No Vacancy' as the entire place was swamped with teenage kids on their schoolies binge.

Isosceles had Google-Earthed the house I was driving to so I knew what to expect: a place that time seemed to have passed by. As I turned into the narrow street, on the headland at Burleigh, where the thick bush was studded with vast black boulders that were known to rumble down into the ocean during monsoonal weather, I marvelled at how millionaires row could be slammed right up next to dumpster town in the same street. It was like the real estate developers had forgotten this little stretch of mountainous land. Trees towered over the road and I crawled along, searching for the right number – it felt like I'd stepped into an African jungle. The sounds of the nearby highway were swallowed up by the dense silence of the forest.

Number 18 was the last house in the street. The road came to a dead end out the front of the building. As I stepped out of the car I was reminded of what Isosceles had told me about the place; that it was an illegal brothel from the 1930s to the 1960s, then a boarding house for war veterans, until a developer took hold of it, did some renovations, went bust and leased it out, room by room. It looked like it had a paint job some time back in the '60s which, compared to some of the Queenslanders up on the Sunshine Coast, is pretty recent. It was a wooden building, with a wide, almost broken-down verandah wrapped around the front and sides. I climbed the wooden staircase that led to the front door, which was locked. I looked back down at the yard. The grass had been mowed recently and while the place screamed dump, it was being maintained.

I knocked on the door, which was, I noticed, made of extremely solid hardwood. A new addition.

From inside there was only silence.

I knocked again. More silence. If Estefan wasn't inside, his mobile phone was, according to Isosceles' tracking of its signal. I went back down the stairs and wandered around the side to the backyard, a vast overgrown jungle of grass and palm trees that backed onto the national park. Beyond that, the headland jutted up, about a hundred metres high, dark and gloomy. None of the windows along the side seemed to be open. I chose the back door as it seemed likely to give me the least resistance. It buckled easily under my weight and within moments I was inside.

This was my second break and enter within a couple of hours. I didn't care. I had a girl to find.

—

THERE WAS BLOOD; I could smell it. As soon as I walked in through the door it hit me – a faraway smell of rotting sweetness that permeated the place. It was almost hidden by the smell of bleach but you can't disguise it easily. It's the smell of death and it lingers.

I stood in the kitchen, a small back room, unrenovated, grey paint on hardwood walls, floorboards stripped back and scuffed by the feet of thousands over the years. The kitchen was clean; there wasn't rubbish on the floor or disgusting dishes piled in the sink. But it had a scrappy look to it. This wasn't the place where Estefan or anyone else for that matter would have been cooking up a bombe alaska or ratatouille – this was strictly a takeaway joint, where the food had been purchased elsewhere; the last time this place had seen any cooking might have been back at the turn of the decade.

As I walked through the kitchen and into a long corridor that spun down the middle of the building, I thought again about the missing Austrian Ida. She was pretty, wealthy, used to a life in a flash ocean-view high-rise apartment in a swank building with its own groovy amenities. I was guessing that when we found out what she drove it would be a BMW or a Saab. This place, supposedly the home of her boyfriend, looked way off key. This was not the sort of place I could picture that sort of girl taking any interest in, unless maybe she was doing sociological research. This place was a dump. The floorboards creaked as I walked along the corridor. It was dark and musty, despite the blast of hot orange sun burning through the windows, with an overwhelming feel of neglect. It was like the house in the plantation scene in Coppola's *Apocalypse Now* or like Miss Havisham's creepy house in *Great Expectations*. It breathed death, and Ida, whoever she really was, seemed to me like she breathed life.

And who was this Estefan guy? Did he really live here? I was starting to doubt whether anyone actually did. I made a note to check the contents of the fridge before I left but, as I passed each room, the doors open on either side of the corridor, it became less of a home or a rooming house and more a series of cells. Each room was the same: a single bed, no sheets or blankets, and a small bedside table. In all there were six of these rooms. Two of the beds had no mattresses on them. Never a good sign.

I hadn't paid much attention to them from the outside when I'd walked along the side of the house but each of the windows had metal bars, painted white, to prevent intruders from getting in. Or to prevent people from getting out.

I turned to look at the doorhandles: they were all connected to sophisticated deadlocks. Most of the house was old and creaky – the locks weren't. Anyone in one of these rooms wasn't getting out, unless they were let out.

The front room on the left was different from all the rest. Larger, it looked like it was lived in. This was, I guessed, where the missing Estefan slept. I went in.

A queen-size bed, unmade, as if it had been slept in recently. The pillows on both sides of the bed had been used and both sides of the sheet that covered the bed had been pushed back by whoever was in the bed when they got up. Two people. Estefan and Ida? The room was a little more cheery than the others, with a large bay window looking back onto the front yard and the narrow dead-end road that led down the hill to the house. At least there were curtains in this room, and no bars. But the walls were painted in a dowdy grey wash and the wooden wall, made up of vertical slats, looked spartan and pretty sad. I couldn't imagine a young girl, vibrant and happy, like I imagined Ida to be, at ease in this place. I just couldn't imagine anyone sleeping in this house unless they were really down on their luck or doing an intensive Edgar Allan Poe research field trip.

I looked in the cupboard and built-in wardrobes. Ordinary guy clothes. Levi's, Converse, Nike. I looked around for a desk – after all, this guy was meant to be a uni student. There wasn't one. Maybe he studied in the living room, which was back next to the kitchen. It didn't seem to have very much in the way of home comforts, only a couch and a flat screen TV.

I went back into the hallway.

This was feeling more and more like a place of incarceration than a place of study and revelry, which is what I'd expected. There was a functional quality to the place; six small bedrooms, all the same, single beds, bars on the windows and deadlocks on the doors. Missing mattresses. This was a jail. And the smell of blood lingered despite someone's efforts to eradicate it.

I thought back to Isosceles' chatter as I was driving along the highway and to his story about the Ashanti and slavery.

I pulled Ida's phone from my back pocket and looked at her recent text messages to Estefan. I brought up his number and dialled.

I heard his phone ring from the bedroom I'd just been in.

As I went back and found it under the covers of the bed, it went to voicemail. I wanted to hear the guy's voice.

I'm no expert in voice recognition but it seemed to me that this was the same man who had told me, in the early hours of this morning, that Ida was 'dead girl sing'.

—

'THIS IS THE guy,' I told Isosceles. 'This Estefan. I want all our resources on him. Can you do that for me?'

He was, after all, officially working for a highly cashed-up US government agency, not a solo warrior out on the streets of the Gold Coast in a bright red Studebaker.

'Of course, Darian,' he replied, 'need you ask? What is it you require, aside from as much personal information as I can find on him? Would you like surveillance?'

'Yep.' I wasn't sure when Estefan was going to be coming back to this place; it did have an abandoned feel to it, but he'd left his phone and his clothes. He'd spoken to me on Ida's phone. He knew who I was and he was probably working on the assumption I'd be coming down to look for her.

But he was cocky. He hadn't bothered to take the battery out of Ida's phone and it was left – by him? – right next to where the dead girls lay in the water. Was he trying to taunt me? Or maybe he was dumb. Not so many killers – if that's what he was – are as smart as they like to think they are.

I hoped he'd be coming back to this place. He wasn't aware that I was so close, not yet. And when he did, with Isosceles' surveillance cameras locked into the front and back entrances, ready to be triggered the moment someone opened either of those doors, I'd swoop on him quickly.

Isosceles had geek friends across the country who specialised in spying on people. They were like a geek spy community, doing favours for each other. No questions asked, no money paid.

'I'll send you a list of all his contacts, details on his vehicle and whatever might be useful from his university enrolment.'

'Can you get his credit card details?' I asked.

'Doing that now. I'll alert you, of course, if and when he accesses an ATM or uses his card in any way. He'll have to run out of petrol eventually, Darian. Then we'll locate him.'

Unless he was paying by cash. But I didn't think so. Something about this guy made me think he wasn't scared.

For the merest of instants I thought about calling my old buddy, Dane Harper, and passing all this information on to him. One thing the cops can do well is flood a territory with a photo of a wanted man. It was for just the merest of instants.

*Only you can help*, she had said.

I didn't call.

# 11

# The Cobweb (i)

I DIDN'T HAVE A LOT TO WORK WITH: TWO DEAD GIRLS, A LOT of missing people and some empty rooms.

I stood on the front balcony of the house and thought about those cell-like rooms. Once they would have been dens for the prostitutes and their clients, back in the dark days before brothels were legalised. At the bottom of a dead-end street, under a looming tower of forest and black rock, this place had been built for the express purpose of avoiding detection. The nearest neighbour was around the corner, up the hill, well away from the comings and goings.

I'd scoured the place and found nothing that could connect it to Ida, let alone Estefan – except for his mobile phone. I couldn't yet join the dots but the two dead girls floating beneath the surface of the water in the Coombabah Reserve and this house were connected. The smell of blood … two missing mattresses …

The house was either being used as a brothel again or, more likely, some sort of holding facility for people. I couldn't get the Ashanti out of my mind; was this something to do with a slave trade? Down here, on the sunny Gold Coast? It seemed unlikely. Did I really need to find out or could I just find Ida, make sure she was okay and get out of here?

I was starting to get annoyed with her. I'd retired from the police force for a reason and this wasn't how I'd imagined my new lifestyle. I thought about driving home and forgetting the whole deal, leaving her to sort out the mess herself.

I remembered the smeared handprint under her laptop and the smell of blood that lingered in the house of cells. Maybe I wasn't looking for a missing girl any longer. Maybe I was now searching for her killer.

I called Austria.

'*Hallo?*' said a woman at the other end of the line.

'Do you speak English?' I asked.

'Yes,' she said tentatively. I guess it's not often you get called in the middle of the night with that opening line. Isosceles had texted me Ida's parents' details. In any missing persons case the first thing you do is focus on the people closest to the one who's missing. I'd been focused on the boyfriend and now it was time to expand the circle outwards.

She sounded nervous. 'Who is this?' she asked.

'I'm sorry for calling you in the middle of the night, Mrs Faerber. My name is Darian Richards. Your daughter, Ida, is missing. I'm trying to find her.'

Telling a person their child or loved one has been murdered is gut-wrenching. You can offer them nothing. You're slamming a door in their face. That, and staring into the eyes of the victim, are the most gruesome parts of the job; the anguish and torment you've passed on seems to travel with you; you never pass on the news of death and walk away without feeling like you're a partner in the crime yourself. To deal with it you vow to enact vengeance.

Telling a person their child or loved one is missing is, by comparison, a walk in the park. There's hope and you're on the case, you're looking. And you've got the reassuring statistics to help: most missing people turn up.

It comes, however, at a cost; you become this person's only hope. This isn't a welcome burden. It's enough of a challenge running an investigation on your own; having a distraught parent on the phone every five minutes wanting updates makes it tiresome.

'What do you mean she's missing?' Ida's mother said. 'I was just talking to her the other day. Where is she?' There was already a note of hysteria in her voice.

'What did she say when you last spoke to her?' I asked.

'Who are you?'

'I used to be a police investigator; I met your daughter last year. She called me yesterday and mentioned she might be in some kind of trouble. I need to know everything you can tell me about her life here on the Gold Coast. Her friends, her boyfriend, where she might be staying ...'

'Boyfriend? She doesn't have a boyfriend.'

Of course the mother would be the last to know.

'Have you ever heard her talk of an Estefan?'

'No. Look, I don't know who you are or what this is about but I want to talk to my daughter.'

I went through it again. Slowly. I tried not to alarm her to the point where she'd be on the next flight to the Gold Coast and trailing my every move. I told her who I was and that I was best equipped to find Ida. Not the police; don't file a missing persons report yet, I said. It won't help.

It might actually bring young Ida a world of grief, I thought – but I didn't mention that. I needed to figure out exactly what her role was in the murders. I was hoping she was an innocent bystander, but I had no way of knowing that, and hey – people are strange.

I didn't tell Mrs Faerber about the blood in her daughter's apartment. No point in her thinking Ida might be dead unless she really was.

She began to tell me about her daughter, her words an urgent, jumbled rush: Ida was loving the Gold Coast, enjoyed the uni, didn't have a boyfriend, loved going on little tourist trips into the hinterland and up and down the coast, had lots of friends but no-one in particular.

It was sounding way too ordinary and very much a superficial portrait.

'Was there any place special that she might have mentioned to you?' I asked, thinking that if she was hiding somewhere, it could be in a place that she'd already mentioned to her mother. 'Like one of the towns in the hinterland, maybe?'

Like the Sunshine Coast, the Gold Coast hinterland is scattered with quaint little tourist towns full of art galleries and coffee shops and antique emporiums. Good places to hide out in.

'Oh,' she said, as if suddenly remembering something.

My pulse jumped. I could feel the surge: I was about to get a lead.

'*Die Spinnwebe*,' she said.

'What is that? Can you translate that for me?'

'The cobweb,' she said. 'I don't know what this place is but she told me she could never forget it, that after being there, it stayed in her mind.'

There was a pause, then after a moment she said, 'I'm not sure it was a good place.'

The cobweb; I had no idea what that was but would ask Blond Richard if it meant anything to him.

'Can you tell me what her mobile phone number is here in Australia?' I asked. She recited it to me and I scribbled it down in pen on the back of my palm. That, at least, was a big lead. Until now we'd been blindly following Ida through Facebook and the contacts on the phone I gave her a year ago, which she'd only seemed to use sparingly. I wanted to start Isosceles on the GPS tracking of the phone's signal. If I was lucky it would lead me straight to her.

Mrs Faerber also texted me Ida's bank account number, which Isosceles had been having trouble finding. It was an Austrian account, but linked to a Visa card. Now I had two excellent leads; tracking a person's whereabouts is easy unless they abandon modern technology – then it can be impossible.

I told Ida's mother I'd routinely check in, then tried to sign off.

'Please find my baby,' she said, bursting into a wail of anguish, one I knew all too well from the many times I'd been on the other end of a call like this.

'Promise me, please promise me you'll find her.'

No, I don't make promises anymore.

'I'll keep you updated. I'm sure she'll be safe,' I lied as I said my last goodbye.

—

'HER PHONE IS off,' said Isosceles. 'Nada. The last signal from her came this morning, from Cavill Avenue in Surfers Paradise. At ten twenty-five. At ten twenty-one this morning her account was accessed at an ATM, also in Cavill Avenue. Five hundred dollars was taken out.'

This morning? At ten twenty-one? Some eighteen hours after she'd called me and pressed the emergency button.

There were three explanations. One: her ATM card had been used by the person who was responsible for her vanishing. Two: she'd used the card herself, under duress by the person who was responsible for her vanishing. Three: she had used the card herself and there was no other person.

I kept an open mind but the third possibility nagged at me.

Cavill Avenue is the main drag through the busy Surfers Paradise strip. The police bunker where I'd been sitting was less than a kilometre away from where someone, hopefully Ida, had left a blink of a signal.

'Keep them monitored,' I said without thinking.

'Of course,' he replied, offended.

'Sorry, wasn't thinking,' I said. Of course he would keep them monitored; I was distracted. Turning off your phone in that way meant actually removing the battery. That's the sort of thing you did when you didn't want to be found.

If it was Ida who did it, then why? After calling me and asking me to help? Of course it was more than possible she was dead and whoever killed her had taken her phone and accessed her bank account. But that theory bothered me; why use someone's phone after killing them before taking out its battery – and why only take out five hundred dollars? Isosceles had told me the account had over a thousand left in it.

I checked my texts and messages. Nothing from Maria, which meant she'd given up on me – or that's what I hoped, even though it was unlikely.

Blond Richard had texted me, though:

*surfers city motel. tell em i sent u.*

And ten minutes later he'd texted me once more:

*aint flash*

# 12

# Your Wife Is Already Here

INDEED IT WASN'T. I DIDN'T MIND, I JUST NEEDED A BED IN A room with a wall for my thoughts. I drove back along the highway as the sun was going down to my left, which I figured must have been west. The sky was vast and pastel blue. On my right, the east, I could occasionally glimpse patches of the ocean down short narrow streets that dead-ended with an expanse of water. In my rear-view mirror I could see dark clouds hovering over a faraway mountain range. Surfers Paradise was up ahead. After passing through Miami and Nobby Beach the towers of Broadbeach loomed ahead, an elegant clutch of modern buildings by the water. The last of the burnt orange sun mirrored off them. To my left was a mega complex called Pacific Fair, a huge shopping centre that looked like it had been designed by Barbie and built with Lego, all pink and purple with useless turrets and fountains. Next door was the casino, one of the first built in the country. It looked like a 1980s Soviet design. Soon I was approaching Surfers Paradise. The highway narrowed into two lanes and on either side were tall hotels facing either the river on one side or the ocean on the other.

I got lost, turned off on the wrong street, despite Isosceles giving me directions. I couldn't believe how many young people, many of them in bikinis and board shorts, thronged the streets. Surfers was pumping and full of action. The kids who came to schoolies all wore a name tag attached to a lanyard around their neck. I guess this separated them from the scammers and scumbags who were down here to prey on their youth and sex.

After driving through a number of narrow one-way streets I managed to find myself out the front of the Surfers City Motel. It was a four-storey pale brick building, L-shaped, so all the rooms, each of which had a balcony, looked into each other. It reminded me of *Rear Window*. As I climbed out of the car I looked up and saw that most of the balconies were full of teenagers drinking, some dancing and smoking. Towels and wet clothes hung over the white metal railings and a discordant mix of rock, hip-hop and rap could be heard from the street. Behind me was the beach and along the street, next to the hotel's main entrance, were shops and cafes and fast-food joints. Across the road was an empty car park which was now home to a gigantic bungee jump. There was a long line of teenagers waiting to burst their guts on it.

The motel looked like it was built in the 1960s in an attempt at some sort of Las Vegas feel. It had seen better days.

The likelihood of sleep during the night was going to be remote.

I stepped inside.

—

LOVE HIM THOUGH I do, Isosceles has a terrible character flaw: he can't lie. This is compounded when the one asking him a question is a beautiful young woman. It gets even worse if that woman happens to have impressive breasts and if she, aware of this childish idiocy, bats her eyelids in a Raquel Welch kind of way, as if to say, *sweep me up, I'm about to swoon, you sexy geek you.*

This character weakness is common in geeks who spend more time in the binary or digital world than with humans. Isosceles rarely ventures out of his top floor apartment in one of Melbourne's tallest glass towers, where he fantasises over Raquel Welch and has sex with high-class hookers – who must be utterly bemused as they step into his weird floor-to-ceiling windowed space overlooking the city for their allotted twenty-six minutes with him. 'Intercourse' requires twenty-six minutes, no more, no less, according to some obscure research that he uncovered while at university. Not being able to lie means that he'd be hopeless as a homicide investigator or, in fact, any sort of investigator. Actually it sort of means he wouldn't be able to hold down pretty much any job these days with the possible exception of postman. And, of course, the job to which he's most suited: geek, analyst, interpreter of digital information.

Normally I don't mind this failing in his character. That's because it rarely has any impact on me. But when it does, it pisses me off big-time and I wish he was just like the rest of us and able to stare into the eyes of another, no matter how pretty, or sexy, and speak an untruth as if it's just as easy as breathing.

'Your wife's already in the room,' said the rat-faced weasel behind the desk in the reception area of the Surfers City Motel.

My wife?

'Blond Richard said nothing about a double room,' he said quickly. His lip was sort of quivering like he was scared. Blond Richard had a reputation. 'I ain't got no double rooms left. They's all gone to the kids, for schoolies. Everything's gone to the kids for schoolies. This place has been booked out for months. You got any idea how hard it was cleaning out a room in a fully booked hotel at this time of year?'

I just wanted to get upstairs and say hello to the wife. For a second I imagined Blond Richard had set me up with a girl but I knew better.

'I had to bribe them kids. Just to get them out of the room. And they reckon they're gunna complain to the cops. Lucky the cops'll tell 'em to get fucked but imagine if this were Greece, mate. In Greece they have tourist police and them guys have power, you hear what I'm saying?'

I leaned over the counter and looked him in the eye.

'Give me my key. Shut the fuck up. Point me in the direction of the lift.'

There was no lift. He gave me the key, lifted a wobbly finger and pointed behind me. I smiled, peeled away from the polished wooden counter and the display of tourist brochures advertising Putt-Putt golf, Sea World, Wet'n'Wild, Movie World and a hundred other local delights, and walked towards the stairwell.

A couple of teenage girls and droopy-looking boys were hanging around the lobby; they watched me as I took out my phone. Why is it that teenage girls always look and act so much older than their male counterparts?

I rang Isosceles as I walked up the stairs. 'Did you tell Maria where I was staying?' I asked. I'd given him the details as soon as I knew them.

'Yes,' he replied.

'Did it not occur to you that I've been trying to avoid her?'

'Yes,' he replied.

I gave up. 'She's registered as my wife,' I said.

'Yes,' he said, 'that was my idea.'

—

MARIA HAD ALREADY begun to cover the wall with a map of the Gold Coast and pieces of paper that described the basic facts, such as 'Johnston last seen here' and 'Dead girls found here'. She was sitting on the end of one of the two single beds, barefooted, in blue jeans and a white T-shirt. Her hair was tied back in a ponytail. She looked like a fresh-faced young kid who might be studying Ashanti history at one of the universities down here.

'Hi,' she said to me with a forced smile. 'I thought we'd get a head start with that wall thing you do.'

When I was hunting Winston Promise, the serial killer on the Sunshine Coast, I had covered my wall with a map of the local area and placed pamphlets and brochures and any sort of tourist or local information I could find on it, to create an entire picture of the area, an area in which the killer was stalking girls. It helped create a collage of his life and it helped bring the history of his crime into some sort of clear pattern, where I could step back and look at where he'd been, where the victims had been taken – it gave me an idea of the ghostly life I was shadowing in order to destroy him. I was planning on doing the same thing now with what little information I had in order, I hoped, to bring these scattered incidents to life with placement and time. Maria had worked with me on the hunt for Promise and would often stare at the wall in my house, as if lost inside the killer's dangerous mind. That's where we had to be.

It was a horrible, dark place, one in which demons and nightmares dwelled and one that I'd managed to step out of. I wasn't sure Maria had.

# 13

# The Girl with Kaleidoscope Eyes

I HAD BEEN WAITING FOR HIM. I WAS LYING IN MY BED WITH an AK47 under the covers. I was twelve. I'd borrowed the gun from one of my friends. Everyone had an AK47. My friend hadn't offered to show me how to use it. Everyone in the favela knew how to use an AK47.

Carlos was sixteen and had just been accepted into Amigos dos Amigos, the gang that controlled our favela. As part of the inauguration each member had to pledge allegiance. Done through blood. The thicker the blood the stronger the pledge. Our parents had both been shot dead many years before so Carlos couldn't kill them.

I was the only target.

He would come into my bedroom, late, when I was sleeping. Asleep I could be killed. He would have to cut my throat. Lately the gang bosses had been asking for proof of the allegiance killings. Severed heads were the most popular. Carlos loved me but his survival on the street was more important. It is for everyone. I would kill him if it meant I would live.

That's survival.

It's different in Australia. Australians don't get it. Nor do

Londoners or Italians who live by the Bay of Naples. The Sudanese get it.

At three, or maybe it was four, but it was still dark, long before the sun came up I heard his footsteps. Carlos is slight. Small, thin, bony, athletic. He could have been a dancer. He's wiry, taut, he moves like a cloud.

He opened the door and stepped inside. In his hand was a carving knife from the kitchen. I'd used it earlier that night to cut up a chicken that our next door neighbour had given me. He hadn't bothered to clean it. He walked towards me. I had the advantage of my eyes being adjusted to the darkness in the room. As he stepped up to my bed I levelled the barrel of the gun against his chest.

'Don't,' I said.

'What?' he asked, attempting to be innocent.

'Don't try and kill me because if you take another step I will pull the trigger and shoot you. It's loaded. I borrowed it from Miguel. I know how to use it.'

I heard the sound of trickling and realised he was pissing his pants. Tough boys aren't so tough when a gun is levelled at their chest.

'I wasn't going to do anything,' he said.

'Liar. Go next door. Kill Papa Gabriel. He's old. He won't even know.'

'But –' he started to protest.

'Tell them he was like a father to you. Tell them that after they shot and killed our parents, Papa Gabriel cared for us, fed us and protected us. Tell them that only this evening Papa Gabriel gave us a freshly killed chicken to eat, instead of eating it himself. Tell them that when you severed his head you wept.'

—

To survive on the streets of Rio a kid has to join a gang. But to join a gang meant that you would die. Eventually. I had plans, dreams. I could have been a good gang member. Sometimes I think I could have been a gang leader. Many of the boys are weak. When I arrived in Australia and started my business I knew I needed help. I couldn't trust the local boys so I made contact with Carlos and told him to come. I told him I'd pay for his travel and look after him when he arrived. I told him I had enrolled him into a university on the Gold Coast and that he had a new name, Estefan Marquez. Estefan was living in Rio; he was eighteen and very smart. He'd applied for a transfer from the Universidade do Estado do Rio de Janeiro to Griffith University. He was studying engineering. I gave Carlos his address and told him to do the rest.

Estefan came home to his parents' apartment one evening, where he lived, to find both of them dead on the floor of the kitchen. Carlos had sat them on the floor and bound their wrists. He told me they pleaded with him and said they would give him fifteen thousand American dollars. He told me he was tempted but knew I'd be mad if he didn't do what I said. He slit their throats and watched TV in the lounge room while he waited for their son to return.

Estefan wasn't alone. He had his girlfriend with him. She was also studying engineering and was, apparently, sad that she was about to lose him to Australia for the rest of the year. Carlos told me they really freaked out when they saw his parents drenched in blood. Carlos told me the whole kitchen floor was covered in sticky blood. He said it was easy to tie them up. They believed him when he said he wasn't going to hurt them like he hurt the parents. He said they believed him when he said he was tired of killing, that slitting a person's throat was a real hassle and that he'd rather not do it again.

Carlos didn't have a lot of time because he'd organised a friend in the police department to come over at five in the evening to help clean up the bodies and then dump them in the hills. Still, he was good enough to call me and ask what I wanted to do with the girlfriend. Knowing about my business he thought I might like to sell her or make something with her. I was impressed. That showed real forward thinking. That showed Carlos was thinking like me. See a person of value and think of her as an asset.

As it happened I didn't want the hassle. He got Estefan's laptop and went on Skype and showed me what she looked like and asked what I thought. I was sleeping at the time and pretty annoyed that he'd woken me up. Still, she was very beautiful, the girl who studied engineering. It seemed a shame to have to kill her too. But she was in the way, of no use really. I could have sold her, I could have made ten thousand for her. She had very thick black hair and a light brown body. I asked Carlos to take off her clothes so I could see her naked. Even though I knew I probably wasn't going to sell her. He did and she had a very beautiful body with large breasts, larger than mine. For a moment I felt jealous and wanted her to die because she was prettier than me. But I have that feeling a lot. It's silly and dangerous, gets in the way of making good business. Luckily I recognise it when it comes. It would be easier if I traded in young men instead of young women but the market's not there. You can make some money selling boys but it's just not as strong as selling girls. Also, there's a sort of stigma about selling boys to men. Some of my colleagues frown on it.

I told him no thanks and signed off, making sure that everything else was okay. It was. He was good.

Carlos told me that he killed Estefan first because he wanted to have sex with the girl but that she was so hysterical it was impossible. He said he actually started fucking her but she was weeping and yelling and begging him. I don't know what for. Anyway he got off her and slit her throat too.

Before that though he sat down in front of Estefan and asked him about his transfer to Griffith University on the Gold Coast. Everything. Estefan was really obliging. Then Carlos said:

'You are me.' But Estefan didn't understand what he meant so Carlos decided to tell him, even though he didn't need to. What does a dead guy care?

With his identity papers, his passport, his letters from the Gold Coast University, Carlos told Estefan that he was going to take his place. He needed to come to Australia to be with his sister but couldn't because of his crime record being with the gang. The Australian authorities wouldn't let him in.

Carlos told me that Estefan said it was a really clever idea. He must have been trying to impress Carlos, maybe thinking that if he was nice and respectful it would make things easier.

His friend in the police department arrived at six. Blamed the traffic. Afterwards Carlos thought that maybe he should have given his friend the hot girl instead of paying him the five hundred dollars but I don't know. I think it was better the way he did it.

He was under my control then.

—

To SURVIVE THIS crisis I have to be calm. That's easy. I've had worse.

'Hi, it's Starlight.'

'Hey, my girl, I didn't expect to hear from you. You're not shipping her out until next week, are you? Or is it my lucky day? Do I get her earlier than expected?'

'There's a glitch.'

There was silence on the other end of the phone. I let the news sink in. It was uncharted territory for both of us. He'd agreed to pay me a lot of money for the girl who was now floating in some lake on the other side of the Gold Coast, all because of Carlos and his dumb sexual desires. We'd made a bit of business together, this guy and me. I'd sold him three other girls. It's not like he was my best client but he was regular and he always paid on time. And really, what was paramount in my mind was my reputation. It's a small, premium business. I grow it with new clients but that's slow – like, a new buyer once every few months. It's all about word of mouth. I had to be really careful and protect my name as a reliable and safe supplier of the most beautiful girls.

But I was calm. It's not like I was sweating or anything. After all he had his reputation to protect too. You dance with the devil once, you're tainted for life. I could so easily destroy him, a married man of forty-six living in Suva, owner of a multinational hotel chain.

We'd have to dance this one carefully, the steps unprecedented but together, in tandem.

I continued: 'The consignment has been destroyed.'

'Oh,' was all he said. I wondered if he'd ask what happened to the girl. Our lines of communication were secure but in cyberspace anyone can hear you talk.

'It will be replaced of course. There will be a slight delay to the delivery and you will, naturally, be appraised of the quality before it's sent.'

'Good,' he said very slowly. I could hear the wheels of his mind ticking over. He'd already fallen in love with his princess since I showed her to him. They all do. He'd been fantasising about what he'd do with her. He'd probably even given her a name. She was like a pet to him. A pet dog or cat that was on its way home from the pet shop. Replacement and delay were going to be hard to endure.

Still, what choice did he have? 'I can assure you, and you have my word on this, that the replacement will be of supreme quality.'

'Of course Starlight. How could I ever doubt you?'

'I'll be in touch.'

'Okay. See you then,' and he signed off. Didn't even express any pity for the girl he'd bought. A perfect repeat customer.

I like to keep a 'to do' list. I make this on my iPad. It keeps my head clear and focused and allows me to sleep calmly, without having to worry and stress about the next day's events.

I ticked off 'Call the buyer and explain situation'. Whew. I was pretty nervous about that. It could have gone really badly. I'll do what I promised though; I'll find him a really top girl. I'll dazzle him with a beauty.

Next on the list …

Carlos.

What do I do about him? What can I do about him? Nothing really. He's on the run but I have to think ahead. Will he be caught?

What happens when the cops find their dead colleague? Will he freak out? And if he is caught will he tell them all about me?

Of course he will. I have to defuse that. Hope that he calls me, begs for my forgiveness – which I will give; pleads to come here, to safety – which I will grant; and he will enter back into my world. Where I can control him once again.

# 14

# Partners

I DON'T LIKE MOST PEOPLE AND I DON'T LIKE SHARING. MARIA was drop-dead gorgeous and most guys would salivate at the chance of spending a night in a motel room with her. Not me. I wanted her out.

That was going to be impossible. On a practical level there was nowhere for her to go and on a personal level there was no way she was leaving. She knew I would have made some inroads – exactly what I wasn't yet sure – and she would be hanging around to find her colleague Johnston.

That was the problem. We were at cross-purposes. I was after Ida whom she didn't care about and she was after Johnston who I didn't care about. Not really; I sort of did but I knew he'd be taken care of. Cops are always taken care of. People like Ida are not.

That sort of disconnection does not make for a solid partnership.

'I'm doing this alone,' I said.

And then she said something that infuriated me, whether by accident or design, I didn't care:

'You can't.'

I didn't say anything, just stared at her as she went on. 'You might think you can but down here, it's different. Nothing like the Sunshine Coast. The cops here are smart and ruthless. They get a sniff of you running a shadow investigation to theirs and they'll come at you with all the force they can gather and believe me, Darian, they will. You can't treat them with the same sort of contempt as you did my lot.'

'Watch me,' I said, immediately regretting the macho posture of the reply.

'This time you really do need someone on the inside. You need me.'

The last time I needed someone was when I was a kid but I didn't bother telling her that.

'These cops are used to crime, hard crime. They can be brutal but they can also get results. They're good. Having me work with you means you get an inside run on their investigation. That's going to help you.'

She paused then said, 'You want to find that missing girl, Ida. If you don't you've failed. Personally. I want to find Johnston. If I don't then I've failed. The same way. And then there are the two dead girls you discovered. No matter what you tell yourself I know you can't walk away. Did you look into their eyes, Darian? Did they speak to you, like the other dead victims you swore to avenge? Have they begun to haunt you?'

Despite wanting to hit her I was impressed: this was a different person from the rookie cop, wide eyed and scared, who I used in my hunt for Winston Promise a year ago.

She was right of course. I wasn't about to tell her that. I turned and looked at the wall board, said:

'Let's start adding the pieces I've found from today. We'll begin with Ida's boyfriend, a guy named Estefan.'

She didn't smile, she didn't nod. No acknowledgment of a battle won; she got off the bed and grabbed a red thumb tack.

'Who's he and where does he live?'

—

AN HOUR LATER we'd added everything that I knew to the wall board – where Ida lived, where Estefan lived, who she'd been calling, where they both went to university. A series of red thumb tacks scattered across the landscape of the Gold Coast, from Coombabah in the north down to Burleigh near the border.

Johnston was a Senior Constable. He'd graduated at the same time as Maria. Although she didn't say it I got the impression they were, for a time, lovers. He'd taken the call from her and after clocking off, took a detour on his way home. To the Coombabah Reserve, to the location she'd given him, that I'd given her, that Isosceles had given me: from where Ida had made her frantic and desperate call saying there were so many bodies.

He didn't arrive home, didn't answer his phone. His wife rang the station and they reacted as they usually do when a cop goes missing: they dropped everything and started looking for him. Accessing his phone records they called Maria in the middle of the night; she told them about Coombabah and when a cruiser went out there all they found was an empty vehicle and no cop. According to Maria there wasn't any blood or signs of a scuffle. It was like he'd been beamed to another dimension.

Did he also stumble across the dead girls?

The dead girls were yet to be identified.

The local cops had asked Maria about Ida, whose call triggered all this. Maria told them she didn't know, to ask me.

They had but they got no answers.

—

MARIA HAD TAKEN out her laptop, hooked it up to the internet and hit Skype. She'd come prepared. Laptop, charger, printer and scanner. I noticed she even had a small overnight bag. It was open and I could see that she'd packed clothes. That was more than what I'd brought which was nothing. She probably even had a pair of pyjamas and a toothbrush.

I was standing back, between the two single beds, staring at the wall, which was covered with information scratched and pinned onto a number of local maps. We'd opened the double doors onto the small balcony. I could see across to the other balconies and rooms of the motel – all of them were brightly lit up and most of them had teenagers draped across the floors and lounging on the balconies. We were the only ones not focused on sex and drink. A myriad of sounds boomed across the L-shaped facade of the motel – Kanye West, Cold Chisel, Led Zeppelin, Lana Del Rey and countless others that made no connection with me. It was night but as this was in the heart of Surfers it was a blaze of neon and streetlights and headlights from cars caught in a traffic snarl below. The bungee jump was lit up and every now and then we'd hear the screams of kids as they hurled downwards through the air, towards the gravel ground, only to be sprung upwards at the last minute. Music and laughter and shouts rose up from the street below. I haven't been to Rio but this was how I imagined the Mardi Gras would sound and feel.

'This Estefan is, I posit, an impostor,' I heard Isosceles say.

I kept my eyes on the wall board and asked:

'In what way?'

'According to the phone and university records his name is Estefan Reale, from Rio; under the student visa scheme he came to Australia in August to start three years of study on the Gold Coast. A few days before he arrived in Australia his mother, father and girlfriend went missing.'

More missing people. These ones in South America, just to complicate the picture.

'They're still missing. Yet Estefan boards the plane and arrives on the Gold Coast and hits the Facebook page as if nothing has happened. Although the Facebook suddenly changes. Where we once had an Estefan Reale who loved reading Gabriel García Márquez and Roberto Bolaño, who studied Shakespeare's sonnets, now we have an Estefan Reale who changes his profile photo to one of Pelé, the soccer hero and posts only about sport and gangsters and crude jokes about drugs. This new Estefan, or might I say "reincarnated" Estefan de-friends pretty much everybody and builds an entirely new friend base with gang members from a favela in Rio and, of course, new friends from the Gold Coast. I'm feeling like Gabriel John Utterson.'

'*Who?*' we both asked at the same time.

'The man who investigated Dr Jekyll only to discover the alter-ego, Mr Hyde.'

I gave Maria a look that said: he always does this, get used to it.

'This Estefan has a sister whereas the old Estefan didn't. She lives on the Gold Coast too. I've been looking at her Facebook page, Darian, and I think she is the one you should be going to visit.'

# 15

# Sifting Through a City of Parents' Fear

THE STREETS ARE ALIVE WITH GIRLS.

Eight glasses of chilled vodka and I'm floating down through the streets of Surfers Paradise. The footpath is like a cloud. Look at all these hot girls. I'm prettier. They notice, they see me, I can feel them watching me as I pass them.

I've never done this before. I'd always left it up to Carlos. But I'm going to enjoy this.

Two girls for me to find, to pluck off the street, take home and sell.

It's schoolies week; it's a gamble taking two girls off the street like this. They'll be higher profile than the usual. Because they're going to be Australian, unlike the wide variety of international girls at the university. Girls with passports, far from home, with parents in another land.

I like Chinese girls best. Their parents live in fear and uncertainty. Growing up in the Cultural Revolution or in its shadow, they're afraid of authorities, afraid of the West; they don't like it or understand it. They send their children to the West to get what they think is the best education but they fear it and its dark influences.

Like me.

This fear creates a barrier for them when dealing with a missing daughter. Uncertain how to proceed, uncertain what to do, uncertain if there's been anything sinister or if, in fact, their worst dreams have come true and their daughter has succumbed to the dark influences of the West. Uncertain what the protocols are, even uncertain if they can get a passport and leave their own country, to search.

And how would they search? Strangers in the dark West, unable to speak the language.

These people are scared of the police because where they come from the police arrive in the middle of the night to take them away to uncertain and unknown places. In these places you avoid the police. Whispers can bring attention. Attitudes can bring on a visit. The police exist in these places to deprive you of your liberty and freedom.

After I take my two Australian girls there will be publicity and a search.

But it's schoolies week and parents are fearful already, fearful of what might happen to their daughters running free and rampant on the Gold Coast, already they fret about what might happen to them. So it's not like it's going to be a surprise when they hear their daughter has vanished. It'll just confirm their fears.

—

I'VE BEEN WATCHING them from my balcony and I've been walking past them in my corridor, standing with them in the lift in my building, driving past them in my car. So many girls, they're all around me.

I could take one when they're drunk in the morning – that might be easiest. But really no-one is going to be suspicious of a girl who's just a little bit older than them. All their suspicions are on guys, older guys and dangerous guys. Male predators. And hey, it's a party and they're all with friends. No-one comes down here alone so they think they're safe. Completely unaware that I'm here. Sexy predator, that's me. I'm here, right next to them, walking between them, smiling at them.

Here's a girl. She's so drunk she's sleepwalking. Alone, head down, hair falling in front of her, she's having trouble putting her feet in front of one another.

'Hello darling. Do you need some help?'

I can't see her face.

'Huh?' she asks from within the fallen head and sweeping hair, her body swaying.

I don't answer. It's not worth the bother. Let's just check her out. I put the palm of my hand under her chin and lift up her head. What does she look like, this girl? Hot? Hot enough for me?

Her eyes are glazed. She's staring at me but has no clue what's going on.

'I'm lost,' she says.

She thinks maybe I'm her guardian angel. They have them down here, during schoolies week; volunteers to help the lost and the drunken, help them get home, get to a taxi, help them to stay safe. That's me, just like a volunteer offering to help.

I stare into her face, step back to appraise her.

She's not that hot. Hard face, big jaw.

'Good luck,' I say as I move on. I can hear her sway and shuffle behind me, on her lost way to who knows where.

I turn into Cavill Avenue, the busy, pumping hot part of Surfers. This is where all the lines into the nightclubs are, this is where you go to be seen, this is where the boys and the girls congregate and promenade to show off. I could be one of them. But I'm the one who's the most hot. I can feel the looks of the boys. Little boys. Idiots. Boys who like to impress with their stories of manhood when they're yet to reach adulthood. Boys with little brains and lots of ideas. Boys who think they can impress with the merest whim of a smile and the dumbest conversation. At times like this I can even feel nostalgic for my Arrivederci, the clumsy lover who I used in my escape from Rio.

I haven't had sex in a long time. I don't need it. I get all my thrills from the job. I'm getting them now, prowling through the throngs of boys and girls waiting in long lines outside the clubs, walking down the footpath in groups, crisscrossing the street, calling out to friends on the other side of the road. I'm surrounded by thousands of girls. All around me. They think I'm one of them. Another schoolie girl. They're smiling at me like we're all in this together.

But I'm the dark needle that's going to plummet two of them into hell. Keep smiling Starlight ...

I've found the first one. She's walking towards me. About seventeen, maybe eighteen. Long brown hair. Round sweet innocent face. Dimples. I'll get extra for a girl with dimples. She's in a group of others. They're heading towards the entrance to Sin City. I can't remove her from the group, not now. Too obvious, too memorable and probably just impossible; this girl wants to go inside and have some fun, enjoy the touch of some 'sin'. She won't come with me, not now. Not unless there's a wild fluke of luck and she has a big argument with her friends as they wait to get inside and she storms off. Alone. But what's the chance of that happening? Can't rely on chance. I know that. If I relied on chance I'd still be in the favela plucking old chickens given to me by a neighbour.

—

All the bouncers know me. I flirt with them and sometimes I fold a hundred-dollar bill into their thick palms. They think I'm a high-class hooker or a teenage madam; they've got no idea. They see me and they think sex. They see my money and they think I must fuck for it.

Doesn't matter; all that matters is that I can walk straight through, past the line, into the club.

And wait for my girl.

But tonight it's going to be special. She's going to be special.

As I'm walking past the line, hearing the cries of 'Why does she get to go in ahead of us?' I turn around and my eyes connect with my girl. I smile at her. As if she's special. She looks confused; is that hot girl smiling at me? she's wondering. I walk up to her, my eyes fixed on hers.

She's so hot. So beautiful and her body is almost perfect. Slim and great hips and long legs and really big tits. I'm prettier but she is gorgeous. I've done well finding her.

'Hey,' I say, 'you wanna come in with me? I don't have to wait, I can get straight in,' I say.

She's confused. Why me? she's thinking. Is this sexy chick a dyke? she's thinking. She's on fear alert: all the girls are on fear alert but no-one's worried about a sexy young girl. Only old guys or drunk angry guys. Dykes are a different matter; girls like this, they don't ever cross paths with dykes; they hear about them and sort of fear them but sort of wish they could fuck another girl at the same time. The forbidden. Girls like this, well brought up, middle-class Australian girls, they like to flirt with the unknown and the sexy thrill of dancing in the shadow. But I can see her hesitating.

'Hey, I'm not a dyke if that's what you're thinking. It just pisses me off about this line. You know, having to wait all fucking night to get in and have one drink that'll cost the price of a car. I saw you, couldn't help but feel sorry for you. Bring your friends.'

She's looking at me with a smile but she hasn't committed yet. There are so many in the line ahead of her and her friends; why did I go to her? Why me? she's thinking again; the curse of every hot girl who frets about whether or not they really are hot and worth the attention.

Not me: I'm stunningly beautiful and I know it.

Men have died over me.

'I dunno ...' she's saying while her friends are all saying: 'Come on, Tina.'

Tina. Like Tina Turner. Tina, soon you'll be mine. All mine. I sort of think I'm gunna rub my body over yours after I've got you under lock and key.

I lean in and whisper into her ear.

'Are you wondering why I picked you out?' I ask. She doesn't reply but waits for the answer.

'Because you are the absolutely most fucking gorgeous girl in this line and girls like you shouldn't have to wait.'

She's laughing now. I have her. She loves me, she loves my honesty.

'Come on,' I say. 'I know the owner, I get free drinks, I stay around the corner. Let me show you and your friends a good time, courtesy of the Gold Coast.'

And we're in.

Stay close, princess, and ignore the men. You're coming home with me tonight.

# 16

# Wonder Woman Takes It Slow

Cops love to hypothesise. They jump at it. As soon as they've got a crime, especially a violent one, they can't help themselves. They look at the victim, take in a few basic facts like where the crime happened or if there's an obviously suspicious connection and they go snap, gotcha. A lot of people get dragged into court on dodgy charges that way and if it starts to go awry with the intrusion of facts then some cops will falsify stuff to entrench their thin supposition made in the first place by a hypothetical that often says more about the cop than the crime.

Once they've got a hypothesis a cop will spend all his or her time working on the facts to bend them so they adhere. A hypothesis is like a one-way dead-end street from which you can't escape. The number of times I've seen a cop hang onto a hypothesis even though the facts didn't support it is huge.

When I ran my squad I told the detectives to beware this sort of behaviour. It's lazy and demeaning. Like the homicide cops who break the speed of sound to get to a crime scene, its pulse is so rapid that evidence, subtleties, crucial information gets lost or ignored.

I was taught to go slow, take your time, examine and observe and never come to a conclusion until it was screaming at you, in the face, with no other alternative. All of this was flooding back to me as I listened to Maria.

After Isosceles had told us about a girl called Starlight, she leapt up off the bed and started pacing backwards and forwards across the room, onto the balcony, as she talked herself into a narrow track of a hypothesis that grew through her own world view and experience.

'There was a big thing up here a couple of years ago; South American drugs being mailed directly to addresses in Queensland … what if this Estefan and his sister are involved in that sort of thing and the girls discovered what they were up to? It makes sense: Rio, the Gold Coast, this Estefan guy … the girls might have been witnesses.'

I thought about calling her an idiot, telling her to shut up, begging her to go home and let me do the work on my own. She'd paused and was waiting for a response.

I like Maria; she's a good cop. I was never this enthusiastically blind but I was a guy, tough and tall, able to use my fists and that made a difference. Female cops get it hard. It's a sexist world out there and sometimes guys like me don't help.

'Start with the actual crime,' I said, 'and work slowly from there.'

She stared at me, either not comprehending or realising she'd bolted out the gate like Wonder Woman.

'The murder of the two girls. What do we know about it? Focus only on that question and then let's take a slow step together and see where it might lead us.'

'So you think my idea about the drugs is stupid?'

Call me sexist but is it only women who leap to the assumption that mild criticism is actually a personal attack?

'No. It's just one of about three hundred possibilities and you lurched to the end without thinking about the beginning.'

'Okay,' she said, drawing in a deep breath. 'You're right. I've solved the crime and we don't even know most of the facts.' She turned to look at the wall. That's where my gaze was centred. Staring at a tourist brochure on the natural wonders of the Coombabah Reserve. Staring at its place on the map. Staring at two hastily printed digital photos of the dead girls that I'd taken this morning when I discovered them.

Initially Wonder Woman had wanted to jump in the car and zoom off to Starlight's, Estefan's sister's, place, an apartment in the Q1, the tallest building on the Gold Coast, the fifth tallest apartment building in the world at around a thousand feet. I'd seen it while I'd been driving around all day; it stood out like a needle-pin beacon.

I told Maria that Starlight could wait an hour as we gathered our information and tried to make sense of the disparate threads of missing and dead people. I needed to get my head across the scattering of events over the past day.

'What do we know about these two girls?' I asked.

'Nothing,' replied Maria.

'Not true,' I said back. I took a step towards the hazy digital image. 'They are young, older than seventeen or eighteen but younger than about twenty-five or -six. What else can we see?'

'They're both really pretty. Does that mean anything?'

I looked at their faces. Even though they were gripped in a frozen terror, their eyes locked onto the very last thing they would ever see – a killer about to squeeze out their life – the girls were astonishingly attractive. They both had a sleepy supermodel quality, luxurious long hair, big eyes, sensuous lips. Their bodies were curvaceous. Did it mean anything?

'Yeah, I think it does,' I answered. I hadn't paid a lot of attention to this fact when I first saw them but now, as I studied the dead girls, it became glaringly obvious, a point to note and consider.

'I'm feeling kinda creepy staring at them like this,' said Maria.

I understood what she meant. It *was* creepy staring long and hard, like a voyeur, at dead people. The longer you did the more they inhabited you and your dreams.

I checked my watch. It was close to eight.

'It's been almost twelve hours since the cops found them and still there's no ID.' I turned to face her. 'Unless we're out of the loop. How close to this investigation are you?'

'Johnston's partner said he'd update me as soon as there was any news.'

'That sounds tenuous; we have to be shadowing them. Give him a call, entrench his commitment.'

She did and I called Isosceles at the same time, moving away from her, onto the balcony.

'Developments?' he asked.

'Can you find a way of tapping into the official investigation? Like hacking into the head of CIB, Dane Harper?'

'With considerable difficulty. Isn't that what the gorgeous Maria is providing: access?'

'Maybe. That's sort of unreliable.'

'Are you talking about me?' I heard, and looked back into the room where Maria was staring, having hung up from her call.

'Unreliable?' She was looking offended.

Partners.

'Not *you*, the information source,' I said.

Holding up her phone she said: 'They still haven't ID'd the girls,' as if to say fuck you.

'See what you can do,' I said to Isosceles and signed off.

'What does that tell us?' I asked Maria.

Her eyes narrowed, not in response to the question but as a reaction to my treating her like a kid at school.

Partners. Especially when one is like a kid at school.

'It tells us they are being slow.'

'Stop being an idiot or I'm going to throw you off the balcony and into the pool.' Even though she probably wouldn't fit as it was looking like a schoolies version of a Roman orgy down there, bodies pressed hard within the water.

'You are such a fucking prick!' she growled, taking a few steps towards me. 'It's your fault we're down here in the first place and now you're treating me like a moron. Stop. I don't appreciate it. Okay?' She was angry, trying to level some breathing in through her nose and out through her mouth. I remembered the time we were lost and driving through the great wasteland of the scrubby desert in the northern reaches of the Noosa River. She got so angry I wanted to fuck her then and there.

I needed to keep a check on that. Maria was my best (and pretty much my only) friend's partner. My morals are questionable sometimes but in that regard I wouldn't ever betray him.

And it's not a good look to be fucking your partner.

'Telling us the cops are slow in making the ID tells us something about the cops. What does it tell us about the *girls*?' Best to ignore the rants and focus on the job.

One of the reasons I really like Maria and one of the reasons I know she'll be a great cop when she gets some experience under her belt is that she can abandon personal emotions in a flash.

'They're not local,' she said.

'Exactly. No missing persons reports to connect them to. Your earlier speculation about them being uni students is probably sound.'

'So that means there's a pattern.'

'Yeah,' I agreed, staring now at the photos of Ida and Estefan. 'With the exception of Johnston, who's a cop we put into the equation, all the players are from elsewhere.'

I stabbed my finger onto the photo of Estefan.

'Killers usually dump their bodies in a place that's familiar to them. These girls were dumped in a national park, out in the open. The killer didn't care about hiding them.' I was thinking out loud. 'That's because it's not his primary focus. Killing, that is. Unless he wants to taunt us. Unless he's about to commence a rampage and this is his opening shot.'

'It's a long way from his place to where the bodies were found,' said Maria. She was drawing a line with her finger, from Burleigh up to Coombabah. She was right – it was almost from one end of the Coast to the other. A hell of a lot of cars and cops and traffic lights and places to get caught over that stretch of distance.

Maria had printed a Google Earth image of both places – Estefan's empty boarding house was nestled directly under another national park. A perfect dumping ground right on his doorstep.

'Can I make a hypothesis?' she asked.

'Go for it,' I replied.

'The girls lived close to the national park, which is also really close to Griffith University. Which has about ten thousand foreign students.'

'And which is where Ida and Estefan are enrolled.'

Her eyes narrowed again. She was staring at a map of the university, which sprawls across a lot of acreage.

'When you mapped out the Sunshine Coast, that first time, as you were plotting the movements of all the dead girls, you told me it occurred to you it was a great place to be a serial killer.'

It was. Winston Promise took advantage of the vast landscape, full of bustling places and remote places, full of itinerants and backpackers, people who dropped in from elsewhere for a weekend or for as long as their money lasted. The fluidity of the population and the topography of the landscape with its mountain ranges and rivers and small villages made it a great place for him to operate.

'Doesn't it strike you that a university is just the same? A great place for a killer to be targeting his victims? Especially if they're from overseas? No family, no long-term friends?'

She was right and in the best style of police work she'd made the point not as a hypothesis but as a cold and accurate observation.

# 17

# Princess

It wasn't as easy as I thought. She wanted to go home with her friends but after a few more vodkas I managed to convince her to come back to my place. By then she trusted me and sort of looked up to me as a big sister. She was really impressed by the way I got her and her friends into the club, past all the others standing in line. She was impressed by the way I got them all drinks.

Of course I lied to them about who I was. I told them I was a schoolie, like them, from Perth. And when we got home Tina laughed and laughed when she watched me take off my blonde wig. She said she had no idea I was a brunette and she told me I looked prettier with dark hair, even though she loved blonde hair. She said I looked totally different, which I know anyway but it was nice to hear her say that; it made me feel just that little bit safer about the photokit image the police would put out of me.

I'm not so worried about the police. If they ever come knocking on my door asking about the missing Tina, I'll just say she came back here and then left. And she will, that's exactly what's going to happen. The CCTV footage will back me up, if they ever get around to seeing it, if they ever get that suspicious of me. But they won't, I don't think.

I've gone through her bag. Her name is Tina MacKenzie and she comes from a place called Coffs Harbour. I think that's down south, on the coast, halfway between the Gold Coast and Sydney. I'm not sure; I haven't really done much travelling around Australia since I arrived here from London. I want to visit Uluru. I hear it's haunted. I've been told that if you take rocks or stones that come from the giant monolith, take them away, then you'll be cursed with bad luck. Carlos told me about it. He said that every year the authorities get thousands of rocks and stones sent back to them by distressed tourists who took them home as souvenirs. I like haunted places. We have lots of haunted places in Brazil and one day, when I'm rich, I'm going to visit them all. I'll have a retinue of people, like slaves, who'll carry me and look after me and get me glasses of champagne and do whatever I want, whenever I tell them to.

Tina left her mobile in her bag, which is very convenient because I'm going to text her mum in a few days' time and tell her not to worry, that I'm doing okay and have met a really cool dude by the name of Daniel. Tina's on Facebook too and like me, she likes to keep lists. I found her list of passwords in her wallet and logged onto Facebook for her.

Later on tonight, maybe at about one in the morning, Tina's going to post how she got really drunk at Sin City and left on her own but, outside, in the busy street, bumped into a sexy dude called Daniel. I think I'll make Daniel come from Hobart. Anyway she's going to post how she went home with Daniel and maybe she's falling in love ☺.

I'll wrap up her mobile phone in a few days' time and send it down to Hobart. I'll find some random address where it will sit for ages, sending out its little signal so that if the police ever mount a search for her they will think she's run away to Tasmania with Daniel to start a new life.

But now I'm going to tape her mouth over so she can't scream and I'll secure her arms and legs to the legs of the bed, then I'm going to send her to sleep. Big long sleep, deep and strong. My little princess in the bedroom. Later, I'll take off all her clothes and oil down her beautiful body so it's pretty and gleaming. Then I'm going to lie down next to her and feel her body. It looks nice, not as nice as mine, but pretty.

But that's later. I have to find another girl first. Busy night for a busy girl.

# 18

# The Devil's Wedding

Q1 STANDS FOR QUEENSLAND NUMBER ONE, A TYPICALLY modest Gold Coast approach to the naming of the tallest building in the southern hemisphere. For a short time it was the tallest residential building in the world but Dubai now has that brilliant honour. Designed to mimic the Olympic torch, the Q1 is thin and graceful, if you're into skyscrapers. It dominates the skyline in a big 'don't mess with me' way. If there were more tall buildings around it, like in New York, it wouldn't look so out of place.

It was expensive. We didn't know what Starlight did for a living; Isosceles had been having trouble finding out very much about her. This caused him grief, making it impossible to ask his standard question when calling: Am I a genius? or, more often, his standard opening line: I am a genius.

I couldn't imagine a girl living in a million-dollar apartment in the most expensive building on the Coast was a uni student but if Ida's Shangri-la poolside apartment by the beach was any indication maybe I was wrong.

But I didn't think so.

All we knew about Starlight was that she was Estefan's sister. Which meant she came from Rio. Not much to go on when you come a calling, seeking answers to questions that are already based on thin factual data, like who were those dead girls and what was Ida's role in all this and what happened to the missing Johnston?

Her name sounded like a stage name or something chosen by an escort. Whatever, it was the sort of name that a person uses as a disguise, as a facade, as a means of presenting a made-up image to the rest of the world.

We were driving along the beach boulevard. For once I didn't need directions. The building was so tall it stood out easily. All I had to do was point the car and drive. Surf was pounding the beach alongside us. It was fully lit up by a series of huge tall lights, the type that are used in football stadiums for night games. The lights created a weird look across the beach – bathing the sand in a ghostly white illumination which spread out to the first clutch of waves. The light then faded, about eighty metres past the water's edge. Beyond was the swell of the Pacific Ocean, entirely black but for the tiny specks of white light that I figured were fishing boats out on the horizon.

For some insane reason I'd agreed to Maria's idea that we drive in my red Studebaker, instead of her boring Toyota. We drove at a snail's pace as the boulevard was dense with teenagers, drunk and yahooing and celebrating, spilling out from the cafes and bars, littering the streets and swelling onto the beach. I figured the huge white lights were a clever way of making sure none of them went drunk-diving into the ocean. It seemed to me that the lifesavers would be of more use during the night than in the day.

The Studebaker was a great hit with the teenage fraternity. We had lots of comments, none of them clever or worth repeating, from guys and girls. I was a cool dude, a toolie (which meant I was an old guy wanting to fuck a female schoolie), a rev-head and a bunch of other things. Sometimes – in fact most times when on a case – anonymity is the better way to go.

The discovery of two dead girls in a forest a few miles away hadn't had any effect on the thousands of teenage kids around us. Usually that sort of thing creates a climate of fear. It certainly would for their parents, wherever they happened to be. But not on the streets and footpaths and on the beach promenade, not with the schoolies kids. These kids were invincible, built of steel and muscle, with nothing to be concerned about. That's because they were a crowd. They'd come here in groups and stayed in groups which gave them a sense of security. If any of them strayed – and of course they would as the point of schoolies week was about individual growth through the rites of passage – then it would be different. But the crowd was providing solace and comfort and, I couldn't help thinking, a dangerously false sense of security.

I looked across at Maria as she sat in the passenger seat, staring out at the throngs of teenage kids. I wondered if she'd come down here when she left school, which wouldn't have been all that long ago. She was still in her twenties. Her hair was flowing freely now. No ponytail. She had the window down, to let in all the moronic music I guess. She was dressed in her standard white T-shirt and blue jeans. She looked hot. She looked like a model.

Watch it, I told myself. Stay focused, Darian.

As if reading my thoughts, Casey rang. I put him on speakerphone.

'Hey Bad Man, is my girl with you?'

'I'm here,' she said, realising her phone had been on vibrate.

'Where's the fucking Turkish bread, baby? I can't find it and I'm starving.'

—

A LIGHT RAIN began to fall as we pulled up out the front a few minutes later. Teenagers were spilling out of the building. Maria had told me Q1 is the most popular place for them to stay during schoolies even though the body corporate freaks out and tries to discourage that sort of guest in the mega-groovy apartments.

Mist blew in off the ocean. It connected with the rain and swirled into whirlwinds among the neon. The humidity was intense. It must have been at least twenty-five degrees, even at this time of night.

We walked inside the building.

—

LOOKING INTO THE security monitor by the front door of my apartment I saw trouble. There was a man and a woman down in the foyer, wanting to come up and talk to Estefan.

And me.

He was tall, really good-looking, in his mid forties I guessed. He wore a black T-shirt and black jeans. He was a cop. I knew it.

Next to him was a girl, a woman I should say. She was older than me but in her twenties. She was hot. She was a cop too.

They were asking if they could come up.

I wanted to fuck the guy; that was my first thought. My second thought was that I wanted to slice open his neck and watch him bleed out, die.

The girl I could sell.

'Come on up,' I said and pressed the buzzer to let them through the glass security doors.

—

'HELLO,' SAID THE man, 'my name is Darian Richards and this is Maria Chastain. Are you Starlight?'

Darian. He's here.

They were standing at my door, in the soft carpeted corridor. Was I nervous?

No. Amused. Delighted, in fact. It had been over a year since I had found myself in a trap and this was far from a trap. This was going to be fun.

'Yes, I'm Starlight. What do you want?' I asked.

'Can we come in?' asked the girl.

'Depends what it is you're wanting. I don't usually let strangers into my place and I'm sure you don't either.'

I was swinging on the door, like I used to do on the seesaw at the beach when I was a child.

—

THE DIFFERENCE BETWEEN a person of interest and a suspect is often said to be one who *might* be involved in criminal behaviour and the other who most likely is; the real difference is that you either have something on them or you don't. Starlight was nothing more than a person of interest. She was young, in her early twenties, maybe twenty-one or twenty-two, younger than Maria. She was extraordinarily beautiful and she knew it; confidence and playfulness oozed out of her. She was hanging on the door to her apartment, not letting us in, smiling at us, her deep gaze switching from me to Maria. She had thick, long, dark brown hair and dusky, almost golden skin. Her eyes were deep blue and sparkled with wit and delight. She acted like a ten-year-old kid in a mature woman's body with the cunning of a UN diplomat. She was half-hidden by the front door but she positioned herself so we could see that all she was wearing was a very small bikini.

Bikini at ten o'clock at night. Either she was going for a swim in one of the pools within the complex or had chosen to divert us with her body. I wasn't sure. I didn't care. Everything about her said danger. At her age I was nervous and unsure of myself, shy and embarrassed, eager to please and awkward. Almost everybody I've met at this age is pretty much the same, give or take a few additions and subtractions; the point is they don't normally radiate supreme confidence like this girl did.

The only people I've met at this age who radiated this sort of supreme confidence were psychopaths, devoid of empathy and completely assured of their genius. Maybe I'd led a sheltered life, albeit one within the confines of murder and destruction, maybe there were people like her at this age, at this point in the second decade of the new millennium, young people who didn't seem to give a fuck or betray any sense of concern.

'We'd just like to come in and ask you a couple of questions, about a girl whose name is Ida Faerber. Do you know her?'

A cold-call interview like this one usually yields little. Certainly not the slam-dunk, being a crim's confession. But what we hoped to gain was some insight; Starlight was the only person who wasn't missing. She wouldn't tell us the truth but we would, probably, get some feel for what she was covering or lying about.

She looked me straight in the eye and said: 'Of course. Estefan's girlfriend. You better come in.'

She stepped back and held the door open and we stepped in, onto a white-tiled floor, into a swank apartment with floor-to-ceiling views of the black ocean beyond. As I passed her she leaned forward and I could smell her, a waft of lemongrass and cinnamon from beneath her neck, from around her shoulderblades. Her body was glistening as if she'd been rubbing oil on it, and I noticed she was wearing lipstick – which I don't think you wear when going swimming in a pool – pale pink lipstick, and she whispered to me:

'What was your name again?'

As if it were to be a secret between her and me, only.

I stopped and stared at her. Hard and into the eyes. I didn't need to remind myself not to stray my gaze downwards, over her body.

'Darian. Darian Richards.'

'Cool name, Darian,' she said with a smile. Her body was just a little bit too close. I could see Maria, out of the corner of my eye, aware of this play that was going on. She'd stepped inside the apartment but I had barely got through the door.

I took a step closer to Starlight, invading her space, as much as she was invading mine. She was using her sexuality to disarm me. I'd match her and raise it.

'Thanks,' I said.

She didn't step back, as most people would have done. She didn't move. She held my gaze. She seemed to be enjoying the game.

'Not as cool as Starlight,' I said and touched her arm, just below the shoulder, and gently squeezed it, as if I was trying to make a pass.

I kept my eyes focused on hers.

She kept smiling.

I could hear the sound of agitation coming from behind me: Maria, no doubt worried that I was about to start fucking the suspect against the door frame. I'd explain myself to her later. For the moment the vibe was all about the girl in the bikini.

'Want to show me in?' I asked.

—

I DON'T KNOW if they expected me to lie and pretend I'd never heard of Ida. Maybe they did. I'm not so sure about Darian. He is smart, too smart. She is young and still learning, I can tell. Not him. He's not that old, maybe forty-five or -six, but he's been around. Be careful, I told myself. Ida said he was a saviour, that he was brilliant, one of the best detectives in the country. So, we'll see.

Long ago I learned that the truth is like a landscape of fields and hills and trees, a big landscape filled with all the elements of your story, and when a police officer or whoever it might happen to be asks you a question you look into that landscape and feel at home there. Stay within the boundary of the truth. Only, sometimes, you might erase a tree or a hill, a piece of information. It's not telling a lie, which is an active and aggressive thing to do, it's modulating the truth, moulding its landscape to fit your story. That way you never look as though you're lying and you're not, not really, you're just not bothering to see and talk about some of the hills and trees. Maybe they've gone for good or maybe they are just, for a little while, obscured by mist and fog.

'I haven't seen Ida for a couple of days,' I said. 'Is she all right?'

'What do you know about her?' asked the young woman called Maria. Dressed in jeans and white T-shirt. Good body. Pretty. Definitely a cop. Only a cop answers a question with a question.

'Before we go on, I think I should ask who you are. Are you police?' Cops never answer that question with a question.

'I am,' said the girl.

'And you?' I turned to Darian. He was all cop.

'I'm nothing,' he said. 'I'm just looking for Ida.'

'You're nothing? Is that right, Darian?' I asked, knowing full well he was an expert investigator and manipulator.

—

STARLIGHT WALKED ACROSS to one of the huge white couches. I'm no expert on furniture but it, and everything in the apartment, looked as if it had cost a few million apiece. She sat on it, crossed her legs and leaned forward, staring at me. I could feel Maria bristling at the body language this girl was using. She was already giving me attitude for the sexy face-off at the door, no doubt stunned by what she'd imagined was extremely inappropriate behaviour. The balcony doors were open and a hot breeze blew in from outside. We could hear the roar of the surf from a long way down below.

'I'm looking for my brother. Estefan. Ida is his girlfriend and I'm really scared that she might have done something to him. He's missing. Can you help me find him?' she asked.

'When did he go missing?' I said.

'Yesterday morning.'

'Was he with Ida?'

'I don't know. I think they might have had a fight and maybe they split up.'

'What were they fighting over?' I asked.

'I don't know. How come you are looking for Ida? Are you her brother?'

'No,' I said. 'Let us help you find Estefan then; tell us about him. What does he do?'

'He's a student. At uni. He studies engineering.'

'Where does he live?'

'Down at Burleigh, in some crazy old house that used to be a brothel.' She smiled at me then slowly turned to face Maria. 'The walls bleed with sex.'

'What does he drive?' asked Maria.

'I don't know, some sort of Toyota, a white car.'

'Do you happen to have the registration?'

'No.'

'Tell me about Ida,' I said.

'What about her?'

'When did you first meet her? And Estefan; how did he meet her?' Two questions in one; not the best approach to interviewing a person. Fuck it, I was rusty. I hadn't done this sort of grunt-level investigative work on a regular basis in ages. My last few years on the force were at the top level; I'd order crews to do what I was now doing. Maybe I could start directing traffic to reacquaint myself with the basic stuff.

—

So I TOLD them a really nice little story about how my brother and Ida were like kindred spirits, from faraway countries, alone on the Gold Coast, at the university, surrounded by all these people who grew up here and who spoke English and how it was hard for them because they didn't. Sometimes, I said, they really struggled with the lectures and the assignments because they didn't understand what the teachers were saying or what they wanted from them, and how that sort of brought them together, and how they were really in love for a while and would go down to the beach at Surfers and swim and how my brother would try to teach Ida bodysurfing. All bullshit but it sounded good. It sounded like a perfect little love story.

I'm not sure they believed it. Maybe the girl did. Not Darian. I didn't care. It sounded romantic. I like stories.

—

IT WAS A bullshit story about her brother and how he met and fell in love with Ida over shared embarrassment at not being able to speak perfect English at a foreign university. I didn't know Ida well but she spoke better English than I did. It wasn't just that, though; she told the story as if it were a bedtime tale. Her eyes were full of drama and poignancy. The girl was good but she still had a bit to learn.

And if she was lying to us about this basic fact then I knew she had more to tell. But I wasn't going to get any further with her like this, in this environment, with Wonder Woman by my side. I'd have to do it alone. Under very different circumstances.

—

LAST YEAR I'D dated a girl called Angie. In fact her real name was Rose. Angie was the name she went by as an escort. That was our relationship; I paid her and we fucked. But it was more than that for me. It grew, to the point where I thought, for the first time ever, I could love someone and actually have a relationship. It couldn't have happened while I was in homicide but I stood a chance, if I was willing, in my new life on the Noosa River. I destroyed whatever chance we had when I put her in Winston Promise's firing line and she was almost decapitated because of it. Since then I haven't seen her – I've stayed away, but I know she's around. Maybe one day I'll summon the courage to approach her. Rose was also a university student, up on the Sunshine Coast, studying writing. As I sat in Starlight's apartment, feeling the mist and hot air blow through the open doors, hearing the ocean far down below, listening to the girl try to fool us, thinking about how I was going to beguile her, I remembered a poem Rose had read to me.

It was called *The Devil's Wedding* and, coincidentally, it was written by a now obscure but then famous Brazilian author, long dead. It told the story of the devil who wanted a bride, a girl, but to achieve this he had to abandon his normal behaviour and appearance. He had to don the cloak of something else, in this case, a human form. He needed to remove and extract all his evil otherwise he wouldn't get what he was after: no girl would marry him. Horns, tail, cloven feet and bad attitude: all had to go. Successful in doing this, he then began to walk the land until he found the beauty he wanted. She fell in love with a guy she thought was a guy. Not the devil. It was more than beguilement he used, it was a transmogrification.

Being the devil he didn't have any qualms about what he was doing. I wasn't quite sure I felt the same ease in adopting the cloak of another persona and I wasn't quite sure if Ida would ultimately prove to be worth it.

—

THE BASIC METHOD of interrogation is to ask questions based on answers you already know and try to trip up the person with a lie. Once you get the first lie you're on a roll, you've got the wedge, you're in. It's a straight cat and mouse game. This was what Maria was doing, asking basic questions that were going to get us nowhere.

There are other techniques, the most popular being violence. I was taught that technique by an old-timer called Aldous. It didn't work, not for me anyway, and certainly wouldn't work on this girl. But there was another option.

Adulation.

# 19

# The Healing Game

'WHAT WERE YOU DOING WITH HER? ARE YOU MAD? YOU'RE trying to fuck a girl who's barely twenty years old *and* a suspect!' We were out on the road, walking across to where I'd parked the Studebaker out the front of the apartment building.

There was no opportunity upstairs to explain my tactics to Maria and I knew she'd take a dim view anyway so I just went ahead and did it. I asked Starlight if she'd take me onto the balcony; I wanted to see the view, I said.

'Sure,' she replied and stood and walked across to the open doors. 'Come on out, have a look. It's dark, but after a few minutes your eyes will adjust and you'll get to see the swirl of the ocean.'

I stood and joined her, leaving the gobsmacked Maria sitting on the couch, wondering if I'd gone totally fucking nuts.

We stood by the railing, seventy floors above the ground. I'd rarely been so high. I leaned in to her.

'This is all bullshit. I got roped into it by her,' I said, indicating Maria. 'People go missing every day. Happens all the time. Ida'll be fine. So will your brother.' Again I indicated Maria. 'She's freaking out. Pain in the butt. I just wanna have a good time.'

'No hassle,' she said, bemused.

Usually I've reached the end of a conversation with a person before I begin – I've figured out the dance steps and guessed how and what they'll do. You get to finetune this art after years and years of interviewing and interrogating suspects, especially callous psychopaths who are only thinking about themselves and how mighty clever they are. I zero in on the person's weakness or strength then juxtapose it with the circumstances they're in with me, then I apply either some flattery or some threat or some understanding and compassion. I haven't used adulation as a tool very often. It can spectacularly backfire on you. I've found it's best used on the vain female who's alone in life and who relies on her body and face to achieve her wants. Or, conversely, the plain female who frets about her appearance and thinks she's ugly. Less so with the latter because, sadly, you can only go so far before they doubt you with the drumbeat of their negative assertion that they are, really, no good, not pretty, ugly – therefore how could a guy be interested in me? They couldn't; it must be a ruse.

The sexier and the prettier the girl is, the easier it is to play with the fires of her ego. It makes them comfortable – they're on familiar ground; it's how they roll through life. I'm not sure which one of these afflictions is sadder. I don't care really – all I care about is getting them to tell me what I want to know.

I said things that I could never possibly say if I meant them. I guess there have been times when I wanted to say these sorts of things, to girls over the years, but never had the courage or maybe the commitment to utter the words.

I told Starlight she was beautiful. I made her feel important, as if she had, suddenly, become a focus for me. I made her feel as if I had suddenly, through her presence and beauty, found that I was revolving around her. I asked her if maybe we could get together later on in the evening.

Maria was watching me through the window like she was Mary Whitehouse or Fred Nile, all rolled into one body of astonished disapproval.

None of this would have had any impact on the twenty-something beauty in the bikini, were it not for the fact two girls had been killed and three people were missing. None of this would have had any impact on her – she wouldn't have even continued listening to me – if she wasn't somehow implicated.

She wanted to control me and I wanted her to think she could. Frankly it wasn't hard. She was used to controlling guys like me with sex and lust.

At the end of it she didn't say anything, just turned away and looked out to the dark ocean.

I touched her. I put my hand on her arm, just below the shoulder. It was close, really close, to her breasts. She didn't move. Didn't say anything. Just kept staring out at the ocean.

'Here's my number,' I said. 'Text me. I'd like that,' I said.

'Maybe,' she said. 'Maybe I won't.'

After I left she'd Google me, discover who I was. Then she'd either run and we'd lose a trail or she'd be tantalised by the possibility she could outwit me. I was betting on the latter. This was a young woman who liked playing games and thought she was good at it; she was, but I was better.

—

'YOU ARE DISGUSTING,' said Maria as we stood out the front of the Q1 building. 'I just don't believe what I saw. What is wrong with you?'

'She has more information to give and she won't be doing it while you're around.'

'So you fuck her to get it?'

Last year, when Maria and I worked as a sort-of team it was because I needed her; I needed an insider within the local police to understand how their investigation into the serial killer was proceeding. I'd cherrypick whatever information I got from her to use on my own private hunt. She was useful; I was using her.

This time around it was different. My job was to find a girl. The search had spiralled beyond that narrow journey, with two dead girls and a missing cop. Maybe I'd get to find out who was responsible for taking those girls' lives – I truly hoped so – but, as I kept on reminding myself, I wasn't back in the game. I didn't want to be playing the one-man police force down here; I didn't think I needed to.

Maria was, therefore, unnecessary.

'Hey, look, I don't need you and frankly, you don't need me. You go find your missing cop buddy and I'll find my missing girl. We can swap notes over a drink back in Noosa,' I said and walked across the road to where the Studebaker was parked.

I got in and drove away.

The street was packed with cars and kids. It was like driving down Chapel Street in Melbourne on a Saturday night: gridlock party time. Maria was walking along the footpath and had easily overtaken me. I felt like a teenage kid myself, fresh from a first love-struck argument over not very much. I turned into the first street I could find so I wouldn't have to see her striding ahead of me.

It was worse. The street was like a car park. Bars and clubs were full neon and music pump. If it could be possible there seemed to be even more kids on the street dancing, making out, vomiting, looking bored, restless, some trying to hail non-existent cabs.

The passenger door opened and Maria climbed in.

'You took the wrong turn. This doesn't take you back to the hotel,' she said.

I drove on in silence. I couldn't exactly throw her out of the car.

'Maybe I was a bit harsh on you back there,' she said. It was a lie but I appreciated the peace offering.

'Maybe I should have told you about my tactics before I embarked on them,' I replied. It too was a lie.

I didn't need her but I was prepared to put up with her. That's what I told myself, anyway.

—

AFTERWARDS, IN THE poem of the devil's wedding, the devil started the process of returning to normal. Time had passed while he was living through his new identity, pretending to be something he wasn't.

It didn't work. Not entirely, anyway. All he could muster were his pair of horns.

He'd changed forever.

# 20

# Arrivederci

I SAW PEOPLE DIE, ON THE BEACH, ON THE STREETS, IN THE slums, anywhere. People were dying all around me. When I went to bed at night I dreamed of fountains of blood. I'd cry in my sleep but my parents wouldn't come to soothe me. They were dead.

I had a name but in my dreams I changed it to Starlight. I had a dream: I was going to go to London and become a fashion designer. I'd be rich and famous and all the guys and all the girls would envy me. People would talk about me. Girls would want to look like me and guys would want to fuck me.

I had dreams but I'm not a dreamer. I'm not like those people who sit and wish. I knew that I had to do certain things to get where I wanted. Action. That's me: I take action. I'm in control. No-one else. No-one's gunna make anything for you. Only you.

So how does a girl get from the slums of Rio to London? How does a girl who dreams while she listens to the sounds of gangs and poor people get to become famous?

Use what you've got.

I'll tell you what I had. A body and a face that men would die for. I knew that from when I was really little. I've always been popular and I've always had men want me. Old men, young men, gang men, tough guys and idiots. Everywhere I went men's eyes would follow me. Girls' too. They'd think *I want to look like her* and the guys would think *I want to fuck her.* I could have stayed there, I could have been a gang leader's girl, maybe I could have run a favela along with him. But my dreams were bigger than that. They were as big as a star bursting all the way through the galaxy with its bright white light.

The Copacabana beach was full of pretty girls but everyone's eyes followed me.

I lived up in the hills, a long way from the beach. The beach was my target. I knew that it was where the wealthy people went, stayed in the big hotels and ate in the expensive restaurants and spent up on their Amex cards. Tourists, people who'd come in and spend big, then leave.

Most of the people in the favela never went there. They were afraid. They thought it wasn't meant for them. Not me. I went there every day. Searching, parading, waiting.

I'd walk or catch the bus. It was a long way. I'd always keep my head down so I wouldn't be seen. Girls like me could get picked up and never be seen again. Only when I reached the beach would I lift up my head and take off my shirt and my jeans. Only then was it time to be seen, to be noticed.

I wanted a wealthy guy to find me and I knew it'd happen. I'd checked out all the girls on the beach and I knew I was the best. I'm not being conceited or anything. You just know from how many people stare at you, follow you. I checked out the other girls. They were pretty and some were really gorgeous but I was the star.

The beach was long and crowded, like really crowded, so I'd hang out near the five-star hotels. They all had special sections for their wealthy guests and I walked around there like I owned the place.

It worked. I knew it would. Because I was beautiful. In a world of ruin and decay, a world of blood, a world where there was no hope, I had one weapon that would help me to survive and achieve my dream. My beauty. That was my weapon.

'Hey you.'

That's what he said to me. Well, I got that all the time, every day. Hey you, come on over here. Hey you, wanna fuck? Hey you. Cheap words that wouldn't take you anywhere. I needed a hey you from a guy with money and deep desire, a guy who'd be wanting to say hey you for a lot longer than an afternoon at Copacabana.

This time the hey you came from a guy who was hanging out by the pool of the Sofitel. An old guy with grey hairs sprouting across his chest and back like razors, his chest of bronze, oiled, his smile of whitened teeth, his hair black and slicked, long and in a ponytail. He asked me to sit with him and offered me a drink; later he asked if I wanted to eat with him.

He was going to fall in love with me. This was more than just a fuck.

And he did. He fell in love with me. Well, he didn't really. He fell in lust with me. Which is what I wanted. He had a black Amex and a passport.

My breasts were large and full. My body slim and brown. My hair golden and my smile genuine, full of love and lust and sex and temptation. His name was Arrivederci, which is Italian for goodbye, but he wasn't going anywhere. Not without me.

What is the art of seduction? I'll tell you. It's about smiling and opening your legs. It's about stroking his back and sucking his dick every morning as he wakes up. It's about dreaming of other things. And smiling while you do. It's about lying. It's deception. It's about the abrogation of your body. Let his wet hands mould your breasts. Just sigh and moan. Let his rough hands slide inside your vagina. Just sigh and moan. Let his bristly face scratch you as he thrusts his tongue into your mouth. Just sigh and moan. Sigh and moan like you mean it. Having trouble imagining you can do that? Here's how you get through: pretend he's Johnny Depp.

I sighed and moaned like a good and generous lover for my Arrivederci. I turned him from wanting me to needing me. I was good at that. He took me from the beach that afternoon when we first met and he fucked me like a stormtrooper in his hotel room that overlooked the beach. He even opened the doors to the balcony and I could hear the sound of the waves. He didn't tire of me, which was good, because I didn't want to return to the slum that night. I wanted to sleep in his bed with white sheets and hear the sound of waves and feel the hardness of his body.

He had an EU passport. He came from Naples. He was a gangster. I imagined that the gangsters in Naples were suave, unlike the gangsters on the streets and beaches and in the slums of Rio. Trigger boys on cocaine.

Sometimes Arrivederci would put on his sunglasses, so dark I couldn't see his eyes, and go 'do meetings'. He'd leave me naked in the bed in his room overlooking the beach and I'd reach into his bedside table and take out his passport and flick through the pages and imagine that one day – soon – I'd have a passport too.

Well, guess what? I did. I got my passport and a one-way ticket to Naples.

Italy. Part of the European Union. I knew all about that. Once you're in, you can cross borders without a visa. Once you're in Naples you might as well be in London.

I sucked Arrivederci for the last time in a squalid, dirty room overlooking the Bay of Naples. After he came he went to sleep. I knew his rhythms. He slept and I ran, passport in the back pocket of my jeans and ten thousand euros in the front. I caught a bus, a bus I was happy to catch, and sat at the back and watched as I travelled through Italy and then France and then down through a long tunnel. Into London.

Ten thousand euros can get you a long way. Ten thousand euros is twelve thousand, eight hundred and ninety-six American dollars. It's eight thousand, two hundred and ninety-three pounds sterling. Ten thousand euros is eighty-one thousand, six hundred and ninety-nine Chinese yuan. This is what it got me: entry into a fashion school, warm clothes, payment of a bond for a little flat in Earls Court and a month's advance rent and six months learning how to speak English. But I knew the money wouldn't last. That's why I had to get a job at Sainsbury's. It's a supermarket. Starlight, the check-out chick. Doesn't sound right, does it? Starlight, the aspiring fashion designer, the girl who turned heads on Copacabana beach, working at a check-out in a supermarket, being stared at by dumb customers and perved on by the store manager, who was barely out of his teens and had pimples all over his face.

I lasted two shifts, got a new job, as an escort. Posted photos of my beautiful naked body on the net and bought myself another phone, dedicated only to the business of providing discreet services to male customers in their London hotels, three stars and above.

Arrivederci was a clumsy lover. I didn't mind. He was a fumbling lover. I didn't mind that either. If the truth be told I hadn't really had any other type of lover. Nor would I. Arrivederci only ever ate kalamata olives dipped in seeded mustard. When he kissed me his breath stank of these things. When he smiled I'd stare at the tiny mustard seeds wedged between his teeth. I wanted to pick them out but I never did. I could blow him but I couldn't groom him. When I left him to his squalid little apartment overlooking the Bay of Naples I told myself I'd never eat an olive again or smear mustard on any of my food.

I'd changed my life. It was scary and sometimes, to be really truthful, I hadn't imagined it would have been possible. Many times I wanted to wrap myself up in my bed back home in the favela and pretend that my ruinous life was great, that I didn't need to make any change. But imagine if I'd stayed there. Would I be dead now? Probably. Would I be pregnant with yet another kid from yet another nameless lover from yet another night that could only have been survived through drink and drugs and sex? Most likely. Would I be here, on the seventieth floor of one of the tallest buildings in the world, living this amazing life? No.

Think positive. Embrace the new life that awaits you and forget about the old. That's how I got here and it's what I tell the girls. Sometimes I tell them my story, bits of it anyway, as an example of why change is so good. I have a really good connection to the girls. I understand them and I know what they're going through. When they first meet me they think I'm a monster but, really, after we've spent a bit of time together, they realise I'm not like that at all.

What does Darian think of me? I guess we'll find out. I'm not so sure I can control him. But maybe; if I can't, it'd be a first.

# 21

# Officer Down

FINDING A MISSING PERSON IS LABORIOUS AND SUCCESS IS NOT guaranteed. It requires a lot of man hours checking their last movements, witnesses and phone calls, incoming and outgoing. I needed this sort of rigour to deal with Ida. I needed a crew. In the middle of the Gold Coast I was on my own but I had contacts – or a contact. I needed to rope in somebody willing to help. I called Blond Richard from the car and asked him if he was hungry. I told him I wanted to take him to dinner. Always best to get someone to agree to something over a meal.

'The oldest joint on the Coast?' he said. 'Fuck man, can't you ask me an easy question?'

'There has to be an old burger joint or a place by the beach that's been around since the fifties,' I said as I drove.

'Nah, everything's been torn down. 'Cept the houses, lots of old houses.'

I like to eat in old places, places that are established, that've been around for ages; I like the idea that the kitchen has been in a family for generations, that the food I'm eating has been cooked on the same stove for over fifty years. I also like the smell and the feel of old restaurants. You walk into the Waiters Club in Melbourne and you can sense that people have been treading the same steps for ages; it's been there since 1947. I was starving, I hadn't eaten in twenty hours, it was late and I needed to get some extra muscle onto the case; Isosceles was ready to put surveillance on Starlight's phone lines, on Estefan's house and Ida's apartment – to check for people both coming and going and for any telecommunications that went in or came out. Estefan's and Ida's places were as dead as doornails but it paid to be thorough. Starlight's place, on the other hand, was going to be a revelation, of that I was sure.

'What about that Thai place?' suggested Maria as we drove past a Thai place.

'What about that Indian place? That looks good,' she said as we drove past an Indian place.

'Holy fuck brother, you know what's the oldest restaurant on the Coast? Dracula's. One of those crazy places where they put on a show at the same time.'

I'd already driven past it. It was a mock Transylvanian castle next to the casino. I guess that about summed up the Gold Coast.

'What about that Thai restaurant? It looks better than the other one we just passed.' Maria said. I kept driving. It looked like a theme park with fairy lights and waterfalls.

'Hey, I've got it man. Meet me down at the Spit, right at the very end, where you can't go no further unless you drive into the sea.'

'What's the Spit?' I asked.

'It's down past Sea World, you can't miss it,' he replied.

'I'll direct you; I know where it is,' said Maria, possibly the worst navigator in modern history. I sort of vaguely knew where to go anyway; I'd driven past Sea World when I was hopelessly lost on my way to Coombabah earlier that morning.

We ended up with takeaway pizza, sitting on the two single beds back in the motel.

—

'You Casey's old lady?' asked Blond Richard as he walked through the door into our motel room, which was bursting with maps and notes and photos, like any task force room.

Maria bristled. At her age I don't think anyone had ever called her Casey's, or anyone's, old lady.

'You know him?' she asked, reaching for the Napolitana.

'Everyone knows Case. Always has the best-looking girls too,' he added before taking a slice of Hawaiian pizza from the tray on my bed.

'But,' he continued, stuffing the pizza into his mouth, 'you'd have to be the absolute best-looker he ever scored with. Remind me to ring him up and congratulate him. How long you been a cop for?' he asked while picking up another two slices. I had the feeling that three large pizzas might not be enough. While I'm not a huge eater, Wonder Woman and Blond Richard seemed to be on an endless gorge.

Maria didn't answer. She was now looking Blond Richard up and down. He was used to that.

As a kid, Blond Richard didn't read much but he had read a book by Ray Bradbury called *The Illustrated Man*, about a guy covered entirely in tattoos, each one telling a different story that came to life. Blond Richard didn't have much of a life before he was known as the Knife Dancer; he was bored and frustrated and shy and awkward. For all of that he was angry. So he covered his entire body in tattoos, just like the character in the Ray Bradbury book, each one telling a parable from the only other book he'd read, Sun Tzu's *The Art of War.*

It was after midnight. If anything the buzz of the party around us had only intensified. The bungee jump had long closed up but the roar of the streets from outside and the din of the music from each of the rooms in the multi-storey motel was reverberating even louder, but we kept the balcony doors open to keep the room from becoming incredibly stuffy. Outside it was still and humid. Sirens could be heard all around us. Police and ambulance. Close and far in the distance, travelling in all directions. I've never heard so many police sirens during the day or night, except for when I was in New York.

—

'I NEED HELP,' I said.

'You want me to cut someone?' offered Blond Richard. I didn't bother to check Maria's response to that.

'No. Thanks.' I handed him three sheets of paper. On them were all the names and phone numbers and addresses from Ida's mobile phone, her Facebook page and the same again from Estefan's phone and Facebook page. I also showed him the list of names that I'd found in Ida's apartment, hidden under her laptop.

'That's a long fuckin' list, Darian,' he observed.

'That's why we asked you over here,' said Maria as she took the last slice of the Hawaiian pizza.

'You want me to call all of these people and what? Ask 'em when they last saw this missing girl chick?'

'No,' I said. 'I want you to go visit them, ask them face to face.'

He consumed another two slices of pizza without saying anything, just looking up and down at the list, as if he were thinking about what old records to buy for his collection.

'Isosceles is going through the Facebook pages and text messages of those who seem to be closest to Ida but, let me tell you: ninety-nine times out of a hundred, a case like this is solved purely by what someone tells you.'

'This is a big fuckin' list, Darian. And mate, these people are fuckin' all over the Coast, from one end to the other and even out in the fuckin' hinterland. I reckon I'm gunna need some help.'

'No bikies,' I said. Two gangs ruled the Coast: the Bandidos and the Finks. They ran all the nightclubs and tattoo joints and a few other businesses as well. Lately they'd been getting a bit of bad press. Well, worse press, as they'd taken to shooting at each other in public places like shopping centres. The Bandidos and the Finks had existed side by side with a clearly marked boundary line in Broadbeach. Each held their territory on either side of their DMZ. Blond Richard would still be floating around these guys although he was no longer actively part of organised crime – or at least I hoped he wasn't.

'Yeah,' he agreed, 'they do like to be noticed.'

'This is totally under the radar.'

'Okay,' he said. 'Geez mate, ain't like the old days when you were king of the eighth floor with all them crews at your beck and call.' He turned to Maria. 'Hey, what's your old man's phone number?' he asked as he took out his mobile.

'He's not my old man and he's got a business to run,' she replied as her mobile buzzed.

'Hello?' she said. And then the tornado struck.

—

A MURDERED COP elicits the same sort of response from cops as a murdered president does from American citizens. Everything freezes in a moment of shock and disbelief. Then, after that wears off, nothing becomes more important than catching the cop killer. And anyone who knows anything that might help catch that person becomes a major AAA target to be brought in, sweated and pumped for information.

That meant me.

# 22

# The Dance Card

SHE'D BEEN EXPECTING NIGHTMARES BUT THEY HADN'T COME. That troubled her more than anything. How can you kill a man and not be haunted by it? Maria had shot Winston Promise as he was running away from her. She'd pledged to herself that if and when they found Promise she would ensure that he was taken in alive. Darian, she knew, as did pretty much everyone in the Noosa Hill police station, was rumoured to have killed over a dozen men, cops and crims. She knew Darian would want to kill the serial killer who'd been haunting Noosa and she was determined to make sure he didn't.

He didn't. She did.

Did she have a choice? She replayed it in her mind, like a YouTube clip on repeat in a playlist, the final moment as Promise broke free and made a dash to the dark forest full of narrow estuaries and creeks that lay ahead of him. 'Stop!' she'd called, watching him run.

'Shoot,' Darian had commanded.

And she did. The crimson explosion from his back, of blood like a hundred ribbons bursting from a piñata, teased her in slow motion without sound every night. But Promise never came to her while she slept, never haunted her like the victims of murder that Darian had spoken of, like the six dead girls did, the ones who'd been taken by Promise, who had begun to creep through her dreams ... before she shot him dead and slept, exhausted, while Darian buried him in a moist hole four feet deep.

How can you kill a man and not be haunted in your sleep? Even if he was a monster. How, she wondered now, walking blindly through the streets of Surfers Paradise at one in the morning, among throngs of teenage kids in the carnival atmosphere of schoolies, could she have been manipulated into pulling the trigger when she'd been so determined not to?

She didn't talk of this to anyone, but a week afterwards, Isosceles, of all people, had sent her a random email about Charles Darwin. In an obscure passage from Darwin's writings, one that only geeks like Isosceles would have read, the great man had recounted his experience in going to see a puff adder snake in the London Zoo. Darwin knew he'd be looking at it from behind thick glass and mentally prepared himself not to exhibit any emotion, fear being the most expected. But when the puff adder lunged at him, Darwin jumped back in fright. He later wrote, 'my will and reason were powerless'.

Isosceles made no comment on the passage, but his point was obvious: when confronted with the actuality of the killer fleeing, her will and reason were powerless, as Darwin's had been. Maria did what she had abhorred, up until that moment, and shot a man dead.

She presumed Isosceles had intended to provide solace, wanting her to know that our primal instincts are beyond our control or, in other words, that she couldn't help it. *So why fret?* Presumably that was his message. If that was the case, it hadn't worked – in fact it only made her feel worse. If she harboured a primal instinct that could lead her to murder, then who was she?

Not the person she'd thought. More like Darian Richards, a renegade with a hero complex who broke the rules and did whatever he had to do to get what he wanted?

Order gave her life meaning – every morning she put on a uniform and went to work as an officer of the law. She was ambitious. She wanted to rise through the ranks and become a chief investigating officer. But at times like this, far from home and now with the chaos of her close friend Johnston found murdered – because of her – everything seemed to be unravelling.

After the call came through she had to get out, leave Darian and Blond Richard and get out, walk the streets, be alone.

'It's not your fault,' was what Chris, Johnston's partner, had said. He'd said it without prompt. Which meant it was on his mind. Which meant he thought it was her fault. She thought it was her fault, in fact she knew it was.

If it wasn't for her, she kept on repeating. If I hadn't called him, hadn't asked him to check out what was most likely a nothing disappearance of a teenage girl, a small favour for a local colleague, a friend. If I hadn't picked up the phone, he'd be sitting at home with his wife and kid.

She had killed him – of that Maria was certain. It was no use blaming Darian. It was her. She did it.

First the killer Promise, now the cop, her friend Johnston. Who exactly was she?

—

JOHNSTON HAD BEEN found in a ditch on the edge of Lake Serenity. It was on the other side of the Coombabah Reserve, pretty close to where the ocean and all its inlets and islands crowd the mainland. Lake Serenity was one of those places where modern and expensive housing estates were being built. An old guy who lived a few streets away had been tramping through the marshes to do his night fishing when he tripped. At first he thought it was a log, but as he reached down in the dark to push it out of the way lest he trip on it again, he realised it was soft and fleshy.

It was only two k's away from where Darian had found the dead girls yesterday morning.

—

SHE'D KNOWN DARIAN wasn't going to wait for her. Even before she turned her car into his driveway and saw that the lights were off, even before she knocked on the door and stood on his balcony with the sounds of the river close by, the sounds of the surf coming in from behind the small narrow island on the other side of the river, as she waited, before she climbed through a window into his garage and saw that one of his cars was missing, she'd known. He'd driven down to the Gold Coast without her. It was because he preferred to work alone, she told herself, but in her heart she couldn't evade the feelings of being, yet again, the girl who came up last on the dance card. The girl who couldn't find a date for the Year 12 formal at school, the only girl in her class who didn't have a boyfriend, the girl who friends forgot to invite over for a party, the girl left behind.

It was like that at work. She was always on the outskirts, watching as the others crowded around a desk and made jokes and swapped war stories. Her life at home with Casey, her lover, was great but she craved more. She knew she was attractive, although she would never admit it and was still wracked with anxiety about her body form and her hair and her complexion and her teeth and basically everything. It wasn't about that. It was about respect and being wanted by more than just one man.

Maybe it was selfish, vain, a hubris desire. Didn't matter; she was always feeling like the one who misses out. Only once, aside from when her whirlwind lover Casey circled her like a goddess, did she feel wanted, needed. Briefly. When she was at the police academy in Melbourne, learning the basics along with all the other year's intake of rookies. A young guy thought she was amazing, clever, skilful, also beautiful. He was dazzled by her intelligence and the ease with which she rocketed through the exams. He'd tell her, on the occasions she'd let him stroke her hair while they lay together, that she'd touch the flag, go all the way, become whatever she wanted in the world of policing. His name was Johnston Connelly.

Was it atonement she was after, for having been responsible for the death of now not one, but two men? She didn't know, and as she walked aimlessly through the narrow streets, ignoring the music and the push of people, she didn't care. She'd find the person who knifed her colleague, who'd slit his throat from ear to ear and folded his head back like a puppet's. She'd ensure that this time justice would be done. Justice her way, the correct way, the way of the law.

Not Darian's way.

She was smarter this time around. She'd learned from him. She knew to take it slow and work her way through the circumstances and arrive at the end point as she was stepping out of the beginning. She'd be ready for him.

Her phone buzzed. It was Darian.

'Where are you?' he asked.

'On the street. Walking.'

'Come back,' he said. 'We don't have the luxury of time to spend on remorse.'

She hung up on him without replying and, after a moment where anger seethed through her, turned back towards the motel.

# 23

# Showtime

THERE'S BEEN SO MUCH SENSATIONALIST PRESS ABOUT SEX slavery and the kidnapping of poor innocent girls off the street and shackling them in chains and then drugging them with heroin or worse so they become catatonic zombies and then shipping them off to wealthy fat Europeans or Indian billionaires. It's all so clichéd. I mean, sure, with some people it's probably like that but with most of us, selling the types of girls that we sell, it's pretty ordinary and like any business really. I mean I have to secure the girls so they don't run away but I'm really kind and I'm really nice. I look after them like they were my sisters. I tell them that where they're going they'll be treated like a princess. They don't believe me, not all of them anyway, but it's true. The way I work, I like to get feedback on my girls and know that they're doing well. The other thing is that I'm pretty choosy when it comes to who's going to take the girls. If I haven't done business with a buyer before, I make sure they have the appropriate means to look after them. You can't just sell them off into any home. I'm also really choosy about my product. It's like any supplier; if your merchandise isn't the best quality then it reflects badly on you. Bad for business.

Not that it really matters but I like my girls to be leaving me with a positive attitude. I want them to be excited about going to their new home. I want them to think about the upside: they'll be living with a man who adores them, so much that he's actually paid money for them. I mean, can you believe that? A guy who pays a lot of money for you? Why wouldn't he look after you, treat you like a princess? Why wouldn't you want that for the rest of your life?

—

'THINK ABOUT THE alternative, Tina. You get married at a young age, to some loser who might start cheating on you, you have a baby, lose all your independence. What I'm offering you is a gift. It's a platinum ride for the rest of your life.'

Tina's not really listening. Like all the girls, she just can't see it. She's crying a lot. I've come into her room with some pancakes which I specially cooked up for her, comfort food, but she won't eat it.

'Please,' is all she's saying, between her tears.

Please let me go. Yeah, yeah, heard it all before, Tina. Frankly, darling, get over it. I'm here with a peace offering and I'm making a big effort to try and help you.

'Please,' she says again.

Sometimes I can feel my anger rising and I want to hit the girls but I never do. I've done some meditation over the past year and I can control these urges. Take a deep breath in, Starlight, and exhale really slowly. Calms you right down, allows you to focus.

See what I mean about all those clichéd portrayals of evil slave-traders? It's just not how it really is, not in real life.

'Look, Tina, I really want you to think about what I'm saying. You're a really beautiful girl and you've got a great future ahead of you ...'

'Please, just let me go. I want to go home.'

'... it's not the future you had planned but believe me, this one is going to be better. You're going to be rich and showered with presents.'

'Please, my parents will pay you. They'll pay you whatever you want.'

I could write their scripts for them. All the girls tell me this.

'Okay. Look, let's make a deal, hey?'

Now she stops crying, now she sits up and looks at me with a sort of expectation, as if I've finally come to my senses. She's thinking that maybe she can get out of here.

'If you don't like it, after a day, maybe two, then you can come home. As long as you don't tell anyone. If you tell anyone, deal's off. How does that sound?'

She's nodding. She believes me. They always do. Any slice of hope and they'll cling to it. I love giving them hope. It's the clincher.

—

IN THE BEGINNING I didn't do any of this stuff. I used to knock them out on Xanax and parade them in front of the guys, sell them – they were barely conscious during the whole process and only when they arrived at their destination did they realise they'd been sold, out of the country or off to another state in Australia, wherever. Then they'd freak right out and beg their new owner to let them go, blah blah blah.

It got to the point where the guys would have trouble with them. Instead of just playing with their new princess, showering her with gifts, they had a basket case on their hands. A couple of those girls, in the early days, well, they got killed. They were just too much trouble. It was my fault. I take the blame for that. I hadn't really thought it through.

So after I had a few complaints and some of the buyers asking me if there was anything I could do to avoid the tantrums when they arrived, I decided to change the whole process.

Now I tell them straight up, just like I've told Tina. I tell them that they've got a new life and that they're going to a new home. I'm even really up-front with them about where they're going. Like with Tina, I've told her she's going to be living in Suva.

Of course all this depends on whether the buyer likes her. We've got a fucked-up situation at the moment, having to replace a girl who's already been sold with another girl. But I'm sure he'll like Tina. If he doesn't that's okay because I'll find her a nice home anyway. I've just got to focus on replacing the two dead girls with Tina and another one. I would have got the other one by now but that whole interruption thing with Darian sort of did my head in. I looked him up. He's cool. He was the ex-cop who made headline news last year up in the Noosa area, with that serial killer hunt. Lucky I'd given Tina a couple of Valium to knock her out before he and the sexy chick arrived. She's slept well now, only a couple of hours but she's sober and the tears are sort of drying up, which is good because I want her to look super-hot for the show.

Hopefully she's going to be a good girl in front of her new owner.

—

TINA THOUGHT: FUCK this shit.

Why am I putting up with a girl telling me what to do? This is seriously fucked up and I'm getting out of here.

By now the sedative had begun to wear off and she was starting to understand her situation a lot more clearly. This maniac of a girl is trying to sell me to some guy in Fiji? This is totally fucking insane. I've got to get out of here. I'm in the Q1 for fuck's sake, it's not like I'm in some prison. I can hear the sounds of the beach, I can hear the sounds of cars down below and sometimes I can hear the sounds of kids screaming with laughter. This is so fucked up. Being held prisoner by some psycho bitch. I am out of here.

Willingly she'd climbed out of the bed. Watched as Starlight undid her hands and ankles. They were really aching. Listened as Starlight told her to go into the bathroom and have a shower, dry herself and then rub oil all over her body.

And then come out naked, 'gleaming and beautiful for your new man'. As if. The streak of rebellion had started as a momentary thought, a daring admission to herself that she could, perhaps, fight back. Then, as she stood under the shower and felt the warmth of the water fall upon her, she became more and more emboldened. As if she was going to take orders from some Spanish chick who was only a year or two older than her. Fuck that.

Tina was eighteen and had never left home, never left the city of Coffs Harbour on the coast until two days ago. She had a boyfriend back in Coffs, who she planned to marry. His name was Aaron and he'd just picked up an apprenticeship with a builder. She wanted her first kid by the time she was twenty-one. Everyone told her she was crazy and that she was pretty much giving up on life by getting married and starting a family so young. She'd smile and say, 'But that's what I want. The other stuff can come later.' She wasn't sure what the other stuff was but it seemed to do the trick when justifying her plans to other friends. She'd been scared about going to the Gold Coast for schoolies but, at the same time, she was incredibly excited. It meant the end of school, it meant a week without her parents, a week of partying with the girls, going to the cool clubs as opposed to the gronky pubs at home, laughing and gossiping about their final year and the teachers and who they hated the most.

Girls' week out on steroids.

She could never have done it without her friends; they all piled into the Greyhound bus and took the long haul along the highway overnight. It was great fun, a real sense of freedom and liberation. She had her best friends with her; they were all staying in a motel apartment in Runaway Bay. It was going to be their last week together as a team, a gang, the group that went through school together – before they all parted and went on their separate ways in life. A time never to forget.

She climbed out of the shower, dried herself and put her clothes back on. Time to give this bitch the Coffs Kiss.

—

'WHAT ARE YOU doing?' I asked.

Tina had come out of the bathroom dressed in the same clothes that she'd gone in with. I'd told her to come out naked. I'd told her I wanted to see her beautiful body oiled and gleaming. I told her we wanted to show her off to her new owner. I told her I'd be waiting for her. I'd given her respect and allowed her to do this stuff on her own.

'I'm not staying,' was what she said in reply. She'd paused at the entrance to the lounge room, where I was waiting for her, sitting on one of the couches. Same one Mister Darian had been sitting on a few hours before. I'd set up my laptop on the glass table and told the buyer that his new princess would soon be on show for him. I told him she was excited.

I've only got myself to blame. In all the haste with finding a new replacement girl I'd forgotten about the stages they go through. I guess I pretended to myself that Tina would be accepting when, really, she has to try and fight back, try and escape, plead and try to bargain. All the sort of stuff that usually takes them a week or maybe two.

Still, I was prepared. Just in case.

'Tina, we talked about this. There's nothing you can do, babe. Please don't make this unpleasant or difficult.'

'You're insane. I'm out of here.'

And with that she crossed the room, heading towards the door. Well, she wasn't to know it was deadlocked so she had no escape, but I really had to take control.

'Tina,' I said, to get her attention.

Without stopping she glanced in my direction. Then she stopped moving.

I was pointing a gun at her. A really big long-barrelled gun. It's a Smith & Wesson Tanaka and its barrel is over six inches long. I use it at special times like now. I stood up with the gun pointed at her heart.

She was full of guts and bluster a second ago. Now she was sagging and staring at the end of the barrel. They always do. They always stop being heroes when a gun's pointed at them. They stop even thinking about being heroes when I show why my choice of gun is a Tanaka.

'Why did you let it get to this, you silly girl?'

'Please . . .' was all she could say.

'Shut up, Tina. Take your fucking clothes off now.'

She did as she was told. I didn't want to get angry but I could feel it inside me. I tried to take some deep breaths but it didn't help.

'Quickly, you fucking bitch.'

She started sobbing. Tears and snot running down her face.

'Lie on the floor, you little cunt.'

She did as she was told.

'Open your legs.'

'Wha–?'

I almost hit her on the side of the head with the end of the barrel. I crouched down over her so she couldn't move and grabbed her around the neck with my right hand. Claw-like, really hard and tight, like I was taught as a kid back home, like some guys would do to me when they wanted to choke me as they fucked me. Hard and full of muscle so she thought she was going to die.

'Don't fucking move,' I said through clenched teeth. I was really angry. I wanted to hurt her.

'Feel this,' I said as I shoved the gun barrel into her vagina. All the way in.

'Can you imagine, Tina, how that would feel if I pulled the trigger?'

She didn't answer me. They never do.

She was scared now but I needed to get total control over her. There was more to do. I needed a girl who'd obey me. I didn't need a girl who'd be thinking she could just walk out, I didn't need a girl who actually really *thought* at all.

I pushed the barrel of the gun in further and leaned down into her face.

'You a virgin, Tina?'

'No,' she said, although I could barely hear her. She was crying a lot. They always do. It's pretty easy to tell the difference between a yes and a no – a person's body language can tell you that.

'Then you'll know how to fuck, won't you?' I said, but she didn't know what I was talking about. I think she might have been more scared about being strangled to death although I'm not sure I could do that. Maybe I could. It takes quite a bit of pressure to strangle a person and while I'm pretty strong and have studied up on some martial arts I'm not so sure I've got that ability.

'Fuck it, Tina. Fuck the gun,' I said as I shoved it in further then pulled it out a bit. She looked horrified but did what I told her to; she moved her arse like she was taking in a guy. I chose this gun specially because it's got the perfect length and width. Don't think the guys at Smith & Wesson ever thought it would be used as a scary dildo, though.

I know how this feels. There's something about the hard metal of the barrel that really freaks you out. But I tell you, what's way worse is knowing that at the end of the barrel is a hole and it's not a guy's cum that could shoot through, but a bullet that would rip open your guts, tearing through the walls of your vagina and everything else down there. What you're thinking about is whether or not you'd die straightaway – you imagine you won't although I think, if you want to be scientific about it, that you probably would. After all the bullet would come out with such a rush and force that it's sure to blow you apart immediately. What you're thinking about is how horribly perfect the vagina is suited to the barrel of a gun and also what you're thinking about is whether, after it tears through that part of you, the bullet will just go straight up inside the rest of your body and fly out through the top of your head.

I dunno. One day I'd like to try an experiment and see what really happens. I've never pulled the trigger when I do this and really, if I had to, I'd be using the air gun pistol with a bullet of ice. I was told about that little method by some weirdo psycho in the favela when I was thirteen. He said it came from a book called *The Arabian Nights*.

Being raped with a gun barrel is pretty much guaranteed to stop you being rebellious. I did it for about five minutes while choking her. At the end Tina was still and sort of lifeless. Exactly how I wanted her.

I climbed off her, held the gun at her face.

'Now are you ready to do what I say?' I asked.

She nodded.

'Good. That's real good, Tina. Because we're running late. We need to get you smiling. You've got to make a good impression. You can do that for me, can't you, Tina?'

She nodded again. Good. It was working. She'd be doing what I said now. They always do. Later I'd be making her some pancakes and telling her how hot she is and what a good life she's about to have and how she shouldn't be scared of change, that a person's plans can change in an instant and that you've just got to embrace that sort of stuff.

Before I do that, though, I want to see the saviour. Darian. I'm going to put little Tina on show for her new owner, make sure he's happy with her, then put her back to bed for a good sleep and invite the hero over.

I'm gunna fuck him in the bedroom, right next to where little Tina will be sleeping.

# 24

# Nights Are Burning

It was nearly four in the morning. I hadn't slept, not because of the sounds coming from outside – the din of the cars down on the boulevard and the endless stream of teenage kids, all drunk and staggering home in rolling boisterous groups, the blast of sirens and the songs blaring from each of the motel rooms above, below and around us – but because I wasn't used to sleeping in the same room as another person. Maria had crashed about two hours ago, a mixture of exhaustion from being up for so long and grief and anguish after she'd been told that her colleague had been found with his head almost sliced off. She felt responsible. So did I. She felt guilt and it wrapped around the inside of her and twisted till it hurt. I didn't. I don't do guilt well.

It had been nearly twenty-four hours since Maria had rung me to say that Johnston had gone missing. Almost twenty hours since I'd arrived on the Gold Coast. Eighteen hours since I'd discovered the two dead girls. Sixteen hours since I'd found Ida's apartment smeared with somebody's blood. Three hours since we learned that Constable Johnston Connelly was officially a victim of homicide.

The cops, especially my old pal Dane Harper, would be looking for me. Thankfully the red Studebaker was parked in a secure undercover car park some distance away from the motel. Unlike Isosceles, who could access a person's mobile phone and track them 24/7, the cops would have to apply for a court order, go through the official channels. They didn't know where I was and they had no way of tracking me, at least for a day or so. In any event, I could go off the radar if I needed to.

The murder of a cop is hardcore and two years ago I would have done everything in my power to get the killer. Now I was withholding important information from the police: the blood I'd found in Ida's apartment, what I'd seen at the house at Burleigh and the identity of her boyfriend, Estefan.

But I wasn't going to contact them. I was going to stay low and finish the search. Do it my way.

I looked over at Maria in the next bed. If she was troubled by her dreams it didn't show; she looked serene, calm, as if she was floating on a bed of whispers. I've slept with girls who snore, I've slept with girls who wriggle and toss and writhe in their sleep, I've slept with girls who gnash their way through apparent nightmares, their faces twisting at the dark phantoms from the recesses of their slumber; Maria slept quietly, softly, as if the torments of the previous day had ebbed away into a faint and faraway haze.

It was quiet now. The teenage cacophony had slowly begun to soften around three. By three-thirty the last bursts of Kanye West, to the right of our room and Michael Franti, to the left, had been silenced. Even the street below us was quiet. I hadn't heard a siren since two-thirty.

It had been over a year since I'd felt the press of a woman's body against mine.

Pushing that thought away and avoiding another glance at Maria, I climbed out of bed. I turned on the bedside lamp and pointed it at the wall, which was covered with the history and geography and the characters of my trek to find a missing girl, now a journey into the death of three others.

Isosceles had sent us the names of the two girls I found in the water. Hannah Wendt, age twenty, from Norway, an international student studying engineering at Griffith University; she lived on campus in one of the dorms there. Allegra Michaels, age nineteen, from Italy, an international student studying journalism at the same uni. I'd recognised their names: they were on the list I found under Ida's laptop.

I was staring at their Facebook pages, flicking from Hannah's to Allegra's. Word of their death had started to seep; friends were beginning to post their grief. Their lives were starting to emerge in front of me and I wished they weren't. I tried to look away from the screen but couldn't.

Hannah loved skiing and had posted about the irony of living on the sunny Gold Coast. Friends had suggested she learn how to surf and she'd laughingly taken their advice. She had a boyfriend named Ethan. Met him at a local pub called Swingin' Safari, where he was a bartender, specialising in martinis. A lot of the postings were to offer him solace.

I clicked onto Ethan's page. Like my two dead girls and so many others the same age he hadn't made his page private. It was completely open for all to see. His friends had posted messages overnight expressing their disbelief and shock and compassion; I scrolled down past them to earlier posts, to the messages Ethan had sent to Hannah. Asking her why she hadn't turned up at his place.

Where was she? Was she all right? And then a message posted to all his friends: Anyone seen Hannah?

She'd been missing, according to her boyfriend, for well over a week, yet she was still posting herself. Ordinary posts about going to the beach and how cute is this dog?

Both Hannah and Allegra had been posting updates until the night before I got the call from Ida. *So many bodies. Only you can help.*

We'd added their names to the list that I'd given Blond Richard. He was going to start knocking on doors at six this morning. Not many of them would be awake then but he'd get their attention. A slow and careful process of asking each of the contacts on that list what they knew about Ida and Estefan, when they'd last seen them and what places they might be hiding out in, was hopefully going to yield a lead.

At the same time the cops would now be on the lookout for me. They'd be doing their forensics on the body and at the crime scene but all this had started with a phone call to me, and they knew it. I was their big lead. Getting me to talk, tell them everything I knew, which by now was quite a lot, would be their major priority. They didn't know where I was and I'd be trying to keep it that way until I'd found Ida myself.

They'd be hassling Maria as well – and while they certainly didn't know she and I were sharing a motel room a hundred metres from one of their bunkers, they'd be on the phone to her soon enough to find out how they could locate me.

Before she collapsed into sleep she'd told me that they'd get nothing from her. On the proviso I accompanied her to pay our respects to Johnston's widow, a young woman named Cathy. Against my better judgement I'd agreed.

—

My phone buzzed with an incoming text.

*wanna cum over*

It was from Starlight.

I got dressed and left Maria still sleeping.

# 25

# I Am the Law

THE FOURTH FLOOR HALLWAY OF THE MOTEL WAS SILENT, ITS carpet sodden and drenched in booze as I walked along to the stairwell. A teenage boy was by the top step. I wedged him to one side and he fell onto the floor. I could almost hear the squelch as he sank into the wet carpet. If he were face down he could die of either alcohol poisoning or drowning.

I walked down to the foyer, if that's what you could call it. There was a different guy on the front desk. He looked at me with a dumb expression, probably wondering what I was doing leaving at this time of the morning, or maybe thinking I was a toolie, out to score a flaked-out girl left on the streets. The toolies were notorious during schoolies week; I'd already seen a few sleazy older guys lounging around street corners perving on the teenage girls. Guys without shame.

I could see the Q1 from out the front. It wasn't far to walk; I don't know why we bothered driving last night. I walked across the road and down a narrow street. The place was empty except for a couple of council workers cleaning up the beer cans and other rubbish from the revelry. In a few hours' time the place would be thronging with the masses again, ready to hit the pubs as they opened.

I reached the boulevard that spanned the length of the ocean. The Q1 loomed up to my right. I walked along the wide footpath by the beach. It would be dawn soon. The sun's rays were already burning up from behind the horizon, casting their glow across the water. Kids were slumped on the sand like broken dolls.

I couldn't get the joyful images of Hannah and Allegra out of my mind; their happy stories of living on the Gold Coast, so far from home; the photos of them with their friends. The last post I'd read, before I logged out and left Maria sleeping alone in the room, was about their funerals. A debate had begun to emerge about whether they'd be held here, where they spent their last couple of years, and where they were murdered, or in their home cities, in Norway and Italy. It was a meaningless debate. The girls were dead. All that was left was for their killer to be found.

I hadn't intended to do anything more than find a missing girl. That was the gig. But it was turning into something else. I could feel the familiar rumbling of anger and determination inside me; to find the killer and kill him myself.

It's not exactly my best character trait.

—

I DON'T GO to funerals anymore. My first was when I was eight. An aunt had died. Her name was Dora, although it might have been Doreen. She was my dad's sister. I don't think he liked her very much but he dragged me along to the funeral anyway. We drove past the trio of depressing mountains, Disappointment, Despair and Misery, along the Western Highway, up to a town called Ararat, where he led me into an old bluestone church, hot and stuffy.

There were bushfires in the area. The fires were sweeping in from the Grampians, a nearby mountain range, and I can remember the smell of burning eucalypts hanging in the air.

People who I guess were relatives patted me on the head between sobs and the wiping of tears. My dad didn't show any emotion but he made me stand and sing the hymns and then drove me, in a long procession of cheap cars, all of their headlights on, occasionally cutting through the brown gloom of smoke from the bushfires on the outskirts of the town, to a cemetery where she was laid to rest. I asked him if his sister was going to heaven and he said it didn't exist.

My last funeral was for a cop, supposedly gunned down in the line of duty. Senior Sergeant Aldous O'Reilly was given a hero's memorial by his colleagues in Melbourne. Aldous had been a copper all his life. Stationed in Northcote, deep in the gnarled inner-city suburbs, he was a highly respected guy. Old school. Young cops would be told that to work under Aldous would be like a stint at police university, if such a place existed. You'd learn more from Aldous than a bunch of instructors could teach in a decade. For me that was irresistible. I put in an application to transfer to Northcote.

Aldous was old school all right. Schooled in taking the law into his own hands while blithely dismissing the actual law, he'd grown to relish his legendary status with young cops like me. He went out of his way to show us how it was done.

'Come 'ere, boy,' he said to me on my second day. He led me down a dark corridor, out into the courtyard at the back of the station where a couple of concrete cells had been built back in the late 1800s. Inside one of them was a scared-looking kid. Maybe he was eighteen. Aldous unlocked the heavy wire mesh door and walked in, gesturing for me to follow.

'This is Dennis,' said Aldous as the kid backed himself into the far wall.

'Dennis likes to break into people's houses, don'cha, Dennis?'

The kid didn't respond. He was terrified.

'Dennis and me, we've had a few conversations in the past, about the shortcomings in his behaviour, haven't we, Dennis?'

The kid said nothing but his gaze darted from the ageing, threatening cop to me.

Help, said the look.

But what was I to do? I was there to learn. Watch, listen and learn. Better than a decade of police instructors.

'But Dennis doesn't seem to be listening. Do you, Dennis?'

Aldous took a step towards the kid and pumped his fist into a tight ball of muscle and bone. It was early in the morning and the sunlight had just begun to cast a glaze of light into the cell. It washed over the kid's bare feet.

'So the object of the exercise today, Darian, is to figure out a way in which young Dennis here will listen.' He turned to me. 'You're a bright, ambitious boy. You got any ideas?'

The atmosphere was becoming pretty tense. The kid was starting to bend in on himself, knowing that he was soon going to be hurt. With every inward flinch of anticipation from the kid came a matching snort of breath, ripple of muscles, grinding of teeth from Aldous.

I didn't say anything. I was beginning to sweat myself. If this was a lesson I wasn't enjoying it and I knew I was sure as hell going to fail.

'Well I do,' said Aldous. 'I've got an idea. It's called: break this little cunt's head open to see if we can penetrate the thick wall of stupidity and let his fried brain see if it can hear the message. What do you think, Richards? You think that's a good idea?'

The kid was starting to whimper. He was a repeat offender. Had probably burgled about thirty homes in the area. He wasn't going anywhere in life but to prison cells, with the occasional holiday back into the world without cells, where he'd smack down a window or a door, rob a place of a TV set or something equally trivial, get picked up and sent home again, home to his real world of incarceration. He was a loser with no hope but I didn't think he deserved to be brutalised by a cop who knew better.

'I'm not sure, sir,' I replied.

I could have told him I fucked his sister for breakfast and his mum for lunch.

'Not sure? I am. Richards, I am. Because nothing else works with scum like this. They don't give a fuck about us, about normal people. They play it their own way and they just don't care. Ain't that right, Dennis? So every now and then we gotta remind them that it's not the way of the world. You ever try and talk to scum like this? Forget it. I have. Haven't I, you little fuckin' cunt? Did you listen? Nah, 'course you didn't. So what's left, Richards? You tell me. What's left?'

What could I say? I said nothing.

'Break his head open,' he ordered.

'What?'

'You heard.'

'I can't do that.'

'Yes you can. Go over to the little cunt, grab his fuckin' head and smash it, smash it against the brick wall. Hard as you can.'

'That's against the law, sir.'

'Don't fuck with me, boy. You want to be a policeman? Do what I say. I am the law.'

—

THERE'S A PSYCHOLOGICAL test, which was banned some time in the 1970s. It's called the Milgram experiment. A person would sit at a machine that had a set of dials, from one to ten. Above the machine was a screen with a video feed into the next room, where an actor was strapped to a chair. The instructor, the person who ran the experiment, would ask the actor a series of questions. If they got the answer to a question wrong he'd instruct the person by the machine to turn one of the dials. Each dial represented a level of voltage of electricity. One meant pain. Ten meant death. The person seated by the machine knew that ten was a fatal electrocution. He or she knew that every increase in the turn of the dial meant greater pain for the person on the other side of the wall.

The deal was that the actor would deliberately give wrong answers and the instructor would tell the hapless person at the dials to give a corresponding punishment. As the dial crept closer to ten the subject of this experiment would become increasingly agitated, knowing they were inflicting increasing pain on the other person. Screams and yells were added in for good theatrics. As the person on the dial began to protest, the instructor's job was to yell and shout, intimidate by any means, so that eventually the subject would hit the ten dial and, as far as they knew, kill the person in the next room.

The experiment was a great success. Pretty much everyone argued, howled, wept and cursed at the instructor, trying desperately not to hit the ten dial and cause death to another person because they were answering questions wrongly.

But most of them did it.

As I stood in the cell with Aldous angrily beckoning me to break open the kid's head, I thought about that experiment. I knew of it because I'd briefly dated a girl called Jacinta, a psychology student at La Trobe University. She'd come home one night, shaken and horrified because, obeying the instructor, she'd let herself inflict extreme pain on another student in an experiment in class that afternoon.

I consoled her but the knowledge that she had it in her stayed with her forever.

'Just fuckin' do it,' commanded Aldous.

And I did. I stepped across the hard concrete floor, grabbed the kid up by his hair and smashed the side of his head into the wall. Blood oozed from under his hair and he went limp under me, collapsing by my feet.

'Good boy,' said Aldous, pleased.

How did I feel? Great. One of the gang. A tough guy. A guy who could be trusted. I'd passed a test, a lesson, I was one of them.

Many years later, though, I stood up to Aldous. He was the first guy I killed and his funeral was the last I ever went to.

—

IT HAD JUST gone five in the morning and I was standing outside the Q1 building. I pressed the buzzer to Starlight's apartment.

The front door latch opened straightaway.

# 26

# The End of the World

CARLOS WAS FEELING SORRY FOR HIMSELF. HE'D SPENT THE night in various bars, drinking beer and tequila, shooting pool and eyeing the young girls who were on their schoolies binge. He was going to stay in the bar until it closed, which wouldn't be until dawn, but on an impulse he'd decided to follow one girl, a blonde who wore a tight yellow dress that showed a lot of leg. He'd been staring at her, falling in love with her. He wanted to go and talk to her but knew his words would come out in a terrible slur. Not a cool look.

When she got up to leave, he did too. Impulse. He was like that; he liked to act on impulse.

He followed her out of the bar. She was on her own, which was unusual. Most of the schoolies girls came in packs, like the gangs back in the favela. He was pissed and almost crashed into a table as he walked behind the blonde girl in the yellow dress. The guys at the table yelled at him as their beers fell to the floor. By then the blonde girl was walking down the stairs that led out of the bar and onto the street, which would be packed with kids. Carlos almost had to run to catch up.

Outside it was hot and the place was swirling. He'd had a lot to drink and was walking in circles as he tried to keep pace with the girl in the yellow dress. He kept his gaze on her behind, just where the line of the dress finished and her legs were revealed as he followed her. She was moving briskly as she walked through the mall. He felt sick from too much beer and not enough tequila. Every now and then he'd bump into someone but he never lost his balance, never fell over. Her retreating body in yellow was like a beacon for him. Stay focused on her, stay close behind and don't deviate from the path. Although he was weaving as he walked his gaze remained hard and sharp.

He'd been staring at her in the bar as he thought about the girls in the house. He kept replaying the moment where he drew out his knife, a long thin steak knife, and pierced them, bled them out, one by one. He had learned how to do this when he was sixteen. One of the gang members taught him. It was part of the ritual initiation process. He liked doing this to his girls – he liked to watch as the energy drained from their eyes.

He was angry with his sister. She'd shouted at him and told him he was an idiot. Then she started to shut him down. She told him to vacate the house in Burleigh, told him to leave behind his phone, told him to stay low. Where? How? There was no place to sleep, all the hotels and motels were full. Did she expect him to sleep on the beach? And then, at about three in the morning, he'd gone to an ATM to take out more money but his card was denied. All his cards were denied. She'd done it. She'd set his cards up, she'd done everything for him and now, because she was angry with him, she'd begun to punish him. Cut him off, shut him down. He needed to be independent. He needed to strike out on his own. The more he thought about his cards being denied the more the rage built up. He kept staring at the girl in the yellow dress as she walked through the crowds of kids, walked with purpose as she turned the corner onto the boulevard that ran alongside the beach. Good, he thought, she was walking away from the busy part, heading in the direction of darkness and fewer people on the streets and footpaths.

His anger began to find a direction: he would take the girl in the yellow dress and slash her, slice her open. Then, afterwards, go to his little sister's big motherfucking apartment up there on the seventieth floor.

All his life she'd been bossing him around. He couldn't recall much about his parents. He remembered the side of his father's face, seen from an angle. Down, low, the angle of a kid. Looking up. But his dad never seemed to be looking at him. Carlos had no memory, none whatsoever, of his father's eyes. Nor of his mouth. Only the curled edges of his lips. Seen from an angle, down and low. The old guy had died soon after his sister was born, when he was four or maybe he would have been five. He couldn't remember. His first memories were of an empty house and a baby crying. Actually the real first memory was of hunger. He just happened to be in their empty house with his little sister crying. He figured she was hungry too. He went into the streets and started to ask people for food. They gave it to him. The favela was a friendly and loving neighbourhood when you were really little. It only got tougher as you got older.

He didn't know how his parents died. People said it had something to do with the gangs and all the relentless fighting over drugs. Maybe. He didn't really care. They just weren't there. He couldn't even remember his mother. There weren't any photos of them so he imagined his mother looked like Pamela Lee Anderson, who was a big hero with the guys as he was growing up.

It should have been up to him; he was the man. But his little sister took over and started to boss him around. She was clever and Carlos got to understand that if there was any chance of escaping the favela and travelling to a new world, a world where he could do what he wanted and make lots of money and live without fear, a world where he'd be tough and people would remember him, then he'd have to follow her. She was always going to be leaving the favela.

Now he was safe in this new world and people were looking up to him, people were remembering him, like the girl in the yellow dress was about to, like the girls he'd floated off into the stream two days ago, like the cop who'd appeared in the middle of the night and said, 'Hey, who are you?', like Ida and now, like his sister.

'Hey, who are you?' the cop had asked.

'I'm Carlos and I am the end of the world for you.'

—

THE GIRL IN the yellow dress thought there was somebody following her. As she walked further and further away from the noise and partying of Surfer's, towards the ocean-view apartment she'd rented with her best friend, about a kilometre up the road in a more quiet and lonely part of the strip along the beach, she heard the drum beat of footsteps behind her. Slow, steady, the sound of someone following.

She stopped and turned to look behind her. A guy who resembled that Latin American movie star, the guy who was in one of the *Zorro* films, was approaching. Sexy. Drunk. Leering. Was he in the same bar she'd just left? Was he the guy who kept staring at her? Yeah, definitely.

Her name was Margaret and she was seventeen. She lived in Brisbane and wanted to be a vet and work with horses. The guy got closer. She could smell the booze on him.

He stopped and stared at her with a big grin. He wasn't quite so sexy up close. He was scary.

'What do you want?' asked Margaret.

'Hey. I'm Carlos and I'm the end of the world,' he said.

# 27

# The Scorpion and the Frog

SHE'D DRESSED FOR THE OCCASION: A THIN PINK COTTON shirt that barely reached down to her legs. Four of the middle buttons were done up, the rest open. Nothing underneath. The shirt flowed and revealed a lot but not everything. It was tease and flirt in cotton. I was reminded of the Dylan lyric about the guy in a topless bar who had to turn away when the girl bent down to do up his shoelaces. Her outfit was designed for maximum effect; to make me look away in embarrassment lest I see her breasts or between her legs but at the same time to make me stare so I could see her breasts and between her legs. It was worn to set me on a tumble, disarm me, enthral me.

'Hi,' she said at the door. 'I wasn't sure if you'd come.'

'Why's that?' I asked as she held the door open for me to walk in. The place looked the same but there was a different feeling to it. I'm not into vibes or anything but you can tell when a room gives you a sinister odour. Or maybe it's the person who's inhabiting the room. I looked closely at her. She seemed drunk. Her eyes were wide open, spacey. She was smiling as if she had a secret.

'Flirting with the devil,' she replied.

'The devil? Is that what you are?'

'Maybe you'll find out,' she said.

She leaned towards me and kissed me lightly on the cheek. Let her body press against me, just for the merest of seconds.

'So what have you been up to this evening?' she asked, walking across to the open kitchen area.

'I've been looking for my missing girl and tracking the hunt for the person who killed two other girls yesterday.'

'Those ones who were found at Coombabah? Floating in the water?' she asked.

'Them. They went to the same university your brother goes to; I wonder if he knew them.'

She shrugged. 'Drink?' she asked, holding up a bottle of vodka. It was almost empty.

'Black coffee,' I replied.

'Have a drink with me,' she said, pulling out two glasses and placing them on the bench.

'I don't drink,' I said.

'Where's the fun in that?' she said as she poured the vodka into both the glasses.

I didn't answer. I was scoping the room. The couch looked messed up and the carpet had been moved since I was last there. I could smell a flowery kind of incense or maybe it was one of those oils you burn over a candle.

'What about you?' I asked. 'What's been happening here over the past few hours?'

'Not much,' she said as she walked towards me with the vodkas. Straight, no ice. Another button of her shirt had been loosened. As she leaned down to hand me the drink her breasts were easily exposed.

'Any word on your brother?' I asked.

'Nothing. Any word on your Ida?'

'Nothing. Yet. But I'll find her today.'

'How?'

'We're tracking her,' I said. I put the vodka down on the coffee table and left it there. I used to be a big drinker and vodka was my hit for the morning, before I cleaned my teeth or had a shower. I don't do that sort of stuff anymore. She knew, of course; it's not hard to spot and she'd be trying to get me to break and knock it back. But I'd rather be drinking rattlesnake venom.

'We're tracking everyone,' I said.

'My brother too?'

'Yep. Him too.' It was a lie but she wouldn't know that.

'So Mister Darian – I read all about you,' she said as she sat back at the other end of the couch, the drink in her hands, and crossed her legs.

It was a Sharon Stone moment. My cue to look between her legs and stare at her magnificent pudendum in all its glory, be magnetised and transfixed. In other words, cunt-struck.

If she was upset that I didn't oblige, she didn't show it. She might have laughed. She was certainly amused.

She didn't cover herself.

'Tell me what it's like to hunt a serial killer,' she said, sipping the drink.

'Tedious,' I said. 'But it's okay when you get to the end and put a bullet in their head so you know their operation has been shut down for good.'

'Is that what you did? You killed him? I read that he's still at large, although there haven't been any reports of similar types of killings.' She leaned forward and for the first time seemed excited, as if the game, the strategy, had been forgotten; she was intrigued by the unexpected.

'No, I didn't kill him,' I said. 'But I'm not expecting him to re-offend. You mind if I get up and make myself a coffee?'

'Stay,' she said and placed her hand on my arm. Didn't move it away. 'Tell me what's important about this Ida for you. Maybe I can help.'

'She's missing,' I said.

'So are a lot of girls. Why her? You're not related. Is she your friend? Or maybe you're a hero, a kind of warrior, like Clint Eastwood.'

'Yeah, the good, the bad and the ugly: that's me. All three.'

'Well,' she said, 'maybe the good, maybe the bad. Not the ugly, Mister Darian. Certainly not the ugly.'

Dreamy eyes. Fuck time.

'Your brother's house, in Burleigh, it's big; I mean, there are a number of bedrooms. Who was living there with him?'

She shrugged.

'Never been there,' she replied.

'But the lease is in your name. You pay for it.'

She sat back. 'Is this an interrogation?'

'Questions, Starlight. That's all. You've got a missing brother, I've got a missing girl. Tell me about the house.'

'Tell me about the Train Rider,' she said. It was a dumb way of trying to disarm me. The Train Rider was a notorious snatcher of girls in Melbourne. He'd ramped up to snatching *and* killing. He was up to number eighteen. He was the guy I could never catch, one of the reasons I decided to resign years ahead of time.

'He's a bad guy. One day he'll get taken down. They always do.'

'Always?'

'Always.'

'By you?' she asked.

'Not necessarily. I've retired.'

'Ha,' she laughed. 'Retired? Not from where I'm sitting.' She reached across to my drink and sculled it in one hit. 'Do you think I'm hot?' she asked.

'Too hot for me.'

I refocused the conversation: 'I'm not the police so I don't do arrests anymore. I just do what I need to. In this case find a girl. I wouldn't mind finding the killer of the other girls and the cop either but frankly I'm not that fussed about that. The local cops are good down here and they'll sort it out. Eventually. Tell me where your brother is and tell me what you know about Ida.'

'And I thought this was going to be a fun time. You're boring, Mister Darian.'

'Sorry to disappoint you, Rosalita.'

She'd got up off the couch and was walking towards the kitchen, for another bottle of vodka, no doubt. She stopped, her back to me, and I heard her laugh.

'Now that is impressive.' She turned around to face me. 'I haven't heard that name for a long time.'

'Since London?' I said.

'No. Good guess, though. Before London.'

She undid the rest of the buttons on her shirt and let it slide from her body. She was, as she well knew, drop-dead gorgeous with a truly amazing body. Guys would go to war over her and I guess some already had.

'Tell me this, Darian: who would you like to fuck this morning? Starlight or Rosalita? It's an interesting choice because they're both very different.'

—

I WAS PLAYING a dangerous game. It's legal for undercover cops to use sex as a means to establish their bona fides. It became a bit of an issue in the UK recently when a copper snuck into a radical green movement, seduced a woman, had sex and fathered a child with her. Only, of course, to leave both her and the kid when the operation was over. I don't know how he dealt with it afterwards but, according to the newspaper reports, the ex and the kid weren't exactly doing too well. It's all based on betrayal and betrayal leaves a deep and nasty pain. Not really erased through time, only through vengeance.

I wasn't concerned about breaking Starlight's heart. I wasn't sure there was one to break. What did concern me was: who was seducing who? I had to remind myself that I was here to achieve something in the hunt for Ida and the killers of the girls and Johnston. Everything was linked and it all connected back to Starlight's brother and, I knew, to Starlight herself. She hadn't invited me into her apartment to watch the dawn and sneak sly glances at her naked body; I was there because I was an investigator and that meant she was involved. I might be vain but I'm not deluded into thinking that I'm sexy enough for a gorgeous twenty-year-old to swoon and say: fuck me now.

This level of calculation and willingness to use herself was unusual. I've been in the company of killers and psychopaths who use their wiles to seduce you into thinking how clever or innocent they are; none though who were this young and few who were women.

I was working overtime not allowing myself to be captured or beguiled by her. The truth was Starlight was unbelievably sexy and she was available. One part of me wanted to lie with her and fuck her; the other part, the guy on active duty, was sending warning bells and trying to focus on the job of finding Ida. I wasn't sure which one was going to win.

I got up and crossed over to her. Held her by the arms and stared into her eyes. Windows to the soul? Give me a break; windows to a dead space. 'Ever heard the story of the scorpion and the frog?' I asked.

'No. What's that?'

'You'll like it. The scorpion walked to the edge of a river. Wanted to cross to the other side but he couldn't swim. He saw a frog, nearby and said, "Take me over," but the frog said no. "Why?" asked the scorpion. "Because you'll sting me and kill me," said the frog. "Why would I do that?" asked the scorpion. "That'd be stupid. If I did that I'd sink along with you and I'd die too." Makes sense, thought the frog and agreed to take him. The scorpion climbed on his back and off they went. Halfway across the river the frog felt a terrible sting and as he started to sink, dying from the scorpion's poison, he said: "Why? Why did you that?"

'"Because that's what I am," replied the scorpion. He couldn't help himself.'

'That's me then?' she asked. 'A scorpion?'

'No,' I said. 'It's me.'

# 28

# Sounds of Silence

THE FIRST SOUND I HEARD WAS A WHIMPER, COMING FROM one of the bedrooms in the apartment. The second sound I heard was a click, coming from behind my ear.

—

AS I LAY on the floor of the bedroom, feeling the ooze of blood on the side of my head, trying to get my bearings, I remembered an elderly firefighter telling me that in the old days, before the firehouse clangers were replaced by computer-generated drones, he'd actually hear, for a split second, the tiny hammer jerk backwards before it started pummelling the round brass bell that signalled a fire. He could be asleep and he'd wake in that split second before the bell went off. The last sound of a silence; that's what I should have been listening for, before I turned around too late, to see the silver gleam of a pistol crash down on my forehead.

Dumb, really. I've been shot, knifed, punched, kicked, beaten with a hammer, even tasered and each time I've vowed to myself that I'll be more alert, more aware, on top of that last moment before the silence ends and the crash of injury explodes inside and around you. Never happens. Don't suspect it ever will. I'm just dumb when it comes to anticipating spontaneous violence. I can pick the aggressive build-up in a guy's face, I'm just useless when it comes to second-guessing what's in the darkness, the shadows.

I listened. The apartment seemed to be empty; aside from the wind through the open doors, all I could hear were the faraway sounds of the beach and the distant yells and laughter of families. I looked at my watch. It was seven-thirty in the morning. The sun was well up and blazing through the windows. It felt hot. It's always hot in Queensland.

I sat up and looked around. The bedroom was empty, but for the dumb guy on the floor. But at least I was still alive.

—

THE FIRST SOUND I'd heard was like a whimper. Coming from behind a door and down a corridor, deep within the apartment. Starlight and I hadn't ventured beyond the dance steps in the lounge room when she'd ramped up the process by deciding to disrobe. A little nudity was, she figured, guaranteed to entwine me inside and around and under her body. Safe within her power.

The whimper was the sound of a person in distress. I knew I was dealing with brazen confidence but this took me by surprise; inviting me to her apartment where she held a girl in captivity. That's called showing off. That's called thinking you're invincible.

I knew what was going on: Starlight was running an operation where girls were taken. What I hadn't figured out yet was whether they were all being shipped off to new homes or killed. Whatever, it was time to shut her down, time to stop the cat and mouse bullshit and take her out of the picture, in whatever way.

I grabbed her. For a moment Starlight thought I'd been tempted and that she'd won. For a moment only; I held her tight, bound her wrists and ankles and carried her back to the couch. Threw her shirt over her and left to check out the room where the whimper was coming from.

I figured I'd keep her captive in her own home until I'd found the brother, Estefan. I'd use Starlight as bait if I had to.

I was expecting venom and some anger from her. But there was nothing. She began to hum a tune. I didn't recognise it and didn't bother to ask what it was. I went down the corridor and checked each of the bedrooms.

—

I WAS HOPING it would be Ida that I'd find.

It wasn't; it was a girl, no older than twenty, half-doped, half-awake, tied to the bed, staring at me with a look of complete helplessness. She was naked under a thin sheet. Her body was gleaming wet, as if she'd been painted with oil. It stuck to the sheet. It was what I smelt when I came into the apartment. The Ashanti slave trade memory flashed through my mind again.

'You're okay,' I said, as I leaned down to undo her bindings.

I heard a click.

By then it was too late; it was the sound beforehand that I needed to hear, that I should have heard, if I'd been on my guard.

—

IT WAS A mistake to remove my clothes for him. It's always a mistake to remove your clothes for a guy if he doesn't respond as you want. It's disempowering and you lose control. I hate that. It hasn't happened to me in a very long time. I haven't been tied up in a very long time either, not against my will.

He placed me – no, he threw me – on the couch and looked down at me as if he was expecting I'd start crying or yelling and kicking. Fuck that. I closed my eyes and hummed my Dead Girl Sing, which always makes me calm, makes me remember that whatever is happening, it could be worse. A lot worse.

After he walked away and down towards the bedrooms I started to wonder what he'd do. He wasn't going to kill me, was he. So I had nothing to fear.

And then I heard the front door open and Carlos walked in. Staggered in, actually. Somebody's blood had sprayed across his chest and face. I couldn't believe the sight. What had he gone and done? Well, it was pretty obvious: he'd found someone, another girl, most likely, and sliced her open. To get back at me, no doubt. To show me who's boss, brag to me about his adventure and then, judging from the look in his eyes, he was going to cut me too. He was a bigger man now. He wouldn't be pissing his pants this time.

I'd been so angry with Carlos over the past couple of days that I'd forgotten why I brought him out here, why I loved him, why he was such a great companion. He was a natural. He took one look at me and didn't say a word. Most guys would shout out something dumb but he didn't. Most guys would freak and run across, untie me and cover me. He didn't; he just knew there was a problem, a danger, somewhere inside the apartment and went searching for it. Silent. Moved like a shadow. I loved him. So clever.

I heard a sort of thud, which I guessed was Darian falling to the floor – or, at least, I hoped it was – and then Carlos came back out. Smiled at me. Wanted my approval, of course, and who was I to deny it? And to find out what he should do next.

'Thank fuck you came and saved me, Carlos. You're a genius.'

He smiled. He likes it when I tell him how clever he is. It's like when I tell the girls how hot they are. They love to hear that sort of thing from me. It's easy and it doesn't cost you anything, so why not?

'You want me to kill him? Who the fuck is he? Is he that guy Ida was talking about? I'll kill him, you want me to do that for you?'

Jesus, Carlos, I thought. The last thing I need – and you, my brother – is another dead body, especially that of an extremely well known and well connected ex-homicide investigator who probably told his partner he was coming to see me. Murdered in my apartment; how would that go down? You don't just kill people, Carlos, it's not that simple. Not here in this country, anyway.

Bodies are messy. Bodies are best avoided, whenever possible. I don't kill, not unless there's absolutely no other alternative and absolutely no chance of being connected to the body. It's called restraint, Carlos. Something you and your impulses need to get acquainted with. Without restraint I wouldn't be here, where I am.

Two, then three, dead bodies is what got us into this. But they're tied to Carlos, a wide enough step away from me. Carlos will wear what he's done. I won't. I'm in trouble, no question, but I'll come through this, free as always.

'Carlos,' I said, 'we have to leave here. For a while, anyway.'

'Until all this gets sorted out?' he asked.

I nodded. He was untying me now.

'I'm sorry for what I did,' he said. Yet again another sorry for what he did, for sending his life and my life into a tumble of chaos. Sending my business against the wall and, hey, don't forget, Carlos: killing a few people along the way just because you wanted to have a fuck. I didn't ask him about the blood spray on his chest and face. Later I'd wipe it off. Now we had to leave.

'Where are we going?' he asked.

'Tell me: is the cobweb safe?' I replied.

He looked pretty shocked; maybe he didn't realise I knew about it.

'Yeah,' he said.

'Then that's where we're going. The cobweb.'

# 29

# Here Comes the Sun

I DREAMED I WAS ON A TRAIN. THERE WAS A MAN, HE WAS old. He'd been killing people for a long time and he was at the other end of a long corridor. Have I jumped away, into another place? Maybe I'm in a tunnel, chasing him, the Train Rider, the killer I couldn't stop.

How do I know he's old? I know nothing about him. Nobody does, except for the girls he's taken, raped, tortured, killed. They know, they know everything but they're not talking or, if they want to, through their spirits to me in my sleep, I'm not listening.

I don't do that sort of thing anymore.

I dreamed I was under the sun. There was a girl. Her skin was the colour of a dusky sky, almost brown with a tinge of purple. She looked like the sky after the sun had gone down. Her body was coloured in pastels and she shimmered. She leaned down over me. I couldn't move and she said:

'Arrivederci' which means, I think, goodbye. Who was she? I don't know, my eyes were closed. I was touching the girl with the blue pastel skin and eyes that sank below the horizon after the sun had set.

I think there was an eclipse of the sun and I think the girl lay down on top of me and pressed her body into mine and maybe we made love. I don't know.

—

I LOOKED AT my watch. It was nine in the morning. I must have collapsed again. I remembered that I'd looked at my watch at seven-thirty. I think I was starting to get up, off the floor, looking around to see if I was alone.

I stood up and rubbed my head where I'd been clocked, knocked unconscious. What an idiot, I told myself. My head hurt like it used to after a three-bottle-of-vodka binge. The bedroom was empty. The girl who I'd found, who'd been tied to the bed, who I'd gallantly told was going to be okay, was gone. I walked through the rest of the apartment. It was pretty much like it was when I'd tied up Starlight, tossed her on to the couch and went searching for the sound of the whimper. The only thing I noticed was that her laptop had gone.

I figured that her brother must have blindsided me. Maybe he was waiting for me, maybe it was a set-up all along. Maybe she got lucky and he came home at the right time. Whatever, he'd taken me out of the picture for over two hours and both of them, with the girl I'd told would be okay, had vanished.

I'd fucked this one up beautifully.

I checked my phone. Isosceles had texted me.

*gofish*

Which meant he had a lead.

Maria had also texted me.

*where are u*

Which meant she was awake.

—

'MARIA'S WORRIED ABOUT you; she thinks you've succumbed to the wiles of our Miss Starlight, aka Rosalita, who is heading in a northerly direction as we speak.'

'Good. Keep tracking her, let me know where she ends up,' I said. I'd made myself a cup of coffee and was sitting on Starlight's balcony, looking out over the ocean from seventy floors up. I'd already texted Maria and told her I'd be back soon, asked her to check on Blond Richard and how he was going with the interviewing of Ida's and Estefan's friends and what they might know of where either of them could be holed up.

'I told Maria not to be concerned,' Isosceles said.

'Good,' I replied, not knowing what else to say.

'By the way, I might have found Ida,' he said.

Isosceles has a chronic inability to tell you the most important information straightaway. It usually comes after a discourse on history or geography, designed to show how brilliant he is.

'Really?' I said. 'That'd be very helpful.' I could hear the urgent sounds of police sirens approaching from somewhere down below on the street.

'Don't be facetious, Darian, it demeans you.'

'Of course. My apologies. Where is she?'

Two squad cars appeared on the beach road in the distance, heading in the direction of the Q1. More sirens were approaching from behind me, also heading in the same direction.

'I can't vouch that it's her I've found but I can vouch for her credit card, which was used at eight-fifteen this morning. A withdrawal, of two hundred dollars.'

'Where?' I asked, getting up from the chair, looking out over the balcony. The four police cars had congregated to a series of squealed stops about a hundred metres away, down on the boulevard; cops were leaping out of the vehicles and running across the grassy area, passing around the pandanus and palm trees.

'A little town called Amity. Do you know it? I didn't. It's on the northern tip of Stradbroke Island. Coincidentally, Darian, it seems that this might be where Starlight, aka Rosalita, is also headed.'

Another two squad cars careered up to the same place. The first lot of cops had appeared on the beach where a group of people had gathered. Aside from the fact that I was seventy floors above the action, I couldn't see exactly what was happening because the thicket of trees between the line of beach and the footpath were obscuring whatever had led them there.

'Isosceles,' I said, 'there's a lot of action on the beach next to the Q1 building; can you listen in to the cops' radio and tell me what they're looking at?'

'I am, indeed, as we are talking. Another dead girl, her throat slashed like the unfortunate Officer Johnston Connelly. She was found about ten minutes ago; apparently she'd been hidden in some bushes. I'll update you as I learn more.'

'Okay. Thanks,' I said, pushing away from the balcony ledge, going back inside.

'One more piece of information, Darian, that might be of good use to you,' he said.

'Yeah?'

'The police are waiting for you at the motel. Don't go back there unless you're ready to be taken into custody.'

I wasn't.

# 30

# Evasion

I TEXTED MARIA:

*at the q1*

Then I stood across the road, under the awning of a bus stop. The sounds of sirens were intensifying. Schoolies week was starting to look like Dracula's picnic. The body count was growing and the nature of the killings was gruesome enough to lure the most lazy of the tabloids. Parents around the country would start going berserk. I'd noticed kids with surfboards passing the throng of desperate cops at the crime scene, not bothering to stop for longer than a few moments on their way down to the surf.

The motel was less than five minutes' drive from the Q1. It took the squad car less than two minutes to pull up out the front. Two uniforms leapt out and ran inside.

Partners. Thanks, Maria, I thought as I peeled away from the bus shelter and ambled up the street, removing the battery from my mobile phone.

The cops would have pressured her. They needed to know everything that led to this catastrophic sequence of events. How had it all started? That's what they wanted to know. Me too.

How had it all started? How do crimes begin? The moment when a person is murdered starts with a trail that's commenced days before, maybe weeks or months before. Nothing just happens, nothing is random, nothing is coincidental. It's all part of some story that, in retrospect, makes perfect sense. My journey here started with the phone call from Ida. *Only you can help. There are so many bodies.* But what led to her making that call?

I could guess, based on what I'd learned. The two dead girls – Hannah and Allegra – were presumably taken by Estefan, for Starlight, who was then going to sell them to some fat ugly buyer in a squalid third-world house, for his pleasure. He would either kill them or keep them; didn't know that yet. Estefan somehow ended up standing over their dead bodies. Bad call for his sister who has to replace them – maybe – then try to curtail the crazy brother who seems to be wandering around the Coast with the smell of blood on him like an intoxicant. The girl at the beach had been killed the same way as Johnston. Violent and thorough. Not an easy thing to do. That's called pissing on your victim. Really letting them have it. The slash across the throat is aggressive enough, the peeling back is just that little bit extra piece of contempt and power that some killers really get off on – it's like an orgasm for these sorts of guys. It's nasty and gruesome; and usually leads to a ramping-up of similar killings. If it was Estefan who'd done it, he was a dangerous guy. He'd need to be taken out forcefully. Not necessarily the type of guy that even the Gold Coast cops could handle. They were having trouble putting some of the more aggro bikies behind bars.

Something bothered me, though: Johnston. Was he just the wrong guy at the wrong time in the wrong place? It could have been that easy but the problem was the timing. Ida's call came in to me during the afternoon. The phone had been swiped out of her hand at around the same time. No later than about four in the afternoon. From the sound and tone of Ida's call it seemed like the girls were well and truly dead by that time.

Johnston didn't turn up until some hours later. Like, many hours later. Why would the killer still be there? What was the point? Some killers go back to the place where they have disposed of their bodies to gloat or to fret …

Maybe that's what he'd been doing. I stopped speculating on that one. It would take me one step too far away from what I knew. Best to leave all that open and close it down more slowly, as more information and evidence came to light. Otherwise I'd be making stuff up, trying to squeeze information into my hypothesis and ignoring the possibility that the square peg wasn't meant to go into that round hole.

—

ISOSCELES HAD TOLD me about Starlight, where she came from, what her real name was. He'd also told me about the Deep Web.

I'd heard about the Deep Web and the Hidden Wiki, a few years ago, when I was still running crews out of the homicide offices in St Kilda Road in Melbourne.

When we hear the word 'wiki' we think of Wikipedia, which I love as a magnificent source of excellent information. The Hidden Wiki is a huge collection of websites, on the Deep Web, accessed by a browser called Tor that was specifically designed for anonymous users. It's what you use if you don't want anyone finding out where you live from the IP address on your computer. Perfect for terrorists and paedophiles. Little of my past work in hunting down killers related to this sort of online secrecy so I needed a guided tour by Isosceles.

He showed me last night, after Maria had fallen asleep, after Blond Richard had left, while the raging party of teenagers was in its dwindling embers, before Starlight had texted me.

'Imagine an iceberg,' he said. 'The Deep Web is five hundred times bigger than the surface web,' he'd said. 'And by surface web, Darian, what I mean is the place where you and I and most everyone else goes; the place of Google and Hotmail and Facebook and Yahoo. The surface web has over one billion documents; the Deep Web has over *five hundred billion* documents.'

I was sitting in front of my laptop. He'd guided me to download Tor and now I was ready.

'The Hidden Wiki is where Starlight works. This is where she puts girls online and sells them. She's not alone. There are hundreds of businesses like hers and dozens of them in Australia. She can't be found down here, she can't be seen. The law enforcement officers are aware of the Deep Web but it's rare that they have the skills or the knowledge, let alone the budget, dear friend, to track these people. Are you ready?' he asked.

'Ready,' I said. I almost felt like I was on board a spaceship, about to enter another galaxy.

I was.

'Oh,' he said, as if remembering something before we started, 'just a warning, Darian. I know you have seen many sides of evil and indeed, sadly, more than most when it comes to the depravity of humanity but what you're about to see down here is worse than Dante's "Inferno". Be prepared.'

I wasn't.

Don't go there, don't do it. I don't like people very much; they bore me. But I've always believed that people, most people, are inherently good. After I went on Isosceles' guided tour of the Hidden Wiki I wasn't so sure about that anymore. It is ugly. This is where you go for anything from child porn to human sacrifices; hand-to-hand combat fighting to the death, between humans and animals; where you can hire hit men or people to do grave damage to anyone; where terrorists lurk; where you can buy or learn how to make drugs. Dante's 'Inferno' was a poem. This is real. On the bulletin boards where people have posted about their experiences trawling through the Hidden Wiki you'll find testimonials from people who have been totally freaked out by what they've seen. You can get lost down there. You just click from site to site; the only way to keep track of your journey into darkness is to bookmark pages so you can go back to where you came from. One guy clicked on a page that freaked him out so much he tried to escape. He couldn't. His computer was locked on the page with its hideous imagery, as if taunting him for having arrived there. He had to remove the battery from his computer then, later, wipe the entire hard drive.

It made me angry and depressed, it made me want to reach out for a bottle of vodka and scull it, it made me want to hammer some people into the ground, pulverise them, it made me want to go and hold Maria tight, walk down the corridor and find the kids who were partying in the rooms of the motel and hold them too, hug them with some form of life-affirmation. I didn't do any of that. I took in a deep breath and waited until Isosceles guided me away from this miasma of horror.

To Starlight's little shop of horrors.

I did all this before she texted me. *Wanna cum over.* Before I stood in her apartment, watched as she tried to lure me with her body, watched as she disrobed, presenting her nakedness to me as a means of seducing me into her web.

I guess that's why I lost it and revealed I knew her real name, that I knew who she really was, that she'd come from Rio and had fled to London before she ended up on the Gold Coast. I was just a hair's breadth away from revealing that I knew about her 'business' of trading in young women.

Before I heard the sound of a whimper.

Before the lights went out, after somebody, probably Estefan, clocked me with something hard and solid, probably a pistol, and I fell to the floor. After I'd told the girl on the bed, tied and bound, ready to be sold, that she'd be okay.

Because I'd arrived.

To save her.

*Only you, Darian, only you.*

# 31

# The Lonely Guy

THE CLIENT IS FINE. I'VE RUNG AND TOLD HIM THAT SHIPMENT might be a day late but he's cool. He was so thrilled with Tina last night. Thought she looked stunning. Told her she was going to be very happy.

She was good. She really responded to me telling her off. She really did well. When I asked her to parade for him, she did. When I told her to blow him a kiss, she did. When I asked her to smile and pout for him, she did. I told her to hold her breasts and squeeze them for him and she did that too. No tears. No tantrums. No complaints. No wonder he's cool. He's got the perfect princess.

A princess who almost got rescued. Lucky that. Now she's back with me and Carlos, in the back seat of our car driving towards the cobweb. It'll be safe there. I'm running behind schedule and I'm down a girl. I need to find a new one. The other client is okay with the delay, he's cool too. My clients are very accommodating.

Most of my clients are just bored and lonely guys, many of them guys who've got contracts for mining companies or oil companies, guys who are stuck in the middle of nowhere, thousands of miles away from a town or, really, any sort of community. The mining boom's been really good for business. Those guys get posted to places where they're so isolated. They get paid heaps of money and they really need a girl. They come to me and I sell them a hot girl, we arrange the transportation and then she's there, with them until they get tired of her and ask for a new one. One of my clients goes through a girl about every two months. He's a regular and it's really good for business when you've got that sort of turnover with repeat customers. Once he's done with a girl he just goes out on his boat and tosses her in the ocean. He uses a wheelie bin so no-one ever suspects anything. It's a really good process. Some of my guys have been stationed on islands. I've got another guy who works on Christmas Island. He does some sort of security with the illegals there. He's been on contract for over two years and says it's the most boring place on earth. He gets so lonely and frustrated. I send him a few girls every year. See what I mean about the clichés? These are just ordinary guys living far from home and far from any place where they can have a good time at night. I don't have many clients in the cities. Not here in Australia anyway. I do overseas; through Asia and India. Over there you can keep a girl locked away and hidden easily. Those cities are teeming with millions of people, cramped and living on top of each other. You're more anonymous like that. Not so in the Australian cities. People tend to notice you a little more.

The business won't last – I've got to be practical about the future. In another ten years, but maybe less, when you consider how fast things are being developed around the world when it comes to technological advances, my girls will all be replaced by sex dolls or robots. I know it sounds insane and Carlos used to laugh at me when I told him about this but it's true. If you look on the internet you'll see there's a sex doll robot called Roxxy that one of my buyers could get for only seven thousand dollars. That's less than what they pay for my girls. But at the moment they're pretty awkward and look stupid. They move like a toy and I dunno what they'd be like to touch. They still look like a sex doll, which in my opinion, are the most random, awful-looking things ever made. Still, they sell. And you know, think about *Blade Runner.* That chick was hot. I'd fuck her. I was going to say 'if' but it's not if – it's when – they get to that level of superior modelling, I'm done. The game will be over. By then I'll be rich, though, and sailing around the world.

Too bad for my girls that they were born too soon – if they were born in another ten years I wouldn't have had to take them and sell them, but then they wouldn't have had the great experience that I'm offering them, being a princess and going on wild and unexpected journeys – even if those journeys are short and end up in the ocean.

—

CARLOS IS DRIVING and I'm in the front seat. Tina's in the back. Sleeping. I've had to give her some Xanax. I need her to be wasted.

I love sitting in the front seat and looking out through the windscreen. You see things you never notice when you're driving yourself. There are cane fields spread out among green paddocks. The ocean is nearby. We're in farming country. Very few people on the road, and all the towns we've driven through have been small and sad-looking. No tourists out here. No cool places to hang out. No hot chicks.

There's time for me to think as well. With Carlos driving he's occupied. His mind is focused on getting to safety. That's good because I don't want him thinking too much about the future and what might happen. If he does that he might get dangerous.

It's not like he came back to my apartment this morning to make me breakfast. I could see it in his eyes. He was going to kill me. He wanted blood revenge. He wanted to hurt me so he'd feel better about all the really dumb things he's done over the past few days. Without me to tell him what an idiot he is, he'd be feeling better about himself.

Those feelings don't go.

And with all that blood spattered across his face and chest, I know he's got the blood lust. He's not going to stop. And where we're going, it's small. People get seen, get noticed. We're going to have to stay low, out of sight for a while.

I should ask him why that blood is there. I'm not going to. He'll either lie to me or he'll go all defensive on me again.

Fuck, I hope he wasn't seen when he did whatever he did, that caused all that blood to spray over him. I hope he was careful. Luckily there are hardly any CCTV cameras on the Gold Coast. That's going to change, I read. Maybe it's time to move on. Maybe even the university will put in CCTV cameras. That'd be a disaster. So much of my work is based around the fact that we can take girls without being seen.

I hate surveillance cameras. I hope Carlos was careful.

The cops can't get him on DNA, on fingerprints; all they could tag him with would be a sighting. Other than that he's off the radar. And he knows it; that's why he's lazy and doesn't give a shit, that's why he thinks he can go round killing people and stay on top of the world, like he was running the fucking favela.

'We're here,' he said.

I looked around and saw the ferry landing coming into view.

# 32

# The Other Woman

'YOU'RE THE ONE WHO CALLED JOHNSTON, RIGHT?' ASKED Cathy.

It wasn't exactly the lead-in to a conversation that Maria had expected and, now that the young widow had shot out the question with thinly disguised contempt, Maria wondered if she should have stayed away.

Despite telling the cops where Darian was, Maria had hung around a while to see if he'd turn up at the motel. He didn't. His phone was off. Dead. He'd gone to ground. 'In the wind' as he liked to call it. He'd be doing it his way and she'd be lucky to hear from him again, until he chose when and where.

She wondered if she'd done the right thing. It wasn't easy giving him up – not that it was much of a betrayal, not really. All she'd told Dane Harper was his phone number and where they'd been staying. Funny, it was barely one hundred metres away from the Surfers Paradise police station.

Then, when Darian had texted her that he was at the Q1, she'd passed that information on to Dane too. But it was a test and she'd failed. Well, fuck him. Her loyalty wasn't to him. It was to the police force, the badge, the uniform, to guys like Dane who actually were police officers, not has-beens like Darian.

Her loyalty, today and yesterday, also was to Johnston. Which was why she'd driven over to his house to pay her respects to his widow, the 23-year-old Cathy, whom she'd never met.

'Yes,' replied Maria. 'That was me.'

And then she said: 'I'm sorry.'

They were sitting in the lounge room. It was a modern house, recently built, in one of those dead, characterless estates, in a suburb called Arundel. Streets that went around in circles. No trees and all the houses looking identical. All brick, one-storey and all with huge garages out the front, as if the garage was more important than the facade of the house.

The sort of cheap and supposedly safe housing estate where first-time home owners buy.

There was nothing on the walls. No books. The furniture looked as though it had been purchased through a catalogue from Freedom or Ikea. It was lifeless before Johnston had been killed and even more so now. It was silent. Cathy wasn't crying. She seemed angry.

'Yeah, me too,' said Cathy.

For the merest of seconds Maria remembered Johnston smiling at her, soon after they first met, in Melbourne; smiling and reaching out to shake her hand. He was a tall, innocent-looking guy, with long eyelashes and eyes that were soft and kind.

'I just don't get the cop thing,' said Cathy. 'Shit pay, shit hours, shit job. And it's fucking dangerous. Who wants to work in a job where you can get killed? Why'd you wanna be a cop?'

'It's just what I always wanted to do,' said Maria, aware of the lameness of the answer.

'Yeah, that's what he said. He thought he was fucking invincible when he put on the uniform, thought he was tough, a man, thought he could do anything, thought he was fucking bulletproof, all because he wore some dumb-arse fucking uniform that never fitted him properly anyway.'

'I'm really sorry for your loss,' said Maria, standing. Time to get out of here, she was thinking. 'I should leave.'

Cathy didn't stand.

'What was the point?' she asked, staring at the pale brown carpet.

'Sorry?' asked Maria.

'You should be able to answer that. You're the one who called him, told him to go out and investigate some missing girl. You're the one who sent him to his death. Why? What was the point?'

'It's just the job,' said Maria.

'Do you make the world safer? Do you bring those poor fucking girls back to life?'

'I should go,' said Maria.

'Yeah. You should,' replied the widow.

—

STANDING OUT THE front of Cathy's low brick home with its gargantuan garage, amidst a world frozen with silence and no movement, as if everyone vanished at eight-thirty in the morning to go to work or were too scared or bored to come out and, frankly, why bother anyway as the suburb was lifeless, more boring and dead than anything Maria had ever seen, she wondered about the other woman's question: 'What was the point?'

She didn't feel like opening the door to the car, getting in. She didn't feel like doing anything but stare, as she was, at the sun-glazed asphalt on which she was standing. The depressing characterless street leading onto another equally flat and boring street in this small place where life seemed to have been drained, didn't help.

Normally she was driven by purpose. The job, the uniform, that was enough. Being a police officer meant something and it gave her a reason for getting up in the morning. It was, to use one of Darian's words, righteous. Even with the office politics and the sexism and her moron boss, Fat Adam, and the guys who would ogle her. There was a fraternity, despite all the differences and annoyances; she belonged.

Now all of that was shaken – by the weird, horrible, confronting experience of talking to Johnston's widow, by his death, her feelings of guilt. What would happen to her? Her mother lived alone; Maria rarely went to visit her. She had nightmares that one day or night, more likely the night, she'd get a phone call or a text or a stupid message on Facebook telling her that her mum had died. Gone without a goodbye, gone without any kind of understanding between them – but what was the point of that anyway? What meaning? What understanding? What more did they need to do but say hello and drink coffee and stare at the ocean once every year or two. Would Maria live in an old people's home? Would there be anyone to care for her; did she want anyone to care for her? Was there a purpose to her life and did it matter anyway? Every day she got up, put on the uniform and went to work, being an officer of the law. Was that it? Was there a purpose to that?

Or maybe she'd die in a ditch like Johnston. There'd be a point to that. There'd be a killer to catch. There'd be a memory, a plaque, tears, there'd be guilt no doubt and remorse and people reminiscing. An early violent death of a young cop: that made sense. That gave everything meaning. Didn't it, she told herself.

And then her phone buzzed. Casey, her lover. For a fleeting moment she thought about letting it ring out.

'Hey,' she said.

'Hey babe, where the fuck are you? I'm here! Me and Arch got the call from Blond Richard last night. We've come down in his fuckin' speedboat. Awesome, babe, awesome. Parked it or whatever the fuck you do with a boat, right next to the Versace Hotel. Can you believe this joint? We're eating a burger right now, darlin'. Ready to help out. Love you, babe. Drop everything, come on over, give your lover a squeeze.'

She laughed.

# 33

# On the Road

I BOUGHT MYSELF A NEW PHONE AND A HUNDRED DOLLARS' worth of credit. I called Isosceles and told him not to pass on the new number to Maria.

'But what if she asks me?' he said, truly perplexed by the conundrum he found himself in.

'Lie,' I said.

There was a silence, followed by: 'All right,' as if I were asking him to sprint up Mount Everest naked.

'Thanks,' I said, as if to offer some salve.

I rented a car, a cheap and anonymous white Holden Commodore. I drove it to the undercover car park near the motel, got out and went across to the Studebaker. I reached in under the front seat where I kept a shoebox; inside was my gun. I slid the Beretta into the back of my jeans and climbed back into the Commodore. As much as I adore my Studebaker with its gear shift, left-hand drive, lack of power steering, antique air conditioning and wind-up windows, I do, every now and then, enjoy the hit from driving a new car with their push-button electronics and zap-control seat adjustments and they even have built-in GPS systems that guide direction-impaired drivers like myself. Driving a brand-new car is, for a guy like me, a guilty pleasure. The downside is you tend to hit the accelerator a little too generously as you're not used to the smoothness of the pedal nor the ease with which these engines burn the mileage.

—

'I FUCKING HATE universities. They make me feel like a fuckwit, all dumb and worthless,' said Blond Richard.

I'd called him to pass on the new number and see if he'd made any progress on the list of names. He'd happily taken the day off, put a sign on the entrance to his record shop that said: *Crime Fighting. Closed for the Day. Maybe Longer.*

'Hey you!' I heard him shout to someone. 'Where do I find the sociology lecture?'

I kept driving as I heard the muffled response to his question, which I guessed would be something like, 'I've got no clue what you're talking about,' and then, after a muffled exchange, I heard his voice again.

'No-one's got no clue about nothing. I'm gunna call that geek mate of yours and see if he can navigate his way round this joint.'

'We've had a hit at an ATM,' I said. 'It might be the break we need to find our missing Ida, but what would be really helpful now is if you can find out if anyone has heard of a place called the cobweb.'

'Cobweb,' he repeated as if writing it down. 'Yeah, rightio. Oh, Casey and that wild fucker, Arch, have arrived; I'm gunna get them on the hunt as well. Okay?'

'Yep, good,' I said.

'Hooray,' he said and signed off. Hooray: is there any other place on the English-speaking planet where that word is used to say 'goodbye'?

I looked at the GPS. It told me I was an hour away from the ferry landing that would take me across Moreton Bay to the town of Amity on Stradbroke Island.

Then Ida's mother, Annie, called.

I'd called and left her a message with the new number.

'Is that Darian?' she asked.

'Yeah,' I replied.

'Good news!' she said.

I turned the steering wheel of the car and ground into the brakes, pulling up abruptly. With that unexpected comment, I sort of knew where this was heading.

'She is safe. She called me early tonight. My time, tonight. This morning with you, I think.'

'How long ago did she call?' I asked.

'About an hour ago. She told me to tell you not to worry, that it was all just a misunderstanding.'

Hell of a misunderstanding. Four people dead and countless girls being sold into some form of slavery.

'Are you certain it was her?' I asked. 'Her voice, her mannerisms; you're sure you were talking to your daughter?'

'Of course.' She sounded offended.

'Where was she calling from?'

'She didn't say but she told me that she is all right and that she's travelling and will be back on the Gold Coast soon. She's looking forward to getting back into her studies.'

'Did she call you from a mobile phone or a landline?'

'It was a payphone,' she said. 'I could hear the coins going in. She is safe, that's all that matters. Thank you for being concerned about her.'

'Did she say anything else to you? About where she's been?'

'It doesn't matter. She told me to tell you it was a misunderstanding. She's not missing anymore. So.'

Much longer on the phone and I think she might have tried to fire me.

'Do you know if she's been at Stradbroke Island?' I asked. 'Someone's been using her ATM card there and I'm hoping it was her.'

'Everything's fine now. Thank you for your concern.'

And with that, she hung up.

My primary reason for coming down here had apparently been resolved. Of course Ida might have made the call to her mother under duress. But I didn't think so. There was a message to me, clear and simple: don't look for me, go home, forget about it.

As I swung the wheel of the car, pulled back onto the highway and started driving in the direction of Stradbroke, I wondered what I was going to find at the end of this journey. It had begun with the desperate plea of a girl, calling me to her aid, who now had only one thing to say to me: stop.

# 34

# The Force

DANE LOVED PRESSURE. THE MORE INTENSE, THE BETTER HE felt.

He was feeling real good right now. Since the discovery of the body this morning – on the fucking beach in full view of the public for Christ's sake – the buzz inside the station was intense. Four bodies in two days. This had to be some kind of record on the Gold Coast; they had their bikie action with shootouts and gang warfare but this was something else. This was a savage killer in the midst of schoolies. The mayor was freaking out, the press were freaking out, parents were freaking out, small and large business owners were freaking out.

Sixty million dollars' worth of teenage spending was in jeopardy. The only ones who weren't freaking out were the schoolies themselves. Thought they were invincible.

It would have been a nightmare, even without the murder of a cop; add that to the mix and the whole place was combustible.

He loved it.

It pumped him. This was why he joined the force.

It used to be called the force, a police *force*. In 1990 it became the police *service*. Dane was two years into the job when the change of name was adopted, in an effort to appease a public whose confidence in the cops was shattered after revelations of deep corruption. There weren't too many cops who appreciated the change. They, and he, didn't want to be a service. No-one joined up to *serve*. They became cops to enforce. They ruled. They didn't serve a public. Fuck that.

He felt good. Now, with this sudden spree of killings, he was back where it felt right: enforcing.

There was just one thing marring his pleasure: Darian Richards. Dane couldn't understand it; Darian had been a top, highly respected police officer. He was, in his time – and that was only a couple of years ago – one of the legends, one of the investigators who younger officers would look up to, talk about, dream of emulating. Why then, was he obstructing their murder investigation? Dane had heard all about the experience the local Noosa cops had a year ago, when they were trying to hunt down that serial killer, and Darian was doing his one-man private thing. He'd even heard rumours about Darian belting a couple of the Noosa officers and breaking another's arm. He'd also heard all the rumours about Darian being a one-man execution force back down in Melbourne, making crims and bad cops disappear off the face of the earth. Although he didn't believe any of that. Even if it was true, it wouldn't explain why the guy was seemingly oblivious to their situation.

Wasn't he aware that a cop had been killed?

That alone should have made him pick up the phone and tell Dane all that he knew. Did he? Nup. Not a fucking whisper. Dane couldn't believe it when he was forced to call Maria Chastain again and harass her for Darian's whereabouts.

At least she understood what loyalty meant.

As far as Dane was concerned it amounted to a massive betrayal. He didn't care if Darian no longer wore the uniform; he didn't care if Darian was burnt-out, if he was cynical, even if he was a prick, if he thought he was smarter than the rest of them, if he was working privately for someone, if he was protecting someone, or even if he was on the take. Dane didn't care what his motivation was; Darian had crossed to the other side.

There are 'them' and there are 'us'; that's what Darian had said in the seminar down in Hobart, that time Dane had sat in the audience and watched a living hero talk about how to conduct a murder investigation. He was describing the immutable fact that evil exists, whether you believe in it or not. There are people who commit evil offences and there are those who don't. Simple. A basic law of the world.

Darian was now, as far as he was concerned, one of 'them'. And when his boys found him and dragged him into the interrogation room, he'd be treated as such. He wouldn't be asking for an explanation, all he wanted was simple information. It's not like Darian Richards was the fucking killer, on the run. He was an ex-cop who'd simply taken a call from some girl in distress. Big deal.

Finding Darian and sweating him for some basic information wasn't necessarily going to break the case even though it would hopefully fill in some gaps in their understanding of what was going on.

They were seriously lacking in leads. No eyewitnesses, nothing in the victims' backgrounds that pointed to specific motivations. One of the two girls found in the water had some boyfriend hassle; they were following up on that.

Always start the homicide investigation by looking at those closest to the victim; that's what he'd learned. The boyfriend was being sweated as Dane helped the homicide crew coordinate the response to the most recent victim, a fourth murder in two days, a girl called Margaret, found just a couple of hours ago.

A schoolie. The other girls were uni students. And Johnston, a cop. Were they linked?

Margaret and Johnston's killer had to be the same person; the method of death was identical. Almost ritualistic. Worst he'd ever seen and he'd seen a lot.

He loved it.

# 35

# The Sociology Lecture

THERE ARE OVER FIFTEEN THOUSAND STUDENTS AT THE Griffith University Gold Coast campus and Blond Richard was getting frustrated looking for one by the name of Michelle De Courcy.

After Estefan, Michelle had received more texts and Facebook messages from Ida than anyone; she appeared to be a close friend, and Darian had put her at the top of the list of people to question. They'd tried to call her but her phone rang out. Blond Richard had gone knocking on her door at six in the morning. No answer. Isosceles had easily hacked into every aspect of her life, from her mobile phone number to her address, and now into her personalised university page where he looked at her timetable. Sociology 1, lecture, from ten to midday. It was ten-thirty and Blond Richard was standing in the middle of the campus, a sprawling series of modern buildings set amidst walkways, open courtyards and narrow roads that weren't meant for a Harley's noise and growl. The campus looked as if it had been carved, about twenty years ago, out of a thick forest of gum trees, many of which were still standing. It also looked as though someone had commissioned an open-air designer to come in and plant as many Australian native bushes in as many places as possible. Everything about the entire place seemed quiet, sedate. Blond Richard had expected to find the place a hotbed of rampaging sexheads and placard-waving protestors. The biggest excitement he could discern, from the posters on the walls, was for formally organised piss-ups at the local pub. Students congregated outside the doors to lecture theatres and on the grass and in the outdoor cafes. No-one had any clue where he might find the lecture theatre for Sociology 1.

'It's in G23,' said Isosceles to Blond Richard.

'What the fuck is G23?' he barked to a small crowd of bemused students.

'It's a building,' said a girl with crimson dreads.

'It's a building,' said Isosceles. 'Had you waited I would've imparted that basic information to you.'

'Jesus, you're weird,' replied Blond Richard, and to the girl: 'Where is it, babe?'

'There,' she said and pointed to the three-storey building behind him.

'It's right behind you, you *baka*,' said Isosceles.

'What did you call me?' asked Blond Richard as he smiled at the girl and began to walk in the direction of the building.

'*Baka*. It's Japanese for dumb arse.'

'I'm a dumb arse? You are one fucking freak, you crazy geek. But thanks for the info. I'm good now, go back to your obsession with Raquel Welch,' he said and signed off.

*I've resigned* was the text that Isosceles then sent to Darian.

—

As soon as Blond Richard walked through the door to the building known as G23 he instantly regretted calling Isosceles a crazy geek and a fucking freak and, truth be told, he also thought Raquel Welch was pretty hot too. G23 was a long building with, he reckoned, standing in the foyer, maybe a hundred different doors that led into study rooms and lecture theatres. At this rate he'd be finding Michelle De Courcy by the time next week's lecture was happening.

Not being particularly strong in the apology department, Blond Richard decided against asking the crazy geek for more help; instead he went from door to door, opening each one and asking, 'Is this the fucking sociology lecture?', to a look of stunned bemusement from the students and teachers.

What the fuck was sociology anyway? he wondered as he climbed the concrete stairs to the next level. Isosceles would be able to tell him, but fuck him.

Seventh door down on the second floor he walked into the right room.

'Yes,' answered a middle-aged gent dressed in tight jeans and a black T-shirt. The teacher. 'Are you part of the class?'

Ignoring the teacher's query, Blond Richard cast his gaze across the students, sitting at desks in rows stretching to the back of the room. He knew who he was looking for; he'd studied her Facebook picture profile the night before. She was plump, about a size sixteen, had short dark brown hair and big cheeks. She would have been called 'chubby' or much worse when she was at school. Blond Richard had looked like an anorexic when he was growing up, and was teased accordingly, so he felt a connection, even though he didn't know her.

She was, as he suspected she would be, sitting up against the back wall, in the corner. That's where the kids who fret about their appearance usually sit; that's where he always sat. It's where he still wanted to sit whenever he went into a restaurant or a public place.

'Michelle,' he said to her across the room. 'I need you, babe.'

Michelle just stared goggle-eyed at him.

The teacher saw her fear and embarrassment, and stepped in. 'Excuse me, this is a lecture. Can you go away?'

Blond Richard turned his gaze on the guy. It was a well-honed look that basically said, 'Shut the fuck up, don't mess with me or else you'll find a significant degree of pain,' and the guy melted away towards the white board.

Turning back to Michelle, Blond Richard smiled. As much as he understood threat and intimidation, he knew all about reassurance.

'It's all cool,' he said. 'I just need to ask you a couple of questions. Just out there,' he said, indicating the corridor on the other side of the door, which had a large glass window in it.

He might as well have asked her to jump off the top of the Q1. She was frozen to her seat and looking increasingly scared.

'Everyone out!' he shouted. Turning to the teacher: 'You. Out.'

Turning to the rest of the class: 'Out! Everyone!'

To Michelle: 'Stay. Don't move. They can watch you through the window; you'll be safe, but you and me, babe, we gotta talk.'

# 36

# The Cobweb (ii)

I TURNED OFF THE HIGHWAY AT THE CLEVELAND EXIT. THE ferry left every two hours and I had to hammer the road if I was to make it. Blond Richard called.

'Yep,' I said.

'I know what the cobweb is,' he said.

—

AT FIRST IT was a war on the other side of the world. But when the Japanese bombed the living shit out of Pearl Harbor that all changed. Within two months they had stormed Singapore, supposedly a fortress from which the British Empire could repel any enemy. The impregnable fortress collapsed within seven days. Four days later Darwin was bombed. The Japanese invasion of Australia was on and very quickly the focus on Hitler and Stalin over in Europe and North Africa, necessary at the time, seemed, for Australia, like an indulgent misstep. There were at least ninety-seven bomb drops on Australian soil; the first bombs landed in Queensland about four weeks after the hit on Darwin.

The locals had been waiting. While the government was doing the Churchill step, fighting the war with orders from London, it was becoming clear that the Japanese might be heading our way. They'd taken over China, Vietnam (then called Indochina) and were hovering above Malaya. They seemed to be on a roll and Australia was at the bottom of the map. The law of gravity suggested they'd be tumbling down on top of us. Anxieties mounted and a protection of the coastline seemed like a pretty solid idea. But, since the previous world war had been fought mostly on land and at sea, they hadn't prepared for planes. This was a modern war; technology caught them by surprise. This was a war started and finished from the skies above.

What was built – a series of fortifications and gunnery points along the shores and islands of much of Australia – was largely redundant against the violent assault.

Most of the fortifications in Queensland were built on Moreton Island, just off the coast from Brisbane, the capital city. There, armed forces and civilian guards sat in concrete bunkers built into the sand and stared out at the Pacific Ocean, in readiness. Just below Moreton lies North Stradbroke Island.

You can only get to North Stradbroke Island by ferry. It's popular like the North Shore up on the Sunshine Coast is popular: with drunken yahoos and fishermen. People love these sorts of places to play *The Fast and the Furious* on the sand and along the dirt tracks that crisscross through the low scrubby bush. It's about 40 k's long. It used to be longer but in 1896 a massive storm literally tore the island apart. Another island, called South Stradbroke, which I'd seen as I was driving along the Broadwater at Labrador, was created. There are three towns on North Stradbroke; Amity, where

I was headed, was the smallest, up at the top end, just a couple of k's away from the once-fortified Moreton.

As I drove like a maniac to reach the ferry before it left the mainland I thought about where I was headed: to one of those wartime concrete bunkers, a fortification built by an isolated group of people who sat staring at an empty ocean while bombs from high above dropped across the country.

—

I ASSUMED IT was because he rarely ventured from his apartment and even more rarely indulged in social interaction with other humans that Isosceles had a tremendously thin skin. He had tendered his resignation on numerous occasions, usually in a bout of indignation at having been slighted – often in the most trivial of real or imagined ways. After I brought him into the homicide squad and got him working along with the crews I realised I'd be having to contend with this distinctive personality trait. Some of the investigators would taunt him like a kid at the playground; I'd reprimand them and remind them how valuable he was and how, frankly, not all crime fighters were tough and burly and rode around in squad cars. Chill it out and don't antagonise the genius, I'd tell them. If ever they got a little out of control, I'd send them down to Livestock to get a dose of the banal. That usually worked. I mean, Isosceles might be difficult but compare him to traffic infringements or cattle and working with him started to seem pretty appealing.

I didn't need to call Blond Richard and ask what'd happened; I figured that the more those two interacted the greater the likelihood of a spat. After I got the text message, which was, I guessed, about the thirty-eighth resignation I'd had from him, I rang and apologised on behalf of the albino, assuring Isosceles that he was indeed a genius and that I wouldn't be able to carry out my work, now or back then, without his extraordinary gift and talent.

It worked. It always did. I wasn't lying. It was true. Sometimes just stating the obvious to a person about what it is that makes them special is all you need.

Back on the job and fit to burst with a newfound enthusiasm, Isosceles was now trying to locate the place I was heading towards. Without success. On Moreton Island the remnants of those old fortifications were still in the sand, easy to see. Tourist attractions. On North Stradbroke they hadn't been officially built by the army; they'd been, we supposed, built by the locals. And no amount of internet searching was bringing them to life.

Michelle knew what the cobweb was, but not where it was. On an island that was 40 k's long and about 8 k's wide, with few paved roads that traversed only a small part of the northern tip, there was mostly just bushland. Added to that geographical challenge, my Holden Commodore wasn't built for driving over scrub and sand and along potholed dirt tracks. There weren't any car hire or 4WD rentals on the island. A little touch of larceny was going to be necessary.

—

DRIVING INTO CLEVELAND was like driving into most Queensland towns that hug the glittering coast between Burleigh Heads and Noosa: a wide modern four-lane highway, vast flashy houses, lots of yachts and powerboats, outdoor cafes and shopping centres. Mall heaven, as if transposed direct from the US of A. Well-manicured suburbs with trimmed grass and bountiful supplies of palm trees. I'd made good time. The ferry wasn't scheduled to leave for another twenty minutes.

As I drove along the main drag, passing shopping centre after shopping centre on either side of the road, I realised just how many 4WDs were being driven around the area. It could have been a 4WD convention. Then again, any trip to any town in Australia – or the States or the UK – is like going to a 4WD convention these days. These beasts are starting to take over the cities. I'd been tailing a Nissan Patrol in the hope it would swing into a car park where I could follow, wait until the driver left, then commandeer it. The driver was a middle-aged guy with a fake suntan and Ray-Bans. He'd driven out of a neighbourhood street in front of me and looked as though he was driving to the shops up ahead. But the streets were awash with alternatives that started to get me excited: a Porsche Cayenne, BMWs, Range Rovers and, for one blistering moment of psychosis, a Hummer. All of those vehicles would be real driving cars, not like the plastic mass-produced numbers from Japan; they go and they go well but that's about it.

I stuck with the Nissan. It was an older model, which meant I'd be able to hot-wire it without hassle. As I hoped, the driver swung the vehicle off the main drag and into one of the smaller shopping centre car parks. Parked, jumped out quickly. He was in a hurry. Me too.

I'd honed my hot-wiring skills while spending time in the Stolen Vehicles Division many years ago. Even though it'd been a long time since I'd had any practice, it came back to me with ease. I was on the road in my '80s Nissan Patrol within seconds.

I turned into the ferry terminal car park a few moments later. The ferry, a large gleaming modern red and white boat, was waiting. I was the last car on board before the engines rumbled and the water churned and the back metal panel rose up. Within minutes we were grinding our way from the mainland through a narrow channel with small outcrops of mangroves and sand, rising just out of the water, on either side. What would I find on the island? Hopefully Ida and answers.

# 37

# The Person of Interest is Assisting Police with Their Inquiries

'THIS RECORD OF INTERVIEW IS BEING RESUMED AT TWELVE thirty-one at the Surfers Paradise police station. In attendance are Inspector Dane Harper and Ethan Hitchcock. Ethan, you've had a cup of coffee and a sandwich during the past hour; is that correct?'

'Yes.'

'And you're happy to continue talking to me about this matter?'

'Yeah, but like I told you before, I don't know anything.'

'Earlier this morning you told me that you and Hannah had been fighting. Is that correct?'

'About nothing.'

'What about, mate? What were you fighting about?'

'Just stuff.'

'Okay. What sort of stuff?'

'I didn't fucking kill her. All right?'

'Yeah, we're just trying to clear a few things up, all right? That's all, mate. Okay?'

'Yeah.'

'Hannah had started seeing somebody else. Is that right?'

'Sort of.'

'Sort of. What does that mean, mate?'

'It wasn't serious. It was just ...'

'Just what?'

'Nothing.'

'But you were pretty pissed off, yeah?'

'I s'pose.'

'You sent her a couple of text messages, on the day she went missing. You want to tell me about them?'

'I was angry.'

'Okay. But what about those text messages?'

'I dunno.'

'I'm going to read one, okay?'

'Yeah.'

'*Don't leave me or else*. What's that mean, mate?'

'Nothing.'

'Yeah, but what's it mean?'

'Nothing.'

'Okay. I reckon it's a bit threatening. What do you think about that, Ethan?'

'This is fucking crazy.'

'Mate, like I said, all I'm trying to do is get to the bottom of what happened. You know? I'm not accusing you of nothing, okay? But you know, like I said before, it's my job to try and figure out what happened to Hannah and her friend Allegra. You wanna help, don'cha?'

'Of course.'

'Yeah, good. So you know – this is a stressful situation, mate. There's no point in trying to pretend otherwise. My job is to find out who did that to those two girls. You haven't been charged with anything, okay? Remember that. Okay?'

'Yep.'

'Good. So we right to continue?'

'Yep.'

'Good. Did you know Allegra Michaels?'

'Yeah. We were in the same class together.'

'The same class as Hannah?'

'Yeah.'

'When's the last time you saw her?'

'Who? Allegra?'

'Yeah, Allegra.'

'It was the same night. That night we all went out together.'

'The night Hannah told you she wanted to break up, right?'

'It wasn't like that.'

'Okay. Allegra and Hannah were pretty close?'

'Yeah.'

'Allegra encouraged Hannah to make the split?'

'The what?'

'The split, mate. The split.'

'It was just a fight, an argument.'

'And then she disappeared.'

'I don't know anything about that.'

'Mate, you texted her ten, maybe even twenty times a day. Leading up to and then for at least a week after she went missing.'

'Yeah. So?'

'Would you say you had an obsession with Hannah?'

'No.'

'But when she started seeing someone else –'

'It wasn't serious. It wasn't like that.'

'– you got pretty pissed off, eh?'

'I don't want to talk anymore.'

'What does that mean?'

'I don't want to answer any more questions.'

'You don't want to answer any more questions?'

'No.'

'You don't want to help me anymore trying to get to the bottom of this?'

'Yeah. No. I just don't want to answer any more questions.'

'All right then, mate. That's your prerogative. I've just got one last question for you, though.'

'What?'

'Did you have anything to do with the death of those girls?'

# 38

# On the Run

TINA'S GONE. WE DROPPED HER OFF AT THE FERRY TERMINAL in Cleveland. There was a town car waiting for her. Her new owner had arranged it. I don't make the travel arrangements. It's too complicated, especially when you've got to send girls all over the place. Sometimes the owners pick them up themselves but that doesn't happen very often. This driver was going to take Tina out to Toowoomba or somewhere so they could get her on a small charter plane without anyone bothering to check the cargo.

I'm not so worried about the second client, though I could tell he was rattled. He'll have to wait. Soon I'll be back at Surfers. Schoolies is on for another week so there'll be lots of girls to choose from. And it's not like the university is a closed shop. I mean I can go there myself and find a girl if I need to. Finding girls isn't that hard, especially when there are something like fifteen thousand students at just that one uni and something like twenty thousand kids who've come to schoolies. Divide those figures in half and you have over seventeen thousand girls. I mean, really, finding one as soon as I get back is going to be simple.

—

I'M NOT RUNNING, I'm not doing that anymore.

I ran from the favela, I ran from the Bay of Naples and then I ran from London.

I'm not running from my apartment on the seventieth floor of the tallest building in Australia to an underground bunker in the sand, built years ago by men who were scared.

I'll stay there for a day. Maybe two. No longer. By then I will have dealt with my immediate problems.

Then I'll return. Darian has nothing. He tried to rape me and I hit him. That's what I'll say if ever I need to say anything. But I won't. He'll search for Ida. He won't find her. He'll return to his home. Done, over. Bye bye Mister sexy Darian.

I don't run anymore. But I know they're still chasing me. They won't find me, I'm certain of that now. I'm safe in my apartment on the seventieth floor, where I'm high above the world around me, where I can see in every direction, where I have locks on the doors and a gun by my side.

But I can feel them and I know they're still looking for me.

Looking for me in my dreams, in my sleep, in my moments of weakness, when fear takes over, for the merest of moments, when I've let myself go back, back to London, back to Soho, back to that night when he came through the door and I didn't even hear it open.

—

IS THERE SOMEONE else in the room? I thought. Has the door opened and I didn't hear it?

I was at the end of the bed in the hotel room, kneeling on the floor with a guy's dick in my mouth. I was naked. I was not in control.

Danger was there; I knew it.

Don't panic, I told myself. Maybe you imagined it. Go back to thinking about what you're going to eat tonight, go back to dreaming about being a fashion designer. Go back to counting how much money you've got in the bank. Go back to the blow job, Starlight, and stop being paranoid.

Then I heard this thud – *whump* – like a fist in a pillow.

It must have been a bullet, I realised, because his legs folded in on themselves as if they'd lost all muscle, and his dick went limp in my mouth. I felt spray, wet, hot spatter. That's his brain, I realised. Someone has come into the room and shot this guy. I'd be next.

What the fuck do I do? I've got to get out of here, now. I'm going to die.

And who would care? Naked twenty-year-old escort, shot dead with a guy's dick in her mouth.

I didn't move. I pretended I didn't exist. Maybe if I kept staring at the carpet, I thought, maybe the shooter would go. Maybe if we didn't make eye contact he'd leave the room and leave me alone. These guys get paid by the kill. He's done the job, I haven't seen him, can't tell the cops anything. He should go.

'What the fuck? Who are you?' I heard. I wasn't going to look up at him. I could hear in his voice that he was African.

'Get up,' he said.

I didn't look him in the eye but I did what he said. There was a gang of Sudanese kids in Earls Court and they were vicious. These guys start killing people by the time they're six. Life in the Rio slum is bad but it's a shopping spree at Harrods compared to what they get up to in Sudan.

I covered myself with my arms but I was naked and covered in the splatter of the dead guy's brain.

He didn't shoot me. He stared at me. Those Sudanese guys, they have dead eyes. I wasn't looking at him. I kept my eyes down. I didn't want to see his face.

He kept staring at me. I could feel his eyes and see that he had the gun in his hand and he was pointing it at me.

He took a phone out of his pocket. It was a yellow Nokia.

I didn't move.

'He's dead,' he said into the phone. 'How do I know? What sort of question is that? I know because I just fucking shot him. He ain't got no head, that's how I know,' he said to the guy on the other end, staring at me all the while with those dead eyes.

'Okay, okay,' he said, and then said: 'Wait a minute.'

He ended the call and pointed his Nokia at the body on the bed. Snap. Using one hand he punched in numbers on the phone. With his eyes staring at me. His gun pointed at me. He dialled again.

'Get it? Good. Next time don't go askin' for proof when you don't need it, not when I tell you that I've done something. You don't need to see it if I tell you. Okay?'

I could hear the guy's voice at the other end but I couldn't hear what he was saying. I was getting cold. Should I talk to him? I kept looking down.

He started to walk towards me. I couldn't see his face but I could see his shoes. They were shiny black leather with sharp arrow points.

'There's a girl here,' he said.

I could feel his eyes staring into me.

'Yeah, she's a pro, was sucking his dick when I whacked him. Funniest thing I ever did see. You tell the Spaniel. You tell the

Spaniel that Wizard God shot off the cunt's head, blew his brains all over his real nice hotel room and when his body, dead and totally fucking headless, falls onto the bed, a girl is revealed. Yeah man, Wizard God is studying his English real good. Hahaha. Tell the Spaniel a girl is revealed, on her knees, all nude and all blonde and is real pretty. Tell Spaniel she got big tits. Yeah, it's true, man. Big tits and she's all nude – naked, man – had the old guy's dick in her mouth but he ain't gunna come on account of him being deceased. You tell the Spaniel.'

He put the gun under my chin and lifted my head up with the barrel.

Our eyes met.

He was smiling at me. Like we had a secret.

'She's real pretty,' he said, staring at me.

'I don't bullshit you, man. I dunno, she looks Spanish or she might be one of them girls from east Europe, you can't tell. All of them white chicks look the same to me–'

He handed me the phone.

'Say hello. His name is Black. He's my boss and I dunno if he believe me or not that you here but he want to talk to the blonde girl with big tits who is nude.'

I took his phone, thinking *I've got to do what he says*. I kept my eyes on the killer man and I said:

'Hello.'

'Who is you?'

'Kelly.'

'You nude?'

'Yes.'

'You got big tits?'

'Yes.'

'That cunt, Wayne, he fuck you?'

'Yes.'

'How much he pay you?'

'Three hundred.'

'Euro or sterling? Or the green? What he pay you in, Kelly?'

'Pounds.'

'Where the money?'

'In my purse.'

'You give it to Wizard God. He give it to me. I give it to the Spaniel.'

'Okay.'

'How old is you, Kelly?'

Lie to him. If you tell him you're really young he might feel sorry for you.

'Fifteen.'

'You young girl.'

'Yes.'

'Why you fuck for money?'

'I don't know. It's all I can do.'

'All you can do? Did you try and get a real job? Did you try and get a job, like at Harrods? Anyone can get a job at Harrods.'

'No.'

'Did you try anywhere? To get a real job?'

'Yes.'

'Where?'

'At Sainsbury's.'

'And?'

'I didn't like it.'

'You left that job?'

'Yes.'

'Now you fuck and you suck for living?'

'Yes.'

There was a long silence and I could hear Black blowing his nose. Wizard God was staring at me, still smiling. He hadn't moved. It was like he was at a fun park.

'But you don't know why you choose to fuck for money?'

'No.'

'No. Me neither. Put Wizard God back on.'

I gave Wizard God his phone and he put it to his ear and said, 'She real pretty.'

He put his gun behind him, in his pants and then his hand came out, the other hand, and he put it on my lips. He rubbed my lips with his fingers, looking into my eyes with his dead eyes.

'I'm gunna fuck her.'

His fingers pushed against my lips and I opened them for him as my body sagged and I stood there while he pushed his fingers into my mouth, deep down my throat.

'No, man, I'm gunna fuck her up the arse, man, I'm gunna fuck her that way then if my missus don't call because she expecting me home for dinner, if she don't call or the kids, if no-one calls me, man, after I fuck this little nude girl here, then I'm gunna tie her up and gag her, yeah, on the bed. Just like back in the desert, man, with them little girls, hahaha, I tie blonde girl up, real tight man, and then I am gunna watch that movie with Tom Cruise in it – that new one, man, it's on the telly here in the hotel, I heard some old cunts talking 'bout it in the lift, they reckon Tom Cruise he real good. No, I dunno what it's called. They reckon he is better in this movie than he was in *Magnolia* and that is saying something, so I watch the movie, nude girl she tied on the bed, remind me of home and old cunt he ain't gunna smell for a while, yeah, I throw him on floor, him and all the blood and all, ain't gunna get my gear dirty, man, and then, you know, when the movie is over if I don't have no phone calls, I fuck her one more time, one for good luck. Yeah, yeah, then I kill her, after that then home to the missus and the kids, man, big fucking day. I want Thursday off.'

If I pretended he's special – no – if I told him I had a child – no, if I told him ...

I'll beg him, I thought I was going to faint, I thought I was going to piss all over the floor, Jesus what could I do to this guy, there had to be something.

He's got kids.

He held out the phone and took a photo of me. Click. Starlight. Look at me now. This is how it will end, with a Sudanese killer called Wizard God who's just sent a photo of me nude and covered in blood and grey brain to a gangster called Black who works for the Spaniel.

'Go in the shower. Wash all that shit off you. Don't dry yourself.'

I obeyed.

'Yeah, I tells you she is pretty, man, this is a bonus, man. I want a nude pro with every execution, man. My price just went up, hahaha. Yeah, I'm not gunna forget her purse, you dumb cunt, you think I'm a dumb cunt? I'm a lucky man.'

He clicked off the phone. He stared at me. I was in the shower, hot water all over me. It felt good but he was staring at me.

'Please don't kill me,' I said to him.

He didn't look away from me as he took off his T-shirt then his pants and his shoes and his socks and then he was naked. He had an erection. He was stroking it. He was smiling.

'Please don't kill me.'

'Get out of the shower.'

I did.

'Don't dry yourself.' I didn't.

'How old is you?'

'Fifteen.'

'How old is you?'

'Fourteen.'

'Nah. You is over twenty. You lying to the Wizard God. Come here.'

I was dripping wet. I walked to him.

'Go in there, lie on the bed.'

Which I did. He reached down to his gun, with its long barrel and silencer on the end and he said, 'Open.'

He waved the gun around and stared between my legs and so I did what he said and I opened my legs.

'Now we play a game,' he said.

He put the end of the gun, the barrel of it, into me, inside me and he said, 'This is the game of click and bang.'

He laughed and looked at where his gun was perched inside me and stared like he was at school and he said, 'You suck it in, like it a dick, you drag it into you, arch your body and pull it in.'

Which I did, obeying him. The cold barrel of his gun went inside me. This was the worst feeling in my life.

'I ask a question and you answer and if you get answer right I ask again, new question and if you get answer wrong I pull trigger.

Bang. You dead. Bullet bang up inside you. This way the cops they know it's the Sudanese who do the killings and they don't come after us 'cause they know we do it to their missus so they leave us alone.'

I hated his smile.

'This is called a signature,' he said. 'I start the game in thirty seconds 'cause I know that you gunna cry and maybe beg and things and it not fair to start game till you over all that.'

I wasn't crying and I wasn't begging. I was looking at him and thinking: this is how I'm going to die. Don't think about anything because if you do then you'll start to cry. Think instead that you are dead. That it's all over. Think the end. Think there is nothing. Close your eyes now. I did. All I could feel was the cold barrel of the gun. I tried to be empty in the head with no thoughts but it didn't work.

'First question. What's the name of Tom Cruise's first wife?'

The end of my life. Did I care? Shoot me now, you prick. So what? What the fuck is there anyway?

'Mimi Rogers.'

'How long Tom he marry Nicole?'

'Just under ten years.'

He looked at me for a long time and he said, 'What's the name of their first film together? Tom and Nicole.'

'*Far and Away*.'

He stared at me. He doesn't think I know this stuff. When you come from the favela you know everything about Hollywood.

'Who the director of *Far and Away*?'

Ron Howard, I thought, and I said –

'Ron Howard.'

'No-one ever got them answers. You clever girl. Now you sing. What song you sing me?'

'I don't know any songs,' I said to him.

'You gotta sing. Dead girl sing. Always sing, always sing before she dies.'

'But …' I started to protest.

He shoved the gun in further, harder and he leaned down to me, so close I could smell the staleness on his breath.

'Yeah. I changed my mind. I kill you anyway, even if you get all them answers right. And I ain't gunna fuck you neither.' He was so close his lips were touching mine as he then said: 'I just wanna kill you. I really wanna kill you.'

I could imagine his fingers tightening around the trigger of the pistol that was wedged into me, pinning me onto the bed while his other hand was gripped around my neck.

'So now you sing. Last words. You die as you sing. God meets you in song.'

I started to cry. This was insane, he was insane. I wanted to beg, plead, do anything, pay him money, tell him my story, make him understand. But I was looking up into the eyes of a dead man.

'Dead girl,' he commanded, 'sing. Sing now, dead girl. I pull the trigger while you sing, bitch. Them gods, they is waiting.'

All I could think of was a nursery rhyme, something I used to hear a mother singing to her baby every morning, every night, in the favela. I didn't even know what it was called.

Then his phone rang.

'Hello,' he said. He listened then hung up. Then withdrew the gun from my vagina.

'You lucky girl. They gunna sell you. Spaniel thinks you real pretty, says he can get twenty thousand for you. They gunna do the auction in a minute. Sit up. Look pretty. You ain't gunna die.'

# 39

# Touch the Flag

'AIN'T COOL, BABE,' IS WHAT CASEY HAD SAID.

Maria had joined him and Arch at the Versace Hotel where they were eating their third cheeseburgers and drinking their eighth – each – bottle of VB. The staff were agitated about the unauthorised mooring of Arch's old, rusty and very large speedboat at the edge of the exclusive five-star resort. At least Casey was wearing jeans, instead of his all-purpose sarong. They looked like two south-seas ruffians, stranded from another time. Maria assumed it was their platinum Amex cards that had quelled the staff's anxieties.

While Arch ambled off to take a call from Blond Richard on the status of their job, Maria told her lover about her recent betrayal of Darian.

It had been bothering her and she wanted an assurance from the man she loved, who stood by her at all times, that she'd done the right thing.

'It was just a call to the local cop,' she said. 'He knew Darian, he was just looking for him.'

'Definitely ain't cool,' he said.

'Case, a cop is dead. A friend of mine.'

'Yeah, get all that, darl. Motherfucking shame it is too. But, you know – it's just me babe, just what I think, but when you're a partner, you gotta stay the course, keep it sweet and do the thing.'

Sometimes her lover, who she adored, spoke in the most obscure ways. This was one of those times. But she got the drift, nonetheless.

'You don't understand,' she said.

'What? Because you're a cop and the bloke you talked to is also a cop? That clan thing? Yeah, babe, I understand that. You and this Dane Harper dude, all puttin' on the uniform, all standin' under the same flag, all workin' to the same code ... but you know it and I know it. Darian ain't a cop, don't wear no uniform, but baby, he is the man for *good.* And you know it.'

Her phone buzzed. She recognised the number.

'Hello,' she said as she got up from the table and left Casey reaching across for another handful of fries with one hand and a new bottle of VB with the other. She walked into the large, ostentatious foyer to take the call.

'You called,' said Dane.

'Yeah. I have some information I think you might want,' said Maria.

'About Darian Richards?'

'No. I don't know where he is.'

'Yeah, right,' answered Dane with a barely disguised sneer.

'The murders are connected to a girl named Starlight. She lives at the Q1 building.'

'Starlight?' he asked.

'Yes. She's about twenty-one, twenty-two–'

'Is that right?' said Dane, cutting her off. He wasn't believing her.

'She has a brother called Estefan–'

'Starlight and Estefan?'

She ignored him and kept on. 'They're running an online sex slave business. They take girls from the unis and sell them to guys around the world.'

'Yeah, she does all this from the Q1, right?'

'I think it's worth you looking into,' she said.

'Thanks for the tip, sweetheart. You see that Darian mate of yours, you tell him I'm looking for him. You tell him I'm gunna find him.'

And then he hung up.

Maria stared at her phone.

'Babe!' called Casey, his yell booming across the golden floor of the foyer. Arch had joined him and they were standing, beckoning her to come and join them.

'Carn. We gotta go be crime fighters. You comin'?'

She had expected to be going to the police station, to flesh out the vital information she had for Dane.

That, clearly, wasn't going to happen. He didn't believe her, he hadn't even bothered to listen to her.

She put her phone on lock, slid it into her back pocket and walked across to them.

# 40

# The Human Factor

I DROVE OFF THE FERRY AND INTO THE SMALL TOWN OF Dunwich. The trip had taken forty minutes across the bay. Isosceles had texted me about the creepy curiosity of some of the local names. There was 'The Dunwich Horror', a short story about monsters by H. P. Lovecraft, who used to freak me out when I was a kid, and *Jaws* was set in a town called Amity, but his personal favourite was a spot down south, in the middle of the island called Black Snake Lagoon.

He'd been tracking the signal from Starlight's mobile phone and she was also on the island. I was following her. Not, thankfully, anywhere in the direction of Black Snake Lagoon. It seemed too easy – simply following a mobile phone signal to find what I was looking for – and it, of course, was. For the past hour the signal hadn't moved. It was coming from Amity, the same town where Ida's credit card had been used.

I drove out of Dunwich and turned left onto one of the few paved roads on the island.

The phone had been left on a wooden picnic table at a small park by the water in the little town. Being Queensland, no-one had thought to steal it. There was a note, written in blue pen on a page of lined white paper, under it.

*Be careful what you seek. You may not like what you find*, it said.

The writing was that of a child's; from what I knew of her past, Starlight wouldn't have spent much time at school. I stared at the round, clumsy writing. It looked like it had been written by a ten-year-old, and the threatening words sounded like those of a fifteen-year-old. Partly a taunt to make me keep going, partly a warning to turn around and go back where I'd come from, and a totally tantalising riddle from someone who thought they had the upper hand, who thought they were in control and had little to fear. A message from a little girl who was thinking she could handle anyone.

—

I WAS ALWAYS a quiet kid. I wasn't shy or awkward, I just didn't have very much to say. It seemed to me, from as long ago as I can remember, that a lot of people did have a lot to say and most of it was bullshit. Words to fill up silence, attitudes or strongly held opinions backed up by very little. A constant cacophony of voices – sounds, really – that meant nothing. I was the kid who stood around and observed. I still do. When I was old enough to make my own decisions about where I'd be spending my time, as opposed to being dragged by my mother to a friend's place, or a family member's place, I chose solitude.

I've been called a snob, an emotional retard, I've been told that I'll die a lonely old man. I've been told I cannot commit, that I must be a psychopath, that I have no feelings, that I can't express myself, that I live on some horrible island, that I'm cold and distant. And maybe some or all of that's true. It's easier to analyse other people than yourself. I don't have children, I don't have parents, I watched my father vanish, off to a booze-sodden, drug-fucked world where he spent his time with Thai prostitutes who'd show him affection in return for the money he gave them. I've been a disaster at relationships and for as long as I can remember, have sought the comfort and warmth of women on an hourly rate.

I'm as happy and content as I've ever been. Even happier now that I've retired, not having to put up with the foibles of the crews who worked for me, not having to put up with the countless interviews with suspects of crimes that made my stomach harden and my anger rise with an almost irrational need for justice that, too often, tipped over into vengeance.

Talking to people is probably my least favourite way of spending time.

I went in to the small Amity post office, a place where, in a town like this, everybody talked and everybody knew everybody else's business.

'Hi,' I said to the lanky guy with a red mop of hair who was partly hidden behind a makeshift wall a few feet behind the counter; it seemed like a jerry-built office, with a desk and a comfy chair for him to snooze in. Business wasn't exactly booming round these parts, specially after the rush hour when the mail had arrived to be picked up by the hundred or so locals who lived in *Jaws* town.

He craned his head from around the side of the wall. I could hear a movie being played, no doubt on a laptop on the desk. He leaned over towards it and the sound went on pause. It sounded like *When Harry Met Sally*.

'Yeah, mate?' he said as he climbed out of his chair, emerged from his little office and strolled up to the counter. 'What can I do you for?'

'I don't know if you can help me but I'm doing some field research on Stradbroke and the military fortifications that were built here during the war. The Second World War,' I added hastily, and hopefully without insult; he looked about eighteen. 'The war' to him was most likely the recent assault on Iraq.

'Yeah, there are a lot of them up on Moreton.'

'What about here, on Stradbroke?'

'Nah, none down here, not that I know of anyway. There are a lot of 'em on Moreton, though.'

Moreton was the next island, up north, not far from where we were standing.

'I don't believe they were official,' I said. 'I also heard they might have been built underground, as in tunnels, along the beach.'

'Yeah? Wow,' he said.

'Is there anyone round here who might have lived on the island during that time? The 1940s,' I added for clarity.

'Trev,' he replied. 'He's old,' he said.

'Where can I find Trev?' I asked.

'He likes to fish,' said the kid.

'Yeah, but do you know where he lives?' Post office workers in small towns like this one know where everyone lives.

'Ballow Street,' he said. 'Right at the very end where it hits the beach. He doesn't have a number and you can't see it from the road. It's on the left-hand side. About fifty metres away from the beach. You can't miss it.'

I wasn't so sure about that.

I held up a photo of Ida and Estefan. I'd taken it from her apartment.

'Have you seen either of these two around here at all?' I asked.

He stared at it a moment then back at me. This didn't seem to be a field research sort of question.

'No,' he replied.

I couldn't tell if he was lying.

'Thanks for your help,' I said. I heard the sounds of *When Harry Met Sally* start up as I stepped out onto the wooden balcony and the searing heat outside.

# 41

# The Kid Who Watched Boats

ANGUS WAS TEN YEARS OLD. HE'D OFTEN SKIP SCHOOL; instead of walking in through the gates, he'd keep going, all the way to the ferry terminal at Cleveland. There he'd sit, by the water, eat his morning tea, his packed lunch, and then an apple for afternoon tea, watching the ferries and the boats as they cruised along and across Moreton Bay, most of them crossing to and from North Stradbroke Island. The sun danced across the surface of the water and Angus wished he had sunglasses but his mum and dad had told him he was too little.

But not too little for a mobile phone. That was different, even though it perplexed him that he was allowed something so grown-up but denied something so basic as a pair of sunnies that would help shield his eyes from the glare of the sun.

On this morning his phone buzzed with an incoming text. He hoped it was going to be from Donna, who he often tried to entice to join him by the docks, suggesting to her that it was way more fun than being at school. But Donna never came, even though she always said, 'I might.'

He checked the text. It read: *your car will be returned to the same place from where it was taken.*

Angus read it again and again. It didn't make any sense. Although it might have something to do with the fact that his dad never remembered his own mobile phone number. Instead he always gave out his son's, Angus's, which was really simple with four eights and three zeroes. Like when he bought their new car, a really old white 4WD, from a second-hand dealer, last year.

'Can't remember my number, mate. Never can,' he'd said. 'Can I give you my son's?'

'No worries,' the car dealer had replied.

Angus remembered it because he'd implored his dad to buy a Hummer but his dad said they couldn't afford it and such cars were a wank anyway.

Maybe, thought Angus, as he sat by the jetty and stared at the weird text message, it had something to do with their new car. Maybe it was the car dealer. Maybe he had to borrow it or something.

Angus decided to call the number that had sent the text and ask what the message was about. That would be the grown-up thing to do and his dad would probably be pleased with him. Might even praise him for 'taking the initiative', which his dad talked about a lot.

It didn't even ring.

It went straight to a message: *This number has been disconnected.*

Far away, at the top of his glass tower in the centre of Melbourne, Isosceles had returned to the job of searching for the cobweb.

# 42

# The Old Man and the Sea

'I SAW A JAPANESE SUB, CLEAR AS DAY. I WOULD HAVE BEEN about ten years old. Out of the water it came, 'bout two hundred yards off shore. No-one believed me. Said I was makin' it up. No-one believes me now. You probably don't believe me. But it's true. Out of the water she came. Clear as day. Saw it with me own eyes.'

I'd driven down Ballow Street, which soon turned into a sandy dirt track with dense low forests of scribbly gum and bloodwood trees. After a couple of hundred metres the road meandered onto the beach; beyond that was the Pacific Ocean. It was hot and the sandflies were out. It was still. There was no wind. It was deadly silent but for the constant sound of the nearby surf. I parked the vehicle under a thicket of banksia trees, all of them bent over hard, blasted by the ocean wind. Climbing out, I looked around me, into the bush. Everything seemed green. I noticed a track leading away from the road and followed it in the hope it might lead to a person or a place – if not Trev then someone who could point me in the right direction.

After a couple of minutes I saw a shack that seemed to have been made out of bits of tin, hessian bags and an odd assortment of wooden posts. Large pieces of what looked like other people's walls were propped up in a haphazard way. It looked like a big man's cubby house in among the trees. As I got closer I saw that it fronted onto the beach. A couple of ancient-looking boats, tin and wood, were assembled in the yard and there were probably about forty thousand fishing rods and sixteen hundred crab pots. I guessed this place belonged to the old guy who liked to fish. Trev.

'Hello,' I shouted.

'Yep?' came a voice as old as the ocean itself. I followed the direction of the voice, walked around the other side of the shack. An old man, wearing only a pair of shorts that might last have been washed back in the 1960s, was lying in a hammock. He was wrinkled with years of living in the sun and his crew cut hair was snowy white. He looked as though he might have shaved a week ago.

He didn't bother to turn and look at me. It seemed as if he was used to visitors.

'You're too late,' he said. His eyes were closed. I think I'd interrupted his midday sleep.

'For what?' I asked.

He rolled around and looked across at me.

'You here for the whiting, aren't ya? Sold out. Gotta be early, mate.'

'Are you Trev?' I asked.

'Who are you?' he replied.

'My name's Darian Richards. The guy in the post office told me you might know about the fortifications that were dug into the sand during the war.'

'Before the war. Not during.'

'I'm looking for one that's called the cobweb.'

'You're a cop,' he said.

'I was.'

'You're from Melbourne,' he said. I wasn't quite sure how he'd gleaned that information; he didn't look like the sort of guy I'd forget nor did he look like the sort of guy who'd leave the shack and the hammock and the beach on Stradbroke. Ever.

'You can always tell. Sydney cops are shifty. Eyes darting this way and that. Queensland cops wear sunglasses and got too much muscle on their arms, but Melbourne cops stand tall and straight and they look you in the eye. I don't like cops,' he added as an afterthought.

'I'm retired,' I said.

'You're too young to've retired. You resigned.'

'Yeah. I resigned.'

Sometimes, occasionally, a person will answer your investigative questions directly. Old people rarely ever do this. You have to give something of yourself – like an offering or a sacrifice – before they're prepared to answer your questions. You expose yourself, revealing something personal, which then allows them to follow suit. Even if it's a basic fact like the location of a seventy-year-old concrete fortification.

'I was in homicide and I got burnt out. Couldn't handle the pressure, I guess.'

His eyes narrowed as he kept staring at me. 'You don't look like a fella who can't handle pressure. In fact I woulda said the opposite. Them old fortifications, they're all on Moreton. Wrong island, mate.'

He was now sitting in his hammock, rocking it back and forwards with his thin knobby legs. I took a seat opposite him, on an upturned antique milk crate.

'I'm looking for a missing girl. I think she's in a lot of trouble. I think she's hiding out, scared, in this place called the cobweb.'

That's when he told me about seeing the Japanese submarine at the age of ten, back in 1940, a good year before the Japanese bombed Pearl Harbor and gatecrashed the war.

'After it surfaced it just sat there in the ocean. I went down to the water's edge and stared, wondering if we were about to be invaded. I was a young boy and there'd been a lot of stories about how the Japanese were coming to kill us all. A few minutes later the manhole, or whatever it's called, opened up. This figure emerged. All in white he was. White uniform. He climbed out of the sub and walked along the top of it. A couple of other sailors followed him out and they joined him. They were all looking at the island, at me. For a moment I thought they were gunna start shooting at me, that I was gunna be the first casualty in the war with the Japs. But they didn't. They just stared at me while I stared back at them. I guess we just stared at each other like that for a little while and then they went back into the sub and a few minutes later it'd gone underwater again. No-one believed a word of it. Not then. Not now. It upset me at first; don't care anymore.'

From where we sat the beach was just in front of us, partly obscured by pandanus trees and bent-over palms.

'It sounds like a true story to me,' I said. 'I've heard a lot that aren't.'

'Bet you have.'

I prefer old people. Generally speaking. They have wisdom and patience, qualities that I respect. That said, I was increasingly aware of the time. I'd been sitting with the old fisherman for almost half an hour and hadn't gotten very far in finding out anything useful. As if he could read my thoughts, he said:

'Have you seen the fortifications they built on Moreton?'

'No,' I said.

'They're small. Holes in the ground mostly. Some were made out of fibro, some were built with concrete. Some were built as machine-gun posts, most were built for blokes to sit and stare and wait; observation posts.'

He stood up and grabbed a crab pot, one made out of twine, not thin metal. It was shredded, maybe by a crab trying to escape its fate, and he began to unpick it, as if it were a woollen jumper.

'The military wanted everything built on Moreton and Bribie islands. This place was left to fend for itself. Or that's how some of the old blokes felt. Back then. I was a kid but I remember everything. Fear does that to you; you'd know about that, wouldn't you?'

I nodded and let him continue.

'So they decided to build their own. Observation posts. Gunnery posts. No help from the government, no help from the military. We were left on our own so we built on our own. They were all pretty ordinary; easy to put up, easy to take down. Built by fishermen, not by soldiers. And that was what happened: when the war was over, the old blokes went back to the sand dunes and took 'em all down. They needed the wood, the fibro, everything these things were built out of.'

I wasn't quite sure in what direction this story was headed but it wasn't sounding too good. But then he said:

'Except for one.' By now he'd disassembled the crab pot and, with a few twigs that he'd picked off the ground, had begun to fashion a new loom. 'You got a photo of that missing girl?' he asked.

I showed it to him.

'Her name is Ida,' I said.

He handed it back to me without comment and returned to the task of assembling the loom; even though his hands were worn and gnarly, he moved with dexterity.

'People were more scared than I'd ever seen. Kids don't expect their parents or any other grown-ups to be scared, so it made an impression, I can tell ya. I started to pay close attention to what the adults were doing, specially the more scared they were. I figured they were gunna be like a barometer; if they really went off their nut, then it would be time for me to do the same and take some evasive action, like run off to Black Snake Lagoon, which I figured was too scary for any Jap soldier. After the bombs started dropping up north and people started talking about the Brisbane Line, how they were gunna let the Japs take part of Queensland just north of Brisbane, hold them on the other side of some imaginary line in the sand, some of the old men got to building a new fortification. They did it quickly and they did it at night. They didn't want anyone to know about it.'

He looked up from the twine and sticks.

'You see, this was to be a place to hide in and the fewer that knew about it, the safer it would be. I watched 'em; I followed them. And after they'd left, round dawn, I'd go down and look at what they'd done.'

His hands had picked up an urgency now. The loom was starting to take form and shape.

'At first it started as a simple tunnel, but circular. Not in a smooth circle, mind, but in straight sections that ended up taking you back to the beginning. They worked fast. The Japs never came but they weren't to know that. They kept on building that tunnel until a year after the bomb dropped on Hiroshima; by then they'd figured that the Japs were never gunna come at all. By then the tunnel had grown into a series of interlocking tunnels; it'd started out by the edge of the sand dunes and had spread inland, underground. I've never heard of "the cobweb" but the tunnel I'm talking about looked like this.'

And he held up the loom, now complete. It was shaped like a perfect spider web, a series of lines making up a circle, connected to ever-smaller circles by numerous bridges. Complex, maze-like – and frightening for anything that would get trapped inside it.

Or, I imagined, anyone.

'I can see what you're thinking,' he said. 'And you're right: you get stuck inside this place and you're most likely not going to be coming out. This is a place best left alone, never spoken of, left to crumble and disintegrate under the sand.'

'Can you tell me where it is?' I asked.

# 43

# Friend Request Sent

ISOSCELES HAD ACCUMULATED 173 FACEBOOK FRIENDS IN THE space of twenty-four hours and he was feeling conflicted.

Firstly he'd used a nom de plume. Instead of his true name, Jack Sullivan, or his professional name, Isosceles Reboot, he'd chosen the name of a hero: Alan Turing, the English computer genius who helped crack the Nazi codes during the Second World War, who built the famed Enigma machine, a brilliant precursor to the computers Isosceles himself was inextricably tied to, and who was then hounded by the very society he helped save, because he was gay.

Isosceles then sent friend requests to a random sampling of people, none of whom he knew and some of whom were dead. George Orwell was a friend. Numerous bookstores and computer outlets were friends. Mark Twain was a friend. Random authors from around the globe were friends. People in Belize were friends, as were some fine-looking young women in the Congo and some interesting musicians from Antananarivo. Porn stars were friends. Lady Gaga wasn't a friend but he'd pressed 'like' on her page so she was part of his growing circle as well. Isosceles had pressed 'like' on 234 pages.

Finally he was feeling conflicted because he didn't really have any friends – as in people who lived and breathed. The closest was Darian but that was a relationship forged through work, usually unpleasant work like sifting through the Hidden Wiki to decipher the words and thoughts of horrible people like Starlight, or chasing after disgusting murderers like Winston Promise.

Despite these hesitations, he was already becoming addicted to Facebook. He went there every fifteen minutes to see what the latest updates were and, more importantly, to see if anyone new had responded to a friend request. With the staggering volume of requests that he was sending out, someone usually had. He felt exhilarated every time he logged on to see the little red markers at the top left-hand corner of the screen – people who'd said yes, you can be my friend.

He kept building, as if he was playing an online game, trawling through the 'People You Might Know' lists and hitting 'Add Friend' for each and every one.

Every time he scored a new friend he'd immediately go to their list of friends and send friend requests to all of them too. It was exhausting.

And, he knew, it was procrastination.

Normally he went at the job, no matter what it was. This time around, he was finding the work a drag.

It was the Hidden Wiki, it was the knowledge that girls had been sold by Starlight, to God knows where, to God knows who ... and that those girls were still alive. Starlight's website had photos of the girls. Testimonials from the buyers. Photos of the girls in every stage of undress; that was before they'd been sold. Photos of them afterwards – not many, but captured within the testimonials page –

in various stages of torment … and they were still alive. Some had been killed, obviously, as their owners had posted new requests, to which Starlight had responded.

He hated Starlight. What would become of her? he wondered. Even though she was on the run, Darian would find her, shut her down. But what then? he wondered. He rarely asked himself these questions; his job was to collate and disseminate information, not to speculate – certainly not to speculate on the future of these sorts of criminals, whether or not the justice system would penalise them in an appropriate way. But this time around he couldn't help thinking about the future, the time beyond her capture. As much as those girls were existing in a torment created by Starlight, in a limbo, so too was she, in his speculative mind.

He just couldn't see Darian killing a beautiful young girl, no matter how evil she was. That was, he knew, part of the problem: the girl was, on the surface, bursting with life and energy; she was ravishing, her body full of glory, her face full of the most captivating beauty. Equating that with her vile actions, equating that with the postings she made on her site in the Hidden Wiki, made it so much harder for Isosceles to endure.

He knew Darian would have thought this through. Darian was always at the end of the game before it had barely begun. He knew Darian would've resolved to hand her over to the authorities or vanish her.

But Isosceles had another idea.

# 44

# Be Thou My Vision

'So this is it?' I asked Carlos.

'This is it,' he said.

We'd driven along really narrow dirt roads, across the island. There are hardly any paved roads. It's like we'd stepped back in time or gone to a faraway wild land. After we turned off the main road and basically just drove through the bush, we didn't see anyone. The place was like empty of people. Good.

Carlos had obviously been before, because he knew where he was going. Me, I would have got seriously lost. All the bush looked the same. Thickets of Australian gum trees and even thicker grasses everywhere. Sometimes you couldn't see further than a few metres past the side of the track. To remind you you're in Queensland there are palm trees and these other weird spiky-looking trees just sort of randomly placed in the middle of the bush.

It was really hot. And really quiet. The only sound was the beach. I didn't know how far away it was but you could hear the surf all the time. The sound reminded me of being back on the balcony of my apartment on the seventieth floor.

We must have driven along dirt tracks for about an hour. It seemed like an hour. Maybe it was less. Anyway Carlos turned off the track at the edge of this sand dune and basically just drove over these stunted bushes for a few minutes and then stopped. We were in a clearing. I got out of the car. I needed to pee so I told him to look away. He didn't, the prick.

'Where do we go now?' I asked.

'It's just underneath us,' he said.

He was looking weird. We'd gotten rid of his blood-soaked clothes and I'd washed his face. He was all right in the car, as he was driving. But now he seemed odd. He was rocking backwards and forwards. Like he was stoned or something.

'Okay, let's go,' I said.

He didn't move.

'Why'd you wanna come here?' he said.

'We needed to get away. I told you. We had to get out of the Gold Coast. Just for a few days.'

'Because of me,' he said.

I really didn't want to have a conversation about his stupid behaviour. Not now. Not any time, actually. 'That ex-cop, the guy you hit, he was on to us. I told you.'

'Yeah but why here? And how'd you know about this place anyway?'

'You told me about it,' I said. He didn't, but as if he'd remember.

'But why'd you wanna come here? You, of all people. You sit up there in your flash apartment, up there on the seventieth floor, all high and mighty, drinking your champagne and vodka, looking down on all of us. Why didn't we go to Brisbane and stay in some expensive hotel? Why didn't we catch a plane, fly somewhere? Why this place? Under-fucking-ground?'

As he ranted he started to walk towards me. He was really angry. All that resentment boiling up, from all those years ago. I guess it even went back to when he pissed his pants that night he was going to kill me. I don't know why *he* was angry. If anyone should've been angry it was me.

'So why here? Tell me!' he shouted.

'It's simple, Carlos,' I said. 'I need a place that no-one knows about, a place that no-one will find. That's this place, right?'

'Yeah,' he said. 'But why?'

'To bury you,' I said.

—

I DON'T THINK anyone heard the gunshot. Carlos flew backwards, onto the sand. The only sound then was his body twitching, his hands scrabbling around in the leaves and dry grass. You could hear the surf, of course, but nothing else, not after he went still.

I'd blown his head off. It's a powerful gun. It sort of freaked me out. I hadn't used it before, not like firing it. I'd made girls fuck it, but only when they'd been bad and had to be punished. But that wasn't too often really. So when I pulled the trigger and used it ... wow.

I was pretty upset actually. I mean, I knew I was going to kill him – he had to die, there wasn't any question about it – but it would have been nicer if his body was still together. You know, I loved Carlos. He was my brother and we'd gone through a lot together. Shared a lot, done a lot. So seeing him like that, without a head, just all these entrails and horrible stuff, all sort of oozing out of him ... yuk, it wasn't right.

I couldn't have killed him with a knife and that bullshit about poison and other exotic things, that's just totally random. Guns or knives, that's it. You gotta make it easy. He would've wrestled the knife away from me. He was strong. Worked out on the beach. The hot chicks loved watching him work out on the beach. He scored pretty well that way. And there are a lot of hot chicks down at Burleigh, where he lived.

I just stood there for a bit. Listening. All I could hear was the surf. People out here, in the middle of nowhere, you know, if they heard a bang that sounded like a gunshot, what would they do? They'd stop and wonder if it was a gunshot. If they'd really heard anything. They'd wait for a repeat to have the out-of-place noise confirmed and if it didn't come a second time, they'd shrug and say to themselves, *must have imagined it* or *it might have been a car backfiring down on the beach* or *maybe there are pig hunters on the island; wouldn't be surprised in a crazy, wild island like this, where hardly anyone goes, just wild boys and their 4WDs and their back seats full of beer.*

—

HE HAD TO die. One way you could look at it, I was doing him a favour.

He'd done some dumb shit and he wasn't gunna stop. By killing him I was protecting another girl from being killed. You can say what you want about my job but do I kill girls? No. I don't. How many people have I killed? Hardly any.

Carlos had it coming to him. He knew it, that's why he was so angry and threatening after we arrived. He was almost taunting me, wanting me to pull the trigger.

And what would have happened to him if I didn't? He'd be caught, charged, he'd go down. For years. He's killed so many people: those two girls, Hannah and Allegra, that cop, whatever his name was, that person last night, whatever their name was – it was on the radio this morning as we were driving here but I can't remember; Mary, or something like that – and then there was the real Estefan and his chick and Estefan's parents. Then there was Papa Gabriel who lived next door to us in the favela, who would give me chickens when I was hungry and there were lots of other people in the favela and probably others that I don't even know about. He had it coming to him. I mean, you can't kill that many people and not get killed yourself, can you? I reckon he was pretty lucky actually, to have lived as long as he did.

I said a prayer for him. We were brought up Catholic.

I know God understands.

There were bits of Carlos's head all over the trees but I left them. I figured that the birds would eat them or they'd be blown away with the wind and rain. I had to dispose of his body so it was time to go down into the cobweb.

From behind me, I heard someone approaching, the sounds of trees and hard dried grass snapping and breaking amongst their footsteps. I turned around quickly.

But it was only Ida.

'Hi,' I said.

She was wearing shorts and a white singlet that really showed off her body. She was looking hot. She has the best legs. I'd kill for her legs; they're so thin and long. She is really sexy.

'Hi,' she said. She was nervous, I could tell.

I went up to her and I put my arms around her and held her tight. I felt the press of her breasts on mine.

'I was hoping you were going to be here,' I said. 'Don't worry,' I said, 'everything is going to be all right now.'

# 45

# I, the Jury

THE OLD FISHERMAN HAD DRAWN A MAP IN THE SAND. WITH A twig. Not being the best at directions in any way, I struggled to follow the little etchings on the ground and translate them into a journey down the beach and then inland over a couple of sand dunes and across fifty metres of dense scrub.

I guess he must have seen my look: he offered to guide me but I declined. I didn't want any witnesses to what might go down when I got there.

I thought I had a solid grip on where I was going. I climbed back into my stolen 4WD and drove back to the main road then on to a small town called Point Lookout. From the cliff tops I had incredible views of the Coral Sea and a long wide beach that swept away from me into the far distance. Clouds of salt mist rolled in with the surf. I eased on to the sand, turned right and drove slowly down towards the water where the grip was firmer. Then I hammered it, driving south, back in the direction of the Gold Coast. Soon all the buildings on Point Lookout became a blur and then they vanished into the haze of surf and the shimmer of heat. The beach was empty, not a person or car ahead of me or in the rear-view mirror. According to Trev, my old guide who I left swinging in his hammock, it would take me about ten minutes of fast driving to get where I was headed then another few minutes of rough driving across sand dunes and through bush. I just had to be certain of my turn-off, which was marked by nothing distinctive; all I could rely on was the distance – I was closely watching the k's click over on the dash – and a narrow, almost-impossible-to-discern track leading through the sand dunes.

I slowed down after ten minutes. I looked at the odometer. I was close. I peered through the window to see if I could make out a track leading up into the sand dunes.

There was a lot of sand.

Isosceles took it upon himself to call me and recite a stanza from one of his favourite poems, which I like, very much, but under current circumstances, found rather annoying:

*But at my back I always hear*
*Time's winged chariot hurrying near;*
*And yonder all before us lie*
*Deserts of vast eternity.*

—

I SHOT ALDOUS O'Reilly in the back of the head as he was walking away from me, after he'd called me weak, on his way back to his car, in the middle of a deserted road among acres of apple orchards a few miles out of the town of Bacchus Marsh. It was cold and windy, a dark afternoon, just before sundown, and he'd been following me for two hours. I think he planned to kill me but maybe he didn't have the guts.

I shot him dead then dragged his body back to his car, threw it into the boot and drove it to an abandoned quarry fifteen k's away, where I rolled it off the edge, down into the pit below. I walked back to my car, which was now covered in apple blossom, climbed in and drove home. I put away my Beretta, had a shower, then a bottle of vodka followed by two more, and slept a monster's sleep.

I didn't regret it for a second and I'd easily do it again if I had to.

—

'IT'S ALDOUS. CAN you help me do something about him, he's making my life a misery and if I don't sort it out I'm going to shoot myself.'

The call came in at my home, soft, whispered, like he was afraid or embarrassed. It was many years after I'd suffered the humiliation of beating up a nonentity, urged on by the great and highly respected cop Aldous O'Reilly. I'd passed the test and in doing so had come to be known as the guy you'd go to for help and advice if you were new to the force and scared and intimidated like I had once been. I was on a trajectory, soon to touch the flag, and I was the 'go to guy', the guy you'd call to help chart the way through the corrupt and venal world that Aldous had woven, snaring all the rookie cops along the way. I'd meet the rookie in a dark corner of a pub, in the middle of Chinatown, along one of the narrow lanes off Little Collins Street. Cops rarely ventured there and we could talk and eat and drink, mostly drink, without being seen. I didn't care but they did. Seeing me was a sign of weakness but a lot of them did it. I'd get them pissed on cheap Asian beer and listen as they told me the familiar story of how they were trying to do their best and uphold the honour of being a cop, wanting to be able to go home at night and still look their girlfriends or wives or kids in the eye and say to themselves that they weren't bad, hadn't been tainted, hadn't become a corrupt cop. Yet every day on the job old Aldous would taunt them, as he did me, pushing them to bash kids or deliver a wad of cash to the Greeks around the corner in one of the dodgy cafes on Brunswick Street. Or worse. It seemed to me, as I heard these tales of woe, as I tried to get them pissed and let them rant without ever really offering any solution, that old Aldous was becoming more extreme. Pushing the rookies further.

And then one day I was told, over beef chow mein and Tiger beer, that he'd asked a rookie cop to do away with someone – a person of no consequence, Aldous said. He was just a name. It might have been a gangster, might have been a civilian; didn't matter to the rookie, who was freaking out, and it sure didn't matter to Aldous. It didn't matter to me either.

I rang him that afternoon.

'Aldous, it's Darian Richards. I'd like to meet up with you.'

'Why would I want to waste my time on a jerk like you?' was his reply.

'I'll meet you at the Farmer's Arms tonight,' I said. It was a pub in Port Melbourne, near the beach, his watering hole, the place he went to after every shift, no matter what time of day.

He hung up without answering. Which was exactly what I expected. I'd already played out the conversation we were about to have in my head – and so I'd already started planning what I would do next.

—

'IT'S TIME TO stop,' I said as he sculled a pot of beer then reached over for a second.

We were sitting at a small wooden table in the middle of what used to be called the Ladies Lounge. That would have been a long time ago; the pub was loud with pokie machines and a television screen that played endless greyhound races at some track on the other side of the country. The bar was full of hard men. Not a lady in sight, not even in the dining room, where blokes groaned over massive T-bones and chicken parmigianas.

'Eh?' he said between gulps.

'I'm sending you a message and I want you to act on it. It's time to stop.'

Years had passed and I now outranked him. Not that he cared. He was an island, his own man, doing what he wanted according to his own rules. He'd long forgotten he was part of a team, acting within a fraternity, let alone having to abide by a code of conduct which was so basic a primary school kid could follow it.

'Dunno what you're talking about,' he said.

'Then let me tell you,' I replied. 'Because, in fact, it's quite specific. The racketeering, profiting from drug deals, stealing from victims and suspects, the fitting-up of suspects; I don't care about any of that.'

His eyes narrowed. Who was I to cast judgement on him? he was thinking.

'That's just stuff you do. You've been getting away with it for a long time and I guess you'll get away with it through to the end. What I'm talking about, Aldous, is the stuff you make other people do. Innocent people. People who didn't sign on to be instructed by you to break the law, to break their moral code, to put themselves at huge risk, not only on the job, but at home and with their future.'

'Are you takin' drugs or something Richards? I dunno what you're talking about.'

'Yes you do.'

There was a silence as he slowly looked away from me and around the pub, no doubt to see if I'd come with others who might be watching, maybe even recording the conversation. His gaze returned to mine.

'Who you working for?' he asked.

'No-one,' I said.

'Bullshit,' he laughed. 'You suddenly become a white fuckin' knight?'

'You're a bad cop, Aldous, and you've had a good run. Time to stop. Maybe even think about retiring.'

'Fuck you,' he said. 'I dunno what you're talking about, Richards, and even if I did, I wouldn't be answering to you. I don't care how much of a hot shot you've become, you got no right to talk to me, none at all.' And with that he stood up, almost knocking over his chair, and strode out. I watched him as he left the pub, walking quickly along the footpath. Through the window, between hand-painted signs advertising the specials for the day and the beers on tap, I saw his sturdy little body, marching away in righteous indignation.

I could have gone to the Commissioner. We were close and he would have listened to me. But he wouldn't have done anything and he would have thought I'd gone soft. No-one wants to know about rogue guys like Aldous. They create an island and it's respected by everyone outside it. No-one wants to deal with a crooked cop, not unless they're forced to because a newspaper has revealed something explosive or a politician goes nuts and tries to expose some corruption in the hope of getting a name for themselves. It's business as usual and don't rock the boat. Kids like I once was, rookies, are expected to deal with it. If it gets too hard, like if a rookie is asked to do something beyond the pale – execute an innocent, for instance – then that's too bad. You either do it and go down or get away free, or you refuse and get ostracised; that's the way of the world and, hey, if you don't like it, go be a fireman.

—

I MIGHT HAVE left it there – I'd shaken him and that could have been a first – but a couple of days later I heard that a young constable by the name of Ashleigh had killed herself by swallowing a bottle of Xanax. She'd worked under Aldous. She'd been bullied and harassed by him.

This I knew because she'd reached out to me, like the others, like the rookie I'd met in the Chinese restaurant the week before, asking for advice and help. I didn't meet Ashleigh, I just told her to grin and bear it, that she'd get through. That we all get through.

I went to her funeral. It was a grim day with much talk about the unfortunate pressures of the job and how young constables, women especially, need to have greater access to stress counselling to prevent the depression and anxiety that could culminate in such a tragedy. Aldous was there, in the church and, later, at the gravesite. Men and women in uniform were there and people spoke in whispers. I caught Aldous's gaze and he winked at me.

Then he smiled at me. *I'm stronger and tougher than you, boy,* was the unmistakable message.

—

HE MADE IT easy for me to kill him. He started following me.

At first I couldn't believe it; what was he trying to achieve: to scare me? Maybe he thought I'd rat on him, drive to a secret meeting with Internal Affairs. He wasn't on my tail all the time. That'd be too inconvenient. But he was there every morning, waiting down the road from where I lived. He'd pull out after I drove away from my house and follow me to HQ. Sometimes he'd appear in my rear-view mirror as I was driving home or driving during the afternoon. He must have had some sort of access to my diary, no doubt from an old mate within the eight floors at St Kilda Road.

On a wet Thursday I drove away from my home and headed out to the Western Highway, the very same road that leads all the way up to the mountains of Misery, Disappointment and Despair, where I grew up. I turned off after about forty minutes, into Bacchus Marsh, a small town that has a long avenue of remembrance where massive oak trees hang over both sides of the road, little name plaques for the men who were killed in both the world wars at their base. I knew the area well. My father used to drive me there when I was a kid; we used to jump the fences and wander through the orchards, picking apples from the trees.

I led Aldous to a lonely road miles from anywhere. In each direction all you could see were apple trees. A storm was coming in and the temperature must have been around zero. I pulled over and killed the engine, shoved the Beretta into the back of my jeans and climbed out to meet him. He'd pulled over behind me.

'I'm gunna destroy you, Richards,' he said. He was drunk, a little unsteady on his feet. For the briefest of moments I felt sorry for him.

'Like you did Ashleigh?' I said.

'Who?' he asked, genuinely nonplussed.

I pulled out my gun. He just stared at it. Didn't plead, didn't fight back, didn't ask for redemption. He just looked me in the eye.

'You're weak, Richards. Always were, always will be.'

With that he turned away and walked back towards his car.

'Aldous,' I called out to him.

He turned back as I was aiming my pistol. He saw it coming and said, 'Son, you don't understand,' then turned back again.

I shot him in the head. A single bullet.

Maybe I didn't understand but maybe I did. Nobody joins the police force to do bad things, to be corrupt, to hurt people. So what happens to those who do?

It wasn't easy killing another cop. It's not easy killing anyone. How did I and how do I reconcile it? My sworn oath is to uphold the law. Beyond that and into what really matters, my place in the world is to ensure justice. My justice.

His body was found a few days later, in the quarry where I left him. A massive search for his killer was mounted, but after a week it became clear there were so many possible suspects, crims and cops, that finding the actual trigger-man was going to be close to impossible. Too many people wanted him dead and too many of them had shaky alibis.

The person running the investigation into the murder of Aldous O'Reilly was me. After two months I went to the Commissioner and told him that we were running down blind alleys, that we'd never find the killer. We could pin it on one of the crims, I suggested, but, frankly, any defence lawyer taking part in the trial would have a field day exposing the truth behind the crooked cop. Let it go unsolved, I suggested. Maybe, I said, it'd be better that way.

He agreed.

—

I STOPPED AND climbed out of the vehicle. I stared at what looked like an incline in the dunes, like a gap between them; it was hard to tell. Most of the dunes were completely smothered in grass and low-lying scrub. Beyond them was a lot more scrub and dense forest. As I walked closer it seemed that a track could be possible. Certainly no-one had driven over the sand recently. The scrub looked pristine; no vehicles had ground across them. I decided to go for it. According to the odometer I was at the right place and my vehicle was going to fit right through the gap between the dunes, even though the concept of a track looked remote.

I climbed back in, swung the wheel and drove up the sand, through the dunes and into scrub. Trev had told me to drive in a straight line for about fifty yards. I was just old enough to remember what a yard was. I did as instructed, bashing branches from blackbutts and pandanus and scraping the sides of the vehicle with hard grass that was at least a metre tall. This wasn't a track but at least I didn't have to drive over trees.

After fifty yards of hard driving I reached my destination. I knew that because, in the middle of a clearing, was a BMW 4WD, and by its rear was a large pool of fresh blood.

I leaned down under the driver's seat and pulled out my small backpack and the Beretta.

It was fully loaded. I didn't want to use it – that wasn't part of the plan – but someone, I guessed Starlight, had already set the precedent and I wasn't going to be caught out.

# 46

# The Shepherd

HARRY HAD BEEN SHEPHERDING PEOPLE FOR OVER TWENTY-five years. First as a taxi driver then, more recently, as a limo driver. He liked his work. He'd met some fascinating people and he'd also met some horrible people. He'd driven rock stars and politicians, businessmen and kids. Some talked. Some didn't. Some gave him tips. Some gave him attitude. He'd driven parcels and dogs. He'd certainly driven a lot of people who slept. Mostly through tiredness or too much booze. Sometimes through too much dope or, on their way to or from hospital, a belly full of medication.

The girl in his back seat seemed to be on some sort of medication. She was out of it. Drugged up big-time.

It bothered him a little, and he kept on casting glances at her in his rear-view mirror. They told him she was ill. They told him she was taking a private flight for some sort of medical procedure. That bothered him too. Most times people didn't tell him anything. He was the driver and where they were going was important, not *why* they were going there.

Since the last financial crash times had been hard. He'd brought his own town car. Aside from shepherding drunken teenagers around the Gold Coast on weekend nights the business had all but dried up.

He jumped at the chance to take this job, no questions asked. Pick up a girl at the Stradbroke Island ferry terminal, drive her to the Chinchilla airport, a few hours west of Toowoomba. It was an all-day drive. They were paying him as if it were an all-week drive. No questions asked.

Fine; not to the guy who hired him on the phone or to the girl who led his passenger out of the car at the ferry terminal, not to the pilot who'd be waiting for him by the plane. But a few questions to himself. Like: what, really, is going on? And: does this girl know what's happening to her?

She was young and very pretty. She reminded him of his own daughter and he wondered where her father was. Did he know what was happening to his girl?

It didn't feel right.

But he kept on driving. He needed the money.

—

IT WAS A smooth drive; he didn't need the GPS, he knew where to go. He stopped just outside Toowoomba and ate lunch, a curried lentil pie that his wife, Eve, had heated up for him and then wrapped in silver foil. He parked by the side of the road and enjoyed the sun. The girl inside was still flaked. She'd fallen down onto the seat, her body bent and twisted, like a doll, because of the seatbelt wrapped tight around her waist.

He stared at her. Her hair had fallen across her face. She was snoring.

For a dark moment he thought about climbing into the back seat, lifting up her dress, pulling down her pants and having sex with her. She'd never know. But as soon as he'd imagined that – as soon as he'd seen the image of her naked sleeping body spread out on the back of his limo – he corrected himself, shaking the bad thoughts away.

—

HE KEPT DRIVING.

Twenty minutes out of Dalby, as the land started to get dry and lonely, he saw up ahead on the straight, empty road a blockage of some sort. It didn't make sense. But there was something.

Spread across the road.

He squinted and eased his foot off the accelerator, as what lay ahead came into view.

A car, white, ordinary. And a motorcycle. A Harley. Parked right across the road, creating a barrier. It looked like something out of an American movie. Like that old film he remembered seeing, *Vanishing Point*. Or that TV show he loved to watch as a kid, *Dukes of Hazzard*.

He slowed down.

What the fuck is this all about? he asked himself.

Standing in front of the bike was this tall thin dude dressed in jeans and a white singlet. Long white hair tied back in a ponytail and his body totally covered in tatts. In his hand was a long thin knife, which he seemed to be spinning on the end of his index finger.

Standing in front of the white Commodore was a girl. Jeans and white T-shirt, hair also tied back. At least she looked normal. She also looked like an A-grade model. While the guy looked like a bleached satan.

—

Blond Richard stepped away from his bike and held his hand up like he was a cop.

'Halt!' he cried. Even though the guy in the approaching car had no chance of hearing what he said. Still, he liked the sound of his commanding voice and thought it was pretty groovy doing traffic cop stuff.

Harry pulled his car to a stop.

He sat inside, staring at these two standing in the middle of the road, their vehicles behind, blocking it.

Has this got anything to do with me? he wondered. And, as soon as that thought crossed through his mind, he said to himself: it's all about the girl.

Blond Richard and Maria walked towards him. She was on her phone.

'We've got him,' she said.

'Well done,' said Isosceles, who'd been tracking the limo since it left Starlight at the ferry terminal.

—

Not for an instant did Harry think about reversing, driving away. Not for an instant did he even bother to think about the money he was about to lose. He climbed out of the car, squinted in the hard sun and said:

‘What’s going on?’

‘We’re taking your passenger,’ said the woman.

‘Yeah. What do I tell my employer?’ he asked.

In a movement that barely registered with Harry, the albino swept down and carved his knife through the air, slicing into his front tyre, the air now whistling from it.

‘Tell him you got a flat. Tell him the chick woke up and did a runner. Scampered her way across the dry earth. Saw her vanishing into the distance. Figured she musta carked it from dehydration. Use your imagination.’

Maria was pulling Tina out from the back seat.

Harry stepped away and watched as Blond Richard moved to them, put one arm around her shoulders and the other under her legs. Whisked her up like a baby and walked back to the white car.

Within seconds they were gone.

# 47

# The Fear

IDA HELPED ME WRAP CARLOS'S BODY IN A TARP. I'D PACKED it into the boot of my car. I was prepared. She helped me drag him down the tunnel into the bunker they called the cobweb. She didn't say much and she did a good job of pretending to be strong. I was impressed actually. I imagined she would have howled and wailed at seeing her lover with his head shot off. But no. She pretended to be okay about it. Didn't really say anything but I knew she was thinking at a thousand miles an hour, wondering what I was doing here and what was going to happen now.

Ida's smart but not as smart as me. Anyway, I know she's thinking ahead, trying to figure out what I'm going to do and if she's safe. Maybe she'll try and run. Maybe she'll try and overtake me, knock me out, that sort of thing. Or maybe she'll do nothing.

That's what I think she'll do. Nothing. She'll just wait for me to act then she'll react.

That works for me because I've got plans for her. She's about to be sold. She's going to replace the dead girl, the sexy dark-haired one that Carlos fucked and slashed. Ida's got a new home, in Jakarta. I'll have to make sure she's subdued before I tell her.

I think her new owner is going to be really happy. After all, she's blonde and gorgeous, curvaceous and busty. She's got an awesome smile and a great arse. I've been wanting to sell her since I first met her but, you know, that was impossible because she and Carlos became close and then, of course, she started working for us, so she was one of the team. Well, those days have gone now. It's just me and it'll be better that way. Just me.

—

IDA HAD BEEN worried about making the call to Darian. It was a mistake. It was impulse. She regretted it. And ever since making the call she'd been thinking about him driving down to find her and worrying about exactly what else he would find.

Her guilt, that's what he'd find.

Her culpability.

It was impulse, a call to a man she barely knew, a saviour, a guy who had rescued her once before, in a moment of desperation, when she needed to be saved.

She hadn't thought about the repercussions. All she'd thought about was the horror that spread out before her, the growing list of missing girls, the deaths and the blood and her lover, a burning need to run away, to flee, to be safe.

—

AFTERWARDS, AS SHE kept on fretting about the call, she realised that Darian would probably have called her mother. That's what cops do when people go missing, and even though she didn't think of herself as a missing person, she knew that's how Darian would be thinking of her.

So she called Annie, her mum, told her she was all right. She didn't need to ask her mum any questions to get information. The first thing she said was 'Are you all right?' and went on to say how desperately worried she was.

Ida had calmed her down and then got her to promise she'd call Darian and tell him everything was okay, that he didn't need to keep looking for her. That it was just a misunderstanding.

She hoped it would work. She didn't know Darian but she did know he was an excellent investigator. And she also knew that he was retired, that he wanted to sit on his deck and watch the river. He didn't really want to be bothered looking for her. That's what she was counting on, his desire to watch the river and live a life of calm.

These worries had been overwhelming her but they'd quickly dissolved when she heard a gunshot and saw that Starlight had arrived.

Now she really had a problem.

—

'WOULD YOU CUT off your arm to save me?' he asked.

'No,' said Ida, laughing.

'No, really: if you had to?' said Carlos.

'Of course I would,' she replied, without hesitation.

'Good,' he said. 'I love you.' And he drew her closer to him, their naked bodies holding each other firm and hard.

'I love you too.'

But she didn't. How can you love a person you're scared of? How can you love a man who dealt with emotions and peoples' futures like the cigarettes he flicked out the window of his car while driving. At first he was charming and dangerous and sexy and compelling, everything she'd missed in her previous men, all of them boys with sprouts of hair on their chests and high, anxious voices and uncertainty pulsing through their veins. At first he was funny and caring and offered to take her out to dinner, to the movies, to the bar at the Q1, the tallest building in the country; he'd buy her flowers and arrive at her apartment unannounced with plans to go sailing or snorkelling. He took her to Stradbroke Island and they had sex in the sand. Later, that same day, she showed him the cobweb, which she'd discovered when researching an assignment for her history class. Holding hands, they walked down the first tunnel. She wanted to show him the core but he was scared, although he pretended otherwise, and told her he was getting claustrophobic. She laughed, teased him, then led him out.

That was the man she loved. Thought she loved. He asked her to teach him German and he taught her how to say 'you are hot' in Portuguese. He showed her how to play soccer and convinced her to follow Brazil. Brazil, he said, had the most awesome soccer teams and stars; giants that an entire nation swooned to. Austria, not so much.

His name was Estefan. Then, a few weeks later, he told her to call him Carlos. He told her Estefan was a name given to him by his family and that he hated it.

She wasn't lonely and she wasn't looking for a lover, nor was she wanting to fall in love; she didn't want a relationship, she didn't want a person to worry about or, when she wasn't worrying, to think about or, when she wasn't even thinking about him, to know that there was, in her life, someone else.

He told her he enrolled in the scriptwriting class to further his English. That was a lie. He was trawling. Looking for pretty girls. He found one: her.

Then he found more.

At first it was a game. It was, really, she told herself. Lately she'd been telling herself a lot of things, telling herself that her part in all this was innocent, that she'd been trapped or conned or hoodwinked. She didn't mean to do any of it. She didn't mean to hurt anyone. It wasn't her, it was them. Carlos and his little sister.

She loved Starlight. She couldn't believe how sexy she was, she couldn't believe how, at almost the same age as her, a girl could be so wealthy. Living in a huge white apartment on the seventieth floor of the tallest building in the country. At first she thought Carlos was lying, trying to impress her. But he wasn't; far from it. Ida could see they were brother and sister just by the way they interacted with one another. He was envious of Starlight, he was even a little bit resentful. She understood. Her brother was always the favoured child of their parents, who said there was no such thing as favouritism. But there was. He was studying law in Boston. He got what he wanted. She rarely did, not from her parents. Like Carlos, Ida resented her sibling. But she couldn't help falling under the trance of his sister. She was fun, no cares in the world, she teased Carlos and made Ida laugh.

Living so high above the ground it was like she was on top of the world.

—

AT FIRST IT was simple. 'Make a friend with her,' said Carlos. 'Invite her out, we all go have a drink.' They'd just come out of a class and he was pointing at one of the students, a girl named Justine. She was hot. All the girls envied her and all the guys stared at her. Once they'd sat together, in a lecture, and Justine had smiled and made her a Facebook friend, then and there, on her laptop, in the middle of the lecture.

She was nice, friendly; Ida liked her. But when Carlos had said that – invite her out, make a friend with her – she was instantly jealous. Did he want Justine over her? Was that what it was all about?

Ida resisted the feelings of jealousy, tried to be grown up about it, and did what he asked.

Justine accepted and they went out to the uni bar. Carlos paid. Didn't say very much. In fact he didn't even seem to be very interested in Justine. He spent most of the time on his phone, texting. That made her feel better and over drinks she and Justine became friendly.

Justine came from overseas, like them. She too was an international student and with that, they all had something in common: annoyed at how the uni was ripping them off, making them pay so much more than the Australian students, lonely sometimes for their home, feeling weird in an amazing place like the Gold Coast with all its beaches and nightclubs and bars but with few friends to enjoy it.

Carlos paid for the vodkas and they all got tipsy. Well, not all of them. Carlos said he had to drive so he should be careful.

She and Justine got pretty drunk. They were meant to hand in an assignment on the Friday but fuck that, they said to each other, after the fourth vodka.

Carlos had told her to ask Justine all about her family and her friends here on the Gold Coast. Innocent questions. At the time. Questions anyone would ask a student from overseas.

As Ida and Justine talked he texted. Ida thought it was rude and when Justine went to the bathroom, told him so.

'I'm telling Starlight about her,' he replied.

And as if that made a difference, Ida nodded and chose not to admonish him anymore. She was impressed by Starlight – so it was all right.

—

THAT WAS SIX months ago. That was the beginning. That was the first time Ida shepherded a girl to Carlos, who introduced her to Starlight, who then sold her to a faceless man on the other side of the world. The first time she didn't know what they were doing and after she was told, after she began to have concerns for Justine, who had stopped going to lectures, stopped taking calls, stopped being at university, after she summoned the courage to ask Carlos what had happened to her, knowing somehow instinctively that he knew, she tried to walk away, tried to cut her ties with him and his sister. But did she tell anyone? Did she report it to the authorities?

No, she stayed silent.

And with her silence came a complicity that he used against her. She was, he said, to blame. It was far too late now for her to say anything.

But then, in the desperate time that followed, as she raged against herself for the role she had played in ending Justine's life, Carlos returned to her. Barged in actually. He and Starlight. They consoled her, told her that Justine was doing okay, that she was, really, happier where she was now living. Starlight told her that it wasn't evil like the sex slavery stuff that everyone talks about. It was more like arranged marriages. Starlight said she was just a broker between charming, wealthy men and single girls, most of whom needed some direction and certainly some love and adoration. And, Starlight said, one thing about these guys was that they adored their princesses. Imagine, she asked Ida, if a man was so in love with you that he was willing to pay a fortune for you – up to fifty thousand dollars, sometimes more? Wouldn't that show how devoted he was? Was that a man to be fearful of? Was that a transaction to condemn?

Ida didn't believe in what she said but she wanted to, she wanted to think that what she'd done wasn't evil, that what she'd done was actually something kind. Reason slipped away, into a shadowy part of her mind, and she heard herself agreeing with Starlight.

As soon as she did, she felt a lot better.

Gone was the guilt. And the fear.

All they wanted her to do was meet pretty young girls at the uni. Introduce herself to them, get to know them, get them to like her, trust her. Then introduce them to Carlos, her boyfriend.

Starlight had confided to her that Carlos couldn't do it alone. Girls didn't trust him, he was a bit too dangerous. She joked that Ida was special. To be Carlos's girl you had to be special.

It made her, fleetingly, feel proud. She was the girl who tamed Carlos.

—

SHE LIVED WITH that deception until last week, when her world spiralled out of control and she was thrust into a pit of darkness. When she discovered Carlos had killed two new girls. She knew them. She'd introduced them to him. By then it was second nature and the thoughts of ramifications had completely vanished from her mind.

'Hey, can you help me move some stuff?' he'd asked her over the phone.

'Sure. What stuff?'

'Ah …' He seemed to have lost concentration.

'Carlos?'

'Oh, yeah. Sorry. Carpets. Two carpets.'

And then Ida heard him giggling. 'I'll come pick you up in an hour, okay?'

—

TWO LARGE ROLLED-UP carpets on the back seat of his car.

Lately he seemed buzzed, kinetic, his eyes dizzying like spinning tops. She wondered if he was on meth. He wasn't the guy she met six months earlier, the soft and charming young man who called himself Estefan. She was starting to fear for herself. He'd be smiling and laughing and making love to her one minute then rampaging the next.

As a precaution she'd taken the pink phone that Darian had given her last year. Charged it up again and kept it on her at all times. Just in case.

When she arrived on the Gold Coast it seemed like a relic from her past, something of no relevance. Instead of throwing it away she dumped it at the bottom of her wardrobe.

As they turned off the road and drove along a narrow park ranger's track, with dense bushland on either side of them, Ida turned to him. 'Where are we going?' she asked.

'There's a lake up here. Somewhere.'

A lake? She turned around to look at the two rolled-up carpets. What was going on?

But she didn't ask. She kept silent.

—

CALLING DARIAN WAS impulsive. Carlos had snatched the phone out of her hand before she even realised what the ramifications could be. But she was innocent. She hadn't done anything wrong, not really.

He threw her phone into the bush and slapped her hard across the face. Then he dragged her back to his car, shoved her into the passenger seat and drove in fury and silence back to her apartment. He pulled up, leaned across her and opened her door.

'Fuck off,' was all he said.

Back inside her apartment she wept.

She wept for herself, she wept for the dead girls he'd left behind in the water by the shore of the lake, she wept for the boy she thought she might have loved, she wept for her stupidity and for having on her conscience other peoples' death and misery, but above all, she wept for herself.

Much later that night, in the early hours of the morning, Carlos returned. He let himself into her apartment. She found him at her desk, on her laptop. His hands were bloody. He was posting updates on Facebook.

About his beloved Brazil soccer team and the World Cup.

'What are you doing here?' she asked.

'I had to go back. I was going to bury them. But there was a cop,' he said, then turned back to her laptop.

'Go,' she said. 'I don't want you here anymore.'

'Okay,' he said. He stood up and walked out. That was the last time she saw him alive. She cleaned up the mess of blood that he left on the desk, on the floor, in the kitchen.

Then she fled.

—

IDA HAD BEEN living in darkness. Underground. That's what fear and guilt does to you. She'd been hiding, too afraid to come up into the sun – sometimes she did – but rarely. Once she'd walked into the nearest town and taken out some money, for food, and even the simple act of receiving cash from the ATM had been familiar and comforting in a world of fear.

'Are you scared?' she heard Starlight ask.

She turned to face her. They were in the main room, the largest space inside the bunker.

'Don't be,' said Starlight as she walked towards her.

# 48

# Darkness Visible

'ARE YOU SCARED?' I HEARD SOMEONE ASK, A GIRL'S VOICE, far away, reverberating along the dark tunnels, off the hard walls underground.

It sounded like Starlight's voice but I couldn't be sure. I certainly couldn't be sure what direction it came from.

'Don't be,' I then heard as I kept shuffling through the dark, my hands outstretched to steady my balance.

I'd been calling it an underground tunnel; I was wrong. It was an underground bunker, sophisticated and set up for some serious long-term hiding in case of an enemy invasion. Isosceles had, by the time I'd driven into the clearing, discovered evidence of a vast network of underground bunkers and tunnels built before and during the war, and that they linked all the way from Melbourne to Townsville, some two-and-a-half thousand kilometres. The cobweb, as Ida called it, couldn't have been part of that network, as it was on an island, and while I was struggling to believe that such a vast underground network of tunnels and bunkers actually did exist, I couldn't imagine there was a link under water, even though the stretch between the mainland and the island was only a few k's.

For that matter, I couldn't have imagined the sophistication of the cobweb. I was expecting a narrow series of squat tunnels, dank and without any illumination, smelling like rotten shoes after a day at the beach, a place where a person in hiding would fold into the earth and pretend they didn't exist. It was nothing like that.

Trev had told me that the entrance was dug into the ground, at the edge of a high dune; he told me I couldn't miss it.

I'd been missing it. There was a long and wide dune, covered in swathes of black wattle, she-oaks and creeping grass. It was a barrier between the clearing and the beach. I didn't know if it was the high dune he was talking about. I didn't actually know what a high dune was; I assumed it was tall. This wasn't.

Coming from the hard city of Melbourne, bush and sand dunes haven't much featured in my investigations; I scoured the immediate landscape for some telltale sign. That yielded nothing. I wasn't sure when Trev had last been here and although my knowledge of sand island undulations is tremendously limited I did suspect that the furious winds from the ocean would, over time, erode, distort and deform the immediate landscape, just as they had bent and twisted the trees and bushes that I'd driven past.

I went over to Starlight's BMW and tried to follow her tracks. They met up with another set of tracks, which seemed to come from the scrub, away from the dunes and the beach. I tracked them back to the pool of blood, where they went around in circles, as if examining it from all angles, then off again, away from the long and wide dune. There were drag marks on the ground, as if a body had been moved.

I lost the tracks within a thicket of bracken and a web of green creeper grass. I kept on walking, in a straight line until they re-emerged when the sand overwhelmed the grass. Up ahead of me was a clutch of large boulders – they didn't look like part of the natural landscape. I walked across to them, shoved one aside and found myself staring into a pit of darkness, the entrance to a small round cave.

—

I'M NOT FOND of being underground. In my waking days it's been a rare experience; the occasional trip into a mine or a large tourist-orientated cave, staring with amazed kids oohing and aahing at stalactites and stalagmites. Creatures like moles and badgers live underground. It's not a place for people.

It's a place of my nightmares. One in particular: a recurring nightmare I had, less so now, when I was hunting the Train Rider. I was always running along a brick tunnel and he was ahead of me. I was chasing him. Along the floor of the tunnel, emerging from the gloom within, every thirty or forty metres, would be a crumpled body, clothes and a tangled mess of arms and limbs awash in blood. His victims. Young girls, their lives ruined by his real-life rampage. They just appeared, like ghosts, as if mocking me. I knew each one of these collapsed bodies, broken and torn, by name. I'd chased their tormentor through the city of Melbourne without any success, and down below, through this tunnel, in my sleep. I was always behind him, always almost catching up to him, then, as if propelled by an inhuman force, he'd burst ahead and beyond my reach. He rarely looked back at me but when he did his features were bland and impossible to distinguish but for his eyes which were sockets of flaming red fury.

Those nightmares stopped once I'd relocated to a safe and quiet life on the Noosa River, abandoning my life as an investigator in homicide. I'd found peace and solace in my sleep. I hoped I'd find peace and solace in my days awake – and most times I did. The abrupt resignation from the police force had worked as I hoped. It allowed me to breathe without a tight band of anguish around my chest, anguish and tension at not having caught him, not being good enough. It had erased the darkness.

I felt as though I was being forced to atone for my abandonment as I stepped into the tunnel, narrow and dank, as I crawled through and into a large corridor, its sides and roof supported by solid wooden beams and roughly hewn planks of timber.

Trev had given me an old Dolphin torch. I switched it on. Its yellow beam was dull and short. I wasn't sure how long the battery would last. I decided to try making my way along the tunnels without it. It was going to be of more use on the way back.

I allowed the darkness to envelop me so I could become accustomed to it, so I'd be able to get my bearings and continue onwards with some degree of vision. Not much came, but enough for me to see ahead, to see that this tunnel ran for about twenty metres and then turned. I could see openings ahead: more tunnels leading off this one, as if it were based on the design of a spider's web.

As I began to penetrate the tunnel I saw that someone had scrawled a message on one of the walls. It was written in large black paint, hastily I guessed, as the words bled with drops screeching down to the floor.

It read: *We are all doomed.*

—

'COME HERE, I'VE got something for you,' I heard the girl say.

Her voice didn't seem any closer.

# 49

# 'For in Hope We Have Been Saved'

IDA IS SCARED. SHE'S TRYING REALLY HARD NOT TO BE, BUT I can see it.

I like it when people are scared of me.

She's trying to be tough. She's trying to be my friend. She thinks that if she's nice to me I'll be nice back to her. I've played that game too; the last time was when I was really nice to the killer who called himself Wizard God. Although he wasn't nice back to me. It didn't work that time.

I hate it when people try to be nice to me because they're scared. It's weak and pathetic. I hate it.

'Ida, don't be scared. What's wrong?' I asked.

'I'm just sort of freaked out, you know, seeing your brother like that.'

—

SHE IS GOING to kill me, thought Ida. I'm going to die in this underground bunker that hardly anybody knows exists. At the hands of a crazy girl who I once admired. She is going to shoot my head off like she did her brother's.

The thought of his body, lying on the ground, his head gone, blood oozing out ... it made her retch. Starlight had made her drag it down into the tunnels, made her dump it in one of the dozens of corridors that crisscrossed the bunker.

I'll look just like him. A headless bloodied body left to rot in an underground tunnel.

—

'YOU WERE BRAVE, babe,' I said. I walked across to her. She wasn't moving. She was just staring at me. Her eyes bug-eyed and staring at me.

We were in this large room or cavern. Ida said we were in the core or the middle of the cobweb. I guess it's where the spider would live, if this were a real cobweb. It was pretty cool. Whoever built this place sure expected to be living here for a long time. Nothing like those underground bunkers the English built during the Second World War, in their backyards, where they hid as the Nazis dropped bombs on them. I learned all about that when I lived in London.

This place was solid. The walls were made out of rocks, bricks, pieces of timber. And it wasn't like you had to crouch or anything like that. I could raise my hands and still not touch the ceiling. And it wasn't like we were in darkness either, not here, not in this room. Whoever built this place added in electricity. They were planning to live here. It had something to do with the Japanese invasion and then it had something to do with all that crazy wacko stuff where people thought the world was going to blow up in a nuclear world war.

—

IDA WAS FROZEN as Starlight walked towards her. They were in the largest of the spaces underground; she was at least ten metres away and walking slowly. The room was wide and circular. There were eight portals leading back to eight separate tunnels. Each of them was cut across by another eight circular tunnels, spreading outwards. Ida knew that this entire place was at least a hundred and fifty metres wide.

'What are you going to do to me?' she asked.

'Nothing, babe.'

'We should go. I don't think we should stay here any longer,' Ida said.

Starlight stopped walking. Smiled. 'I think so too,' she said.

—

I PULLED OUT my gun. I'd wedged it between my belt and shorts. I don't know if Ida had seen it before but she must've known I was carrying it. After all, how else did I kill Carlos?

'Turn around, Ida,' I said.

She did as she was told.

'Kneel down, on the ground.'

She obeyed me.

'Don't kill me. Please,' she said.

I laughed. 'I'm not going to kill you, babe. You're way too valuable for that.' And I pulled out a small roll of plastic wire. Totally the best to tie up a person's wrists.

—

IDA DIDN'T BELIEVE her. *I'm going to die. I'm going to die. I'm going to die.* The four words kept repeating through her mind. With her back to Starlight, kneeling on the hard cold floor, quivering, furious at herself for being such a dumb fucking idiot, she thought: *There is no hope.*

The absence of hope. Exactly what she needed. Hope is what sent the Jews to their death in the concentration camps. She remembered hearing that when she was at school. They didn't rise up, because they were hopeful, didn't strike back at their guards. They did nothing. Because they were consumed with the hope that they would survive.

She heard Starlight's footsteps drawing close, then she felt the girl's hands reach down to her.

# 50

# Fairytale Ending

The voices stopped and then I heard what sounded like a scuffle. I heard what sounded like a distant scream of pain.

'Fuckin' bitch,' I heard.

I was shrouded by darkness but there seemed to be some light up ahead. As the tunnels were circular, with intersecting tunnels every ten metres or so, it was hard to get an accurate fix of how far I'd penetrated and where the light was coming from. It was dull and hazy, like a shady pocket of pre-dawn silver within a black sky.

I was deeply uncertain I'd find my way through the dark tunnelled maze. Before I'd come down into the cobweb I'd stuffed my backpack full of pieces of white coral that I'd seen scattered across the ground up above. Like Hansel and Gretel in the fairytale, I dropped a piece every ten or fifteen metres along my journey. I felt like something of an idiot but I knew I was bound to get lost on my way back to the entrance. I kept turning left, then right, hoping I was edging my way closer to the centre of the web, which is where I assumed the voices were coming from, where I assumed Starlight, and probably Ida, were.

The voices had stopped. I thought I heard footsteps running away from me. I couldn't be sure.

I turned into another tunnel and, about thirty metres ahead of me, was a rectangular glow of light. Trev, the old fisherman, had told me that one of the locals had wired up the place back in the mid 1960s, at the height of the Cold War.

—

I STEPPED INTO a wide circular room with eight doorways. The room was bathed in a dirty yellow light, coming from an ancient fluoro that swung from a piece of wire coming out of the ceiling.

Starlight lay on the ground, crumpled and bloody. Next to her was a gun, a mean-looking Smith & Wesson. I guessed it had been recently used but I hadn't heard the sound of a gunshot down here so Ida was still alive.

I crossed over to her, rolled her onto her back, checked her pulse and the head wound around which a thick ooze of blood was congealing.

Her eyes fluttered open and she tried to say something.

I didn't bother asking what it was. I rolled her onto her front, pulled her arms behind her, put one knee into her back and twined a coil of tape around her wrists.

'Ida!' I called. 'It's Darian!'

I heard the sound of my voice booming around the circular walls of the room. But I didn't hear anything else.

—

IDA HAD STOPPED running.

It had been a blind bolt into one of the tunnels. She'd caught

Starlight off-guard, dragged her to the ground, grabbed her hair, pulled her head up and then smashed it back into the solid floor. Starlight had been stunned. Ida could have run then but she didn't. She saw Starlight's gun, yanked it out from under her belt and brought it down hard onto the other girl's head. Then she ran.

Through the first opening, down a tunnel, into another one turning left, into another, turning right, down that and into a third. Then she stopped.

She heard Darian's voice, muffled, distant, calling out to her.

The shame and the guilt and the knowledge that she would be held accountable for her actions made her want to keep on running. The desperate urge to be free made her turn back in the direction from which she'd come.

That direction was clear until she reached the first intersection where another tunnel crossed over. Had she turned left or right? What was the correct way back? She closed her eyes and tried – calmly – to piece together the route she'd taken.

*Left. I turned left*, she said to herself.

She turned in what she thought was the correct way.

Moments later she realised she was lost.

—

I HEARD IDA calling out to me. It seemed like her voice was a long way away. I called back, hoping the sound would anchor a route back for her. But the next time she called she was even more distant.

Starlight was laughing. She thought it was amusing that Ida had gotten herself lost in the maze of tunnels. I wanted to kick her in the head to shut her up but I restrained myself.

I called out one last time.

And there was no response.

I had no choice. If I'd gone searching for her I too would have gotten lost. I dragged Starlight to her feet and pushed her ahead of me.

I left Ida in there.

# 51

# Saved

'You do this to all the girls?' I asked.

He didn't answer. Just kept on binding my already-tied ankles to a metal bar under the passenger seat of his vehicle. My arms were tied together behind my back and he'd put the seatbelt on. I couldn't move. I guess he was worried that I might have kicked at him while he drove.

I would have.

'I don't know what you think's been happening but I'm the victim here,' I said. 'Ida was the one who picked the girls, she was the one who ran the whole thing. I was working for her. You won't find anything that connects me to criminal behaviour.'

Still he didn't speak. Oh well. Have it your way.

'I found my brother. Ida killed him with that gun that was next to me down there. She's evil, Darian. I think you did the right thing leaving her down there. Did you see the writing on the wall as you went in? That's Ida. She's doomed.'

—

It's a really pretty drive along the beach. I think Stradbroke is underrated. At first I thought it was boring but that might have been because I was so stressed out. I think I could spend a bit of time over here, lie in the sun, get a really good tan. No distractions, that's what's good about it. Maybe for a week. No longer than a week. I'd go insane if I had to spend more than a week here.

Darian saved me. Really. I don't think I would have been able to find my way out of that place. I sure couldn't have relied on Ida to help me, not after she realised what was happening to her.

—

'You is saved.' That's what the black guy who called himself Wizard God said to me.

Saved from being shot, yeah sure, but about to be sold into some sort of slavery.

The first bid was for six thousand dollars. Is that all I'm worth? I thought. Is that the sum total of my body, my experience, my abilities? Is that how much the rest of my days are to be valued at? Six thousand dollars?

But shut up, these are the thoughts of a victim, I told myself. Victims die, I told myself. I'm not like that, I haven't come all the way from Rio to die or be sold, not me.

So I did, I shut up and stopped thinking like that, feeling sorry for myself. Instead I thought about how I was going to get away. I wasn't dead, I was saved.

First rule of the survivor is this: watch and observe, know your enemy by keeping your eyes open and your mouth shut.

Second rule: never feel sorry for yourself. That makes you a victim again and remember what I told you? Victims die.

He told me to stand up, to look at him while he put me on Skype. He told me that this is what his great-great-grandfather and grandmother went through, standing in front of prospective buyers, in a market, being sold as slaves. Naked like me. He laughed and said, 'Swings and roundabouts, sister, how about that? What would my great-great-grandparents have thought if they knew I was doing the same thing to a white girl?'

The Spaniel told him to tell me to cover my breasts with one of my arms and place the other between my legs, as if I was scared and wanted to hide my nakedness. He said it looked better for the customers. They didn't want a brazen naked girl. They wanted a scared and humiliated naked girl. The Spaniel told him to tell me to move away from the bed. The dead guy's spattered body was in the background of the shot.

I did what I was told and as I heard the bids of distant voices from scattered parts of the world – the voices of men who had been woken at a minute's notice for an online auction of a naked girl found in a London hotel room – I thought about the options. I thought about how I was going to escape. Being auctioned was good because it meant I had a value. I was important to them, I was income and guys like these love their income. That's all they live for. I know. I'm like that too.

I stopped listening to the bids, stopped thinking about my life's worth valued by these creeps and thought only about the angles, how to jump this guy. He was stupid but he was vicious and he had the gun.

—

I WAS SOLD at twenty-two thousand euros to an Indian man who lived in Calcutta.

'Now we is gunna get you ready. You get dressed, girl. Then you and me, we is gunna wait till Jackie arrives.'

'Where?' I asked.

'What?'

'Where are we going to wait?'

He thought about it for a moment then said, 'Here.'

'We should go downstairs, wait in the foyer,' I said as I indicated the dead guy on the bed. 'He told me he was expecting someone to come and see him really early in the morning.' It was just five, another hour until dawn.

Wizard God stared at me, wondering if I was trying to trick him, wondering what the downside was, wondering if I was going to try and do a runner. I was and maybe he knew it but he had to get me out of the room, down the corridor, into the lift, into the foyer and out of the hotel. He had to gamble on that risky journey either now or later.

I stared back. I'd been staring into his dead eyes for over two hours now. Stare into a person's eyes for that long and you'll get a sense of who they are, how dangerous they are, maybe you'll also get a sense of where their weaknesses are, when they look away, blink, when they're thinking or when they're reacting on instinct. He was dangerous and he'd kill me with brutal pleasure, that I knew. But I also knew he wasn't sure of himself, not in all circumstances. He would smile at me as he told Spaniel how he'd fuck me then kill me, he'd smile at me as I was in the shower naked, he'd smile at me as he slid the barrel of his gun into my vagina, he'd smile as he boasted how he'd shot the dead guy on the bed, he'd smile as he boasted about finding me, wanting more money, how clever he was. But he was also anxious – when he tried to connect to Skype before the auction, when he was told to manoeuvre me away from the bloody background, and now, when I was telling him someone was coming to the room in the hotel. He might be chief of the kingdom in this room but he wasn't in the corridor or in the foyer. Me, I breathed easy in these sorts of hotels, from the three-star to the five-star. I knew how they worked and they didn't intimidate me. But Wizard God wasn't used to them. He was a pub guy. Once he had me out of the room I had my chance, my only opportunity. Once he had me out of the hotel, on the street below, waiting for the car driven by Jackie to arrive, he had me again. But I had the upper hand as soon as we walked out the door of the room, from there to the front glass revolving doors downstairs. It was enough time, there were enough places, I had my chance and I knew where I was going to take it.

What would he do? Shoot me? In the corridor? In the foyer? Not him. Not the Sudanese Wizard God. This isn't the desert, black boy, and I'm not a native girl trembling beneath you. Not anymore.

I looked him in the eye. He hadn't been staring at me with that hateful lasciviousness anymore. Now I was worth twenty-two thousand euros I wasn't as attractive, wasn't good for the fucking and torture and killing he had himself all ramped up on.

'We should go downstairs and wait in the foyer,' I said.

He didn't reply, which meant he'd do what I suggested. I could tell. His dead eyes had glanced towards the door to the room. Even though there was a 'Do Not Disturb' sign hanging on it, he was vulnerable. Downstairs in the foyer was safe, even if it meant leaving the sanctuary of the room with me as his hostage. He'd have people around him, desk staff, bar-room staff. He'd be anonymous down there, not the big black dude with the gun hanging on his hand in a room full of blood.

'Get dressed,' was all he said.

He thought he could control me. They all do. Everyone does.

He thought I was scared. He thought the fear would make me do what he said.

—

As soon as we stepped out of the lift, into the lobby of the hotel, I was home free. In the movies you see bad guys hustling poor, scared people out of lifts, across the floor, through all the bustle of the hotel, out into the street. Bullshit. The second the lift doors open the guy with the gun has lost everything. All he can rely on is fear.

As soon as the lift doors opened, I wrestled myself out of Wizard God's grip and walked straight across the floor into the open bar area. I knew it'd be full. It doesn't close. Smart guys from the city hang out there all night, telling each other stories about how much money they make and what sort of fast cars they're going to buy and how many chicks they'll fuck on their next holiday to Majorca.

I walked straight up to a bunch of five guys. All wearing suits, ties loosened, lounging at the bar. They were smashed and laughing at each other's brilliant jokes.

'Who'd like to escort me home, boys?' I asked.

If they hadn't been so pissed it might have been a little more difficult. But they just looked at each other, back at me and moved forward like a scrum.

All of them, that's who wanted to escort me home.

Wizard God just stood watching, totally fucking helpless, as the guys almost carried me out of there, through the front doors and into one of the cabs parked outside.

I let them touch me all over until we got to Earls Court then, when the cabbie stopped at a red light, I opened the door and ran.

A couple of them ran after me but soon gave up. I got home, packed my stuff and left. Wizard God and the Spaniel would be looking for me and it wouldn't take them long to find me through the escort agencies. I figured I had a couple of hours.

I took a cab to Heathrow and bought a ticket to the furthest place I could think of. Australia.

Free. Saved. I don't know what Darian thinks he's going to do with me but the cops won't be able to find anything. Not down there in the Deep Web. And that's the only place I do my business.

I think about Wizard God and the Spaniel every now and then. To be honest they still scare me. I know they're looking for me but I know they won't find me. Not now, not on the Gold Coast in Australia. I guess I have to thank them. You know, if it wasn't for that online auction I would never have thought to go into that business. Funny, huh, how life works?

# 52

# Crime and Punishment

'WHERE'S STARLIGHT?' ASKED MARIA.

We were standing in the car park of Dreamworld. It's the largest theme park in Australia. Carved out of bushland in the 1970s, it was built by a bunch of guys who'd also designed Disneyland. A thick forest of towering gum trees surrounded it. The sun radiated a baking heat from the flat asphalt and the thousands of car windscreens lined up in rows that seemed to stretch forever.

I could hear the screams and yells of kids, mostly teenagers who'd taken some time out from the essential drinking activities of schoolies week. Among them was Casey, riding what's known as the most 'menacing' ride of all, the BuzzSaw.

I'd chosen the Dreamworld car park because it was about twenty minutes away from Surfers Paradise, the hub of current police activity. I wasn't going back there. I had asked Casey to hot-wire the Studebaker and drive it out of town, to this car park, told him I'd meet them there.

Maria was waiting for me, leaning against the bonnet, eating from a bag of fairy floss. She didn't offer me any.

'Where's Estefan?' she said. 'And Ida? Did you find her? Where are they? What the fuck has been going on, Darian?'

She was angry. Aside from my direction to Isosceles that he guide them to rescue the girl Starlight had been holding captive, I hadn't been communicative. Reception on Stradbroke had been an issue.

So too was the fact that Maria had almost put me in Dane Harper's hands. Low-level betrayal, sure, but betrayal nonetheless.

'Estefan was the killer. He murdered Johnston, the two girls in the lake and the girl down by the beach,' I said. 'I don't think that's his real name either. I think it's Carlos. As far as we can tell he killed the real Estefan, his parents and girlfriend, back in Rio, took his identity and came out to work with his sister under the assumed name. We'll probably never know. The police in Rio don't seem to care. It's just another unsolved multiple murder to them.'

'And?' she replied. 'Where the fuck is he? Estefan or Carlos or whatever his name is?'

In the distance I thought I saw Casey waving at me, at the top of the crazy ride, in the middle of what looked like a death spiral.

'Darian?'

Never talk to cops. Basic rule of interaction between civilians and uniforms. Gets ignored all the time. By them and us.

I turned and walked around the car towards the driver's-side door.

'Darian? What have you done?' she yelled.

I opened the door. Threw my backpack onto the passenger seat.

'Darian?' She'd thrown the bag of fairy floss onto the ground. Weird how some people you think you know go and do something you'd never imagine them capable of, like littering.

'What the fuck happened to them? Did you kill him? Did you execute him? Did you play the hero again? The one-man judge and jury? Because if you did ...'

And then she stopped, seemingly aware of the hollowness of her threat.

I drove out of Dreamworld, leaving Maria standing in the car park, turned onto the highway and headed home.

—

THE TRANSACTION WAS effortless.

The second client had become extremely impatient. First, the girl he knew as Starlight, who'd been so totally reliable in the past, rang him in Jakarta to say the shipment had been destroyed.

What? Destroyed? How in God's name did that happen? And what exactly did that mean, destroyed? Destroyed how? He owned a construction business that erected shopping centres throughout Asia, based in Indonesia. His world was bricks and mortar. You get sent plans, you sign off on them, you build. Simple. He liked doing business with Starlight because she had the same approach. His transactions with her so far had been completely straightforward. He ordered a girl, was shown a few possibilities – and they were always of the highest quality, really premium stuff – he made a decision, paid, organised shipment and it was delivered within forty-eight hours. Simple.

Now, this. A mess. After hearing that his new girl wasn't available anymore, he was told she'd be replaced immediately. The very same night. Didn't happen. Then Starlight told him her mobile phone number was being suspended and to use another one, which irritated him, then he was told he was to get a lovely blonde girl. He saw the photos and approved. She wasn't what he really wanted but he just needed someone. He could replace her in a few months' time.

She was Austrian and, of course, she was gorgeous with a great body. He just wanted something different. It was hard to explain.

Then nothing. With every passing hour he grew more and more impatient. And angry. He wanted his girl.

Then, finally, he got a message on the wall.

—

ISOSCELES TYPED:

*hi*

Then he waited for the response, which came within seconds:

*about time. was getting worried. what's happening?*

*got a new girl,* he replied. *totally awesome. wanna see pics?*

*yes. PLEASE. send now*

*click on the link.*

—

HE DID. Wow, he thought. She's magnificent. Dark hair, golden skin, full, beautiful breasts, quite the most stunning girl he'd ever seen. She certainly wasn't a blonde from Austria – that was good – she looked like she was one of those supermodels from South America.

*awesome. love her,* he typed back. *whats her name?*

*rosalita*

*when can i have her picked up?*

*now. immediate delivery. OK?*

*yes. pick-up address?*

*ferry terminal car park, cleveland, between gold coast and brisbane*

—

Isosceles waited, and then:

*car's on its way. be there in an hour. OK?*

*an hour's good. she'll be waiting. tell driver to look for 1980s Nissan 4WD*

*thanks so much*

*you're welcome*

*can't wait to have her under my control* ☺

Isosceles couldn't help himself; he typed back:

*she'll like that*

—

I drove off the ferry, parked and waited. Not for long. A black town car eased its way into the car park and paused. I guessed the driver was scoping out the place, looking for the 1980s Nissan 4WD that he'd been told to find. After a few moments the vehicle began to move in my direction.

Starlight hadn't said very much on our journey along the sand, across the island and onto the waiting ferry. She'd been silent as we churned over the water. Now, as the black town car was slowly approaching, she began to talk.

'What's that?' she asked.

I didn't answer. I climbed out of the driver's seat, closed the door and walked across to greet the driver.

'You've done this before, right?' I asked him. I knew he had.

'Yeah, man,' he replied.

'So you know the score?'

'Yeah. Have you replaced Carlos? He was a pretty cool guy.'

I ignored the question.

'This one's not on Xanax. She might be a bit vocal,' I said.

'No drama. I get paid big money to do what I'm told, ask no questions and keep my mouth shut. And if she's noisy, my ears are closed.' He laughed.

I laughed along with him.

'Bring your car next to mine. Back seat to my passenger side. Open the door, I'll open mine. That way no-one can see the transfer as I put her in.'

'Cool,' he said.

—

'WHAT THE FUCK do you think you're doing?' asked Starlight.

I was unbuckling her seatbelt. The town car was easing in next to us.

'I'm sending you away,' I answered.

For the first time, she looked concerned.

'You think you can get away with that?' she asked.

'Did you?' I asked back.

'Ready when you are!' shouted the driver. He'd parked the car and leaned over to open his back door. With both doors open, a metal curtain had been created. No-one would see me lift her across.

'Please,' she said to me with urgency. I looked at her and saw a little girl, but below the surface, not very far below, was the woman who'd preyed on dozens of unsuspecting girls.

There was no point dropping her off at a police station. The cops would have had a huge challenge trying to find evidence against her. Tor had made all her transactions anonymous. The case wouldn't even have made it to court, if it had made it past first base with the cops anyway.

I had no intention of killing her. I didn't want to go to that extreme and Isosceles had a brilliant resolution anyway.

Maybe she'd escape, one day. Maybe she'd have time to reflect on her actions. Maybe the guy who was about to take possession of her would get busted and she'd be freed. I didn't care. I wanted her off my hands and out of my sight.

I lifted her up and swung her across into the other car. I snapped the seatbelt shut, leaned in to the driver.

'Good to go,' I said.

He started the engine and put the car into gear as I slammed the door shut. I saw her staring up at me.

She was crying.

—

IDA HAD LOST all track of time. How long had she been lost down here, in these tunnels? It felt like days but she knew it could only have been a few hours.

She'd stopped calling out to Darian long ago. He was gone, she knew it. She was on her own. Somewhere, in one of the tunnels, was Carlos's body. She prayed she wouldn't trip over it as she stumbled through the maze.

She also prayed for forgiveness.

As a child she was taught the Bible. She was sent to Sunday School and was confirmed at the age of eleven. She believed in God but, lately, hadn't given it much thought. He, and everything she had learned from the Bible, seemed highly irrelevant to her life over the past couple of years. Perhaps, she thought, she had turned her back on Him, in order to get out of bed in the morning, in order to make her way through each day, in order to sleep at night, in order to survive.

She wasn't going to survive. She knew that. She was going to die. It might take a few days, but this was to be her grave.

She deserved it, she told herself.

Still, in order to finally atone, she recited sections of Psalm 51, which she still knew off by heart:

*Oh loving and kind God, have mercy.*
*Have pity upon me and take away the awful stain of my transgressions.*
*Oh, wash me, cleanse me from this guilt. Let me be pure again.*
*For I admit my shameful deed.*
*It haunts me day and night.*
*It is against you and you alone I sinned and did this terrible thing.*
*You saw it all, and your sentence against me is just.*

—

IDA DREAMED THERE were men coming to save her. They carried torches and had come from the sea. She dreamed they were calling her name. She dreamed their voices carried through the tunnels and that their footsteps were drawing close.

She watched as one old man, who led the others, leaned down to her and said, 'You're all right now, love. You're safe.'

She watched as another old man reached down to her elbow and gently lifted her up. The one who spoke said, 'We're taking you out of here now.'

He put his arm around her waist, so she could lean on him.

She watched as they began to move and she saw that they were carrying her.

She watched as they climbed rough stone steps, the steps that led out of the cobweb, outside, into the world above.

As the sun washed over her and the light burned her eyes she dreamed she'd been saved.

When she woke up she was lying in an old hammock in a rough garden beside a wooden shack next to the beach. Fishing rods and crab pots were strewn across the ground.

The old man from her dream was cooking fish on a barbeque made out of stone and brick.

'How did you find me?' she asked.

'There was a fella looking for you. Said you'd gone missing. Said you might've been hiding out in those tunnels. He came back a few hours later. Told me you were down there. That you'd got lost. Smart fella. Ex-cop from Melbourne. Asked me if there was anyone on the island who had the know-how to get down there and find you, without getting lost themselves. Lucky he asked the right bloke.'

'What else did he say? Did he leave a message or anything?' asked Ida.

'Yeah. He said: "Find your own way home".'

# 53

# Age of Innocence

I DISCONNECTED THE MOBILE PHONES I'D GIVEN THE GIRLS. They were all different bright colours, each one to remind me of the person making the call, should she need to, should she be in distress, should she be in danger and in need of someone to come and rescue her.

*Only you can help, Darian, only you.*

Ida's plea, spoken to me in the heat of the moment, only a couple of days ago, seemed like a mocking refrain in my head.

I climbed up onto the wooden beams in my web-like roof space and grabbed the cardboard box that held them, pulled the charge lead from each of them. As an afterthought I flipped open the backs and removed the batteries.

I'd driven home without stopping, leaving Maria behind in the Dreamworld car park without having answered any of her questions. I didn't need to. It was done. All over.

Or so I thought.

—

TINA HAD BEEN returned to her parents.

Starlight had sent, as far as Isosceles could tell, seventeen girls to new homes. He'd alerted the various authorities but I wasn't sure there was going to be a happy ending for many of them. A number seemed to have gone into the hands of vicious sadists and in some countries, like India and Indonesia and Kenya, the local cops didn't show a great deal of interest. All the girls who'd been sent to Australian 'homes' had been rescued.

Charges were pending for the guys who'd bought them.

There was only one guy with one girl who we didn't bother contacting the cops about; he was in Jakarta and she was called Rosalita.

She'd destroyed the innocence of some and the lives of others. I thought it was a fitting end for her, to experience the torment and enslavement that she had so willingly, and without any shred of guilt or remorse or concern, delivered to others.

—

ON MY DRIVE home, as I was nearing Brisbane, I saw a familiar car ahead of me. The same blue Holden, packed full of six young girls, now on their way home.

Schoolies week hadn't yet finished on the Gold Coast. But the calls from tens of thousands of anguished parents across the country had reached their crescendo in a singular demand: come home *now*.

I could see that the graffitied messages of 'YAY!' and 'OFF TO SCHOOLIES!' were still visible on the car as I drew closer but they had, over the couple of days, begun to fade.

The same girl was driving with the same intensity, eyes firmly on the road ahead, hands gripping the wheel, rigorously observing the speed limit, terrified of potential hazards on the highway.

As I began to overtake them, I cast a sideways glance. They'd shouted and sung and yelled and waved at me on their way down. Now the enthusiasm was gone, the sense of adventure lost. I could see it on their faces. They all sat in the car, staring ahead, not talking, not singing, not waving to passing motorists or swaying to the beat on the drive back home.

It hadn't been the schoolies week they were expecting.

Another girl had gone missing. She'd gone missing on the Sunshine Coast, a long way from the Gold Coast and schoolies but it didn't matter. Her sudden vanishing just reinforced, to parents and maybe, after the carnage had begun to sink in, to the teenagers themselves, the unknown danger that flows around us.

This new missing girl had caught a train from Gympie, at the far northern end of the Sunshine Coast. Somewhere between that town and her destination, Nambour, about twenty minutes from where I lived, she disappeared. The police were suggesting she was a runaway and quoting the stats about the vast majority of missing people who eventually come home safe. With all the grim news from the Gold Coast, her parents weren't listening to the cops – and who could blame them? – and, in their terror and grief, had snared the attention of a hungry press.

Fear permeates.

—

AFTER IMPLYING TO the media that Ethan, Hannah's boyfriend, was a lead suspect in the four murders, Dane Harper quietly dropped that line of pursuit and let the kid walk out through the back door in the middle of the night. The murders remain unsolved but the latest is that they might be bikie gang–related.

That always works.

—

I PUT A Buckwheat Zydeco LP on my old but highly reliable record player – music from another culture, music from far away, from the Cajun world in the deep south of the US, music to dance and laugh to, to drink and eat to, music about love and sunshine – and opened the doors to my front yard, a patch of grass with palm trees, a hammock that swung lazily by the river's edge, next to my wooden jetty which jutted out into the sparkling azure Noosa River, full of guys in tinnies catching fish, families in putt-putt power boats, having picnics and letting the incoming tide float them upriver, kids in canoes, their shouts and laughter carrying like fading echoes across the gentle surface of the water to the uninhabited narrow island on the other side, dense with mangroves and strangler figs and towering eucalypts, the thumping surf of the Pacific Ocean on the beach just a mere stroll through the bush. I let it all in, embraced the warmth and the calmness of home. I lay in my hammock, ignored the pelicans who'd gathered nearby, wanting food, and closed my eyes.

On the third day I succumbed and fed them. I'm a sucker for expectant pelicans.

—

On the fourth day I heard footsteps approaching. Soft and tentative on the gravel drive out through the side gates, leading into the front yard. I wasn't expecting her, but I knew who it was.

'Hello,' said Ida.

'Have a seat,' I said, and she did. She sat in one of the creaky wooden chairs that Casey had given me out of sympathy, and to prompt me to socialise more.

Her hair was tied back and she looked gaunt – nothing like the happy girl in the photo on her apartment wall, smiling for the camera alongside her boyfriend, Carlos.

'I'm sorry,' she said.

I didn't say anything. It was brave of her to come. I just let her talk.

She told me everything. I'd guessed most of it; her mother's call telling me to abandon the search had confirmed it.

'I did bad things. I did terrible things,' she said. 'I hurt people.'

She was staring at the ground. She'd hardly looked at me but then she did, looked up, held my gaze.

'Do you forgive me?' she asked.

'Do you forgive yourself?' I answered.

'No,' she said, still staring at me. Her eyes were bloodshot, large and round, as if frozen with a horror she couldn't shake. There was a scared kid inside the woman.

'Then one of us should,' I said.

# Acknowledgements

I'd like to thank Claude Minisini, Lucio Rovis and David de Pyle for their advice, guidance and feedback regarding the world of criminal investigation. This is a work of fiction and I've no doubt stretched the realities beyond the boundary of what's normal; any mistakes or incredulities are entirely my responsibility.

Thanks to Ross Macrae, Stefan Wern and Dean Barker for reading early drafts and giving me great feedback. Also to Carlos Nunes for answering my questions about life in Brazil and adapting to the English language.

Thanks to my brilliant editor, Elizabeth Cowell. Thanks also to everyone at Hachette Australia for their guidance and support, specifically Kate Stevens for her additional editing and especially to Vanessa Radnidge.

Thanks to Jasin Boland and David Franken. To my beautiful children, Scarlett, Charlie and Delaware and finally to Rachael for her love, help, guidance, support and positivity at every turn and in all of the fleetingly dark corners.

Tony Cavanaugh has written for *The Sullivans*, *Carson's Law*, *The Flying Doctors*, *Fire*, *Adrenalin Junkies* and *Clowning Around*. He was nominated for the Victorian Premier's Literary Awards for the screenplay *Father* and the Queensland Premier's Literary Awards for the screenplay *Through My Eyes*. His first novel, *Promise*, was critically acclaimed. *Dead Girl Sing* is his second novel.